Empyrean Love

Oksana Dubrova

iUniverse, Inc.
New York   Bloomington

Empyrean love

iUniverse books may be ordered through booksellers or by contacting:

iUniverse
1663 Liberty Drive
Bloomington, IN 47403
www.iuniverse.com
1-800-Authors (1-800-288-4677)

ISBN: 978-1-4401-6510-8 (pbk)
ISBN: 978-1-4401-6511-5 (ebook)

Library of Congress Control Number: 2009933800

Printed in the United States of America

iUniverse rev. date: 8/6/09

For an American film-star, the most charismatic "pirate" of modern cinematography **(2006).**

I would like to express my great thanks to my mother and brother, whose invaluable support enabled me to write this book.

"Fathers and teachers, I ask myself: What is hell?
And I answer thus: The suffering of being no longer able to love.
Once in infinite existence, measured neither by time nor by space, a certain spiritual being through his appearance on earth, was granted the ability to say to himself: I AM and I LOVE."

F. M. Dostoevsky - 'The Brothers Karamazov'

Heaven in His Eyes

Fixing her aquamarine eyes toward the enigmatic infinity of the frosty, star-filled, January sky, Sarah intuited a sublime heavenly reality that, while beyond her comprehension, nevertheless engaged her young imagination.

After several hours of practicing the piano at the academy of music, her heart was still filled with the divine music of Bach. The distant stars shimmered overhead, conveying alluring hints of unexplored worlds.

As she gazed upward, contemplating the wonders of the night sky, an indistinct silhouette resembling a man appeared suddenly, as if it had materialized from the nebula before her eyes, defying all laws of nature.

"What's this?" Sarah said to herself. She winced and moved away from the hazy phantom. "Nonsense!" She shook her head, vainly trying to clear her mind and calm her thoughts. "Some childish fancies ..." Yet Sarah could not ignore the illusion.

Usually, the twelve-year-old girl was convinced that earthy reality was beneath her contempt. She eased her natural sentimentality with great difficulty. Sarah had developed a cynical attitude toward the ill-disposed, sublunary world. Even her few friends found the girl unpardonably haughty.

Now the apparition inflamed Sarah's curiosity. But the dogs' unexpected yap, which resounded from the yards of some rickety huts, dispelled the mirage. After catching her breath, the girl advanced confidently.

The ramshackle, log houses propped up one another like decrepit old men, and a single street lamp faintly lit one small area of the bumpy road. Centuries-old, huge pines showed black along the other side of the road. Drooping over a small, slimy pond coated with ice and immersed in winter dreams, the trees were almost invisible in the pitch-darkness of January night. Indeed, the residential area of this provincial Ukrainian town resembled an impoverished countryside village.

The winter dusk intensified Sarah's sensation of danger, and she quickened her pace. Sparkling snow scrunched under her worn-out boots, but the girl slid over numerous ice-covered hummocks, regardless of the impressive winter fairy tale unfolding around her.

The windows of multi-storied uptown flashed with electrical light in the distance. Sweet home at last ...

Having raced up the several front steps, Sarah bounced into her flat, which was on the ground floor of a five-story building. A bit out of breath from running, the girl leaned against the slammed door with her back. Her home's warm air felt delightful.

She knew both her younger brothers were already sleeping by now, but her punctilious parents still sat at the small table of their kitchenette, waiting for their incorrigibly nonchalant daughter. Her entrance turned their attention to the same small hallway, where the girl stood taking off her tin-pot overcoat, which was made of thick cloth, and her black toque, from under which Sarah's dark-brown curls cascaded over her shoulders.

After removing her boots, Sarah came into the kitchen and crossed its creaking wooden floor. She listened wearily to her mother's loud complaints and her father's more reserved disapproval of her gadding about the town so late. The girl's eyelids grew heavy. Her parents—and the world beyond—faded from the sphere of her perception. After a sip of tea, prepared for her hours ago and now cold, Sarah wended her way to her bedroom without saying a word.

After removing her dark-brown school uniform, which she had to wear all day—from grammar school to the music academy—Sarah was happy to put on her pastel flannel pajamas. She was steeped in slumber as soon as her head touched a soft pillow.

Another drab day concluded; the dreams began.

... Slowly opening her eyes, Sarah cast a vacant glance upon some bright, snow-white light. The girl closed her eyes again, turning from side to side and nestling her body upon a smooth surface.

Suddenly, she tumbled down.

Half-awake, Sarah sat up, gazing around and slowly realizing she was not at home. She laid upon a shiny floor that was blood-warm to the touch. The strange room produced a blinding light that pained her watery eyes.

At first sight, the room looked like a hemisphere with its streamline. Its base would be the floor, on which the astonished girl now sat, cross-legged. The arched walls of the hemisphere sloped upward to create a gigantic, domed vault. The room had no furniture, no windows, and no doors. Sarah looked over the unusual structure again and stood up with a sense of misgiving.

At the same moment, as if in response to the girl's intuition, the room melted into space. Sarah found herself surrounded by the boundless black of the universe. Choking with terror, she cried out. Never believing in supernatural, the girl now clutched a small, silver cross, which was on her breast. Her mother had almost compulsively put the cross on Sarah. The girl's steely atheism could not accept what was happening.

Fearing for her life, Sarah sensed an invisible, firm footing. The hemisphere reappeared, and now she realized that the dome-like structure didn't vanish: it had become transparent.

Terror-stricken, Sarah didn't notice that her left hand was still squeezing the cross on her breast with inconceivable strength. The symbol of religion so alien to the girl dug into her palm. Now blood trickled from tiny wounds in her flesh.

Suddenly, the ambient light became brighter, and Sarah momentarily shielded her eyes. However, she paused cautiously, studying her hurt palm.

Now there was no wound ... only a faint, cross-shaped scar.

Sarah sensed another presence in the room. She looked up and, utterly surprised, stood motionless. Dark eyes of superhuman beauty gazed down at the girl.

It seemed that the entire bliss of Elysium had fused with the wild, Plutonian passions of the lower world, sparkling in those marvelous, dark eyes. They were possessed by both mad, Asian ardor and cold, Nordic self-control. The fiery look penetrated the most secret places of Sarah's soul, where they left an indelible mark of sadness.

Sarah was dazed. Her thoughts dispersed like the beads of a broken necklace.

The Stranger with such exotic eyes stood in the middle of the shining hemisphere. His flawless shape was dressed in a baggy-sleeved white shirt, slightly unbuttoned on his chest. Lacy cuffs gently covered his elegant hands. Brown trousers were tucked scrupulously into his jackboots. To Sarah, he seemed a hyperbolical fancy of a medieval nobleman.

The man's straight nose with slightly widened nostrils added excitement to his expression. But his coquettish lips compensated for his slightly demonic allure by softening the exalted melancholy. As a beaming smile played over the Stranger's face, reflecting in the magic abyss of his eyes, a romantic aura shrouded Sarah like an energy net. There could be no salvation from this entrancing power.

The girl backed away to protect her defenseless soul. But having stumbled with her back upon the shining wall, Sarah stopped and nervously straightened her pajamas.

The Stranger stepped jauntily toward the girl. He tossed back his slightly disheveled, deep-brown, gleaming curls, which touched his dimpled cheeks and high cheekbones. His features, manly and chiseled, captivated Sarah. She'd always considered herself strong-willed, but she couldn't resist the profound stare of this unknown man.

A thrill overwhelmed the girl: her body trembled and her heart leaped. Apparently wishing to calm her, the Stranger cast down his eyes, standing silent and motionless. But after a mere blink of his splendid eyelashes, his impassioned, dark look overwhelmed Sarah again.

She found herself so close to the man that their breaths mingled, confusing her thoughts. The Stranger's tapered fingers brushed her deep-brown locks, which quite resembled his own. The man followed his gesture with a languid look, as if wishing to remember it forever. Suddenly, Sarah surrendered her composure, grabbing the man's caressing hand and covering it with fluttery kisses.

Instantly, everything was plunged into pitch-black darkness. With the final fragments of her failing consciousness, Sarah felt the man's safe arms catch her collapsing body.

'I'll never see you ... I'll never forget you ...'

(From the rock opera 'Juno and Avos,'
based on Andrei Voznesensky's poem)

In May of 1985, an undistinguished municipality in northeast Ukraine was buried in the emerald ocean of spring verdure, storming with crests of blooming gardens. Warm air rushed through opened school windows. Standing before one of them, Sarah was covered with the confetti of cherry petals. Intoxicating the girl with its floral scent, the balmy wind tousled her long, curly hair.

Sarah closed her eyes. The spring zephyr tenderly disheveling her tresses suddenly brought back the inexplicable events of three years earlier. As before, it was much easier to pretend that the mysterious Stranger had been just a dream on a starlit winter night 1982. However, after scrutinizing the delicate, cross-shaped scar on her left palm, Sarah once again pictured the eagle-eyed, dark stare that had foredoomed her heart with true pangs of love.

"Dear, one more piece of music is necessary for tonight's school party," the form-master said from behind the girl, making her shudder. "Your musical education always pulled us from such troubles ...Do it again!" The teacher's wish ringing like some hollow sweet talk was, in fact, an order that could not be denied.

Sarah made a fist of her left hand, thereby hiding the scar

from the teacher's curious eyes. She couldn't ignore her form-master's request, and so she reluctantly glanced at an old, broken piano standing not far away in the spacious assembly hall. Sarah wondered how it was possible to play piece of lumber that was so out of tune. The girl adored music, but she hated to express her feelings in public. Sarah had realized, bitterly, that she would never become a true musician because of her unconquerable introversion.

"Sure, I'll do it." Most of all, Sarah was longing to see the back of her form-master, who had been still standing behind the girl. When she heard the fading steps of the teacher, moving away and being satisfied with her agreement, Sarah breathed with relief. She about-turned, leaning back toward the window. Sarah examined the familiar faces of senior pupils, now slowly filling the hall.

The teenagers clustered near the walls. They glanced with slight irony toward two young teachers on duty, who sat on leatherette tip-up seats. The delicate female teachers tried to impose discipline with their cool gazes, searching out any outsiders among the crowd of pupils at the school. But the school administration's efforts were useless. Sarah smiled at them sarcastically. The undesirables would come with the beginning of the promised discotheque, under the cover of its darkness—and, as usual, nobody would spot them.

Suddenly, an amateurish presenter announced Sarah's name. Amplified by the audio system, it reverberated throughout the hall. She startled. Restraining her nervousness, Sarah bustled through the crowd of pupils that now packed the hall.

When she reached the piano at last, Sarah opened its scarred cover and took a seat on the low, maladjusted music stool. Her long, black skirt spread with the graceful sweep of draperies over the parquet floor. Yet something distracted her: the lilac chiffon blouse. Sarah had sewn the blouse herself, but unskillfully. Its nondescript shawl collar hung with formless folds over the girl's breasts and was secretly pinned. The vexing clothes hampered her motions. But Sarah could afford nothing better, as her family barely made ends meet.

Trying to euphonize dissonant chords with her gentle voice, Sarah rushed her fingers along the range of sticking keys. The melancholy romance of the first Soviet rock opera, "Juno and Avos," invariably touched people's hearts: they were moved by the tragic love story of a Russian count and the daughter of the governor of Spanish California, which was set almost two centuries ago. The song plunged listeners into a world of broken hopes and impossible wishes.

Teardrops glistened in Sarah's eyes, misting all before her with a fluctuating shroud. Straining to avoid sobbing before the audience, which was already moved by the drama of her singing, Sarah now regretted accepting her form-master's desire to revitalize the girl's unrealizable musical ambitions. Upon ending her performance, Sarah abandoned the piano amidst stormy applause that rewarded her apparent artistry. Yet she felt she was a third-rate actress, just expressing the feelings that had tormented her heart during the last three years.

Having hidden in a distant corner of the hall, Sarah sat on a fold-up seat, discretely wiping away tears that trickled over her cheeks.

"Oh! You are already here! The ball comes to the player!" A familiar, round voice provoking her with its presumptuousness sounded not far from Sarah. She looked at the boy, her eyes sharp as daggers.

Having reclined against the backrest of the seat beside her, the boy studied Sarah with the sly almond dark eyes of the Grand Mogul's scions. Pertly smiling and biting a long, dark lock, he whispered mockingly, "Indeed, it's a pathetic song. But to tell the truth, your hips impress me more than your foolish melancholy.

How did you like my hands under your skirt ...yesterday, near the cloakroom?" Sarah sensed the boy's hot breath over her shoulder, even through the fine-spun chiffon of her blouse.

Seeing that Sarah ignored him, the boy grew even more impertinent. Suddenly, he clapped sarcastically, as if cheering her again and attracting more attention to the girl with the tear-streaked face.

"Tinhorn buffoon," Sarah whispered. She was taken aback by the smiles of those who now looked upon her. Unaware of the spreading mascara on her cheeks, she tried to nonchalantly smile at her schoolmates. At the same time, Sarah was peeving inwardly, recollecting the incident of which the boy had so rudely reminded her.

The irrepressible admirer was Sarah's neighbor, Andrew. In spite of their living in close vicinity, having grown up in the common yard of their five-storied block of flats, Sarah and Andrew's relations left much to be desired. Andrew had made advances at the girl with all his hot-blooded, Asiatic machismo. But his efforts had collapsed; despite her vulnerable nature, Sarah feigned indifference. Accepting the futility of his efforts—Sarah was the only girl who had rejected him so coolly—Andrew now harassed her out of pique.

Haunting Sarah day after day, he made an ambush in the most secret corners of the three-storied building of the school, watching there for the girl, exactly as he had the day before.

Having spied Sarah approaching the mirror hanging on the wall in front of the cloakroom, Andrew had remained close as Sarah brushed her hair. Examining the curves of her feminine figure and her rich, dark-brown tresses streaming along her back, he was wildly attracted to her, as if they shared common Asiatic blood. Barely keeping his desire within in check, Andrew recalled that she was the first girl he'd ever kissed, when he was merely ten. Since then, Sarah's snide laugh at his greenness had constantly echoed in his soul. His grievance was so deep that it obscured his reason completely. So now, having acquired some experience, Andrew hankered to assert his sexiness at any cost to the girl who attracted him as if she were everything unattainable.

After leaping out of his ambuscade, he had grasped the dumbfounded Sarah and pressed her against the wall. Pushing back against Sarah's resistance, Andrew had pawed the flesh beneath her skirt. Laughing at her attempts to evade his tongue, which eagerly licked her face, the boy whispered into her ear: "Sweetie, I'll get you, even if it takes me all my life."

Barely escaping, Sarah again realized h0w strongly she hated that idiot for not leaving her in peace—even though a horde of schoolgirls dreamed of finding themselves in Sarah's place. But sometimes Sarah felt as if she were rather afraid of Andrew's dark, passionate look because it was so familiar to her from her early childhood. His penetrating eyes awakened her latent, Asiatic blood. Still, Sarah remained cool and did not forgive Andrew's abandon.

Having seen a teacher wending along the school corridor, Andrew had let Sarah go, following her with his vexed look. He did not want more problems with the school administration, which had for years found fault with the boy's behavior.

Now, at the school party, Andrew continued to pursue Sarah.

"What the kind of raggery did you dress up in?" The boy brushed against the tip of Sarah's improvised surplice collar with his fingers. His face expressed simulated distaste. To Andrew's surprise, the funny formation hardly resembling the collar of Sarah's blouse came apart, drooping over the girl's bust and baring it.

"Get lost!" Sarah hissed through clenched teeth. Her green eyes flashed like a wild cat's. But for all that, she wasn't in a hurry to cover her naked breast, which now captured Andrew's attention. He was surprised by the shamelessness of the girl, who always treated him like dirt. Seeing lust in Andrew's squinting, bleary eyes,

Sarah smirked malevolently, feeling she had gained revenge. She knew that Andrew, who'd already had the last admonition from the school administration, wouldn't dare be brutal with her on school grounds.

The lights were turned down, and colors flashed wildly on the walls and ceiling to the rhythm of new wave music. The flickering of a rotating laser light snatched dancing silhouettes out of the darkness, rendering their smooth movements erratic and abrupt. The rumble of the audio system overpowered all other sounds, including Andrew's indistinct commentaries concerning Sarah's clothing, which he was still mumbling as he wondered inwardly at her unblushing conduct.

The boy moved toward his mates, who were sitting across a gangway, beckoning Andrew and screaming with laughter, having observed the couple's amusing conversation.

When she had installed her collar at its fixed place, Sarah pinned together its parts as before. She lolled in her tip-up seat and closed her eyes, dipping synchronously with all fibers of her soul into the harmony of sounds. The girl, immersed in a musical trance, looked over at an approaching, slim boy with long, lily-white hair. Just when he stopped in front of Sarah, having shaded the play of light with his graceful pose, the girl glanced languidly at him.

Even in the twilight of the disco, she could see the boy's black suit, in contrast to his white shirt and a narrow silky tie, which seemed ruby-red in the beams of the laser. In that musical pandemonium, roaring with decibels and absorbing the abusive language of teenagers, his solemn costume and romantic blond hair, which reached the middle of his torso, looked as out of place as Sarah's long skirt and homemade blouse.

Sarah curiously measured the blond from head to toe, concluding that he wasn't from her school of 3,000 pupils. It was impossible to imagine a Soviet school administration tolerating a boy attending classes with such a defiant hairstyle. He was an "outsider," and therefore potentially risky. But Sarah was struck by his almost angelic, well-groomed curls, which suddenly enveloped her with the unobtrusive scent of some expensive hair spray. Now the blond stooped to her ear and asked affably, "May I invite you to dance?" The boy astonished Sarah not only with his manner of dress, but also with his urbane parlance, which was so at odds with the slang of her circle of teenagers.

Andrew, sitting not far from Sarah and still struggling to contain himself, glanced nervously as the dazzling blond touched the girl's face. Sarah's neighbor felt the sudden rise of wild jealousy. He vociferated at the top of his voice, addressing the fair-haired masher and nearly shouting down the loud speakers, which were rumbling like a jet engine.

"Hey, dude! The miss chooses rather without any ceremony!"

With those words, Andrew rushed up to Sarah, shouldering the blond and opening the girl's ill-fated collar with one brusque motion of his hands. It was ineffectual in the darkness, but the clasp-pin that had been helping keep Sarah out of trouble now bounced with a clink under the feet of the dancers. Furious, Sarah leaped up as if she had been stung. Suddenly angry, she slapped the wrongdoer's face.

Sarah knew that Andrew would not put up with such disparagement. Without waiting for his reaction—her heels clicking and her long skirt tangled—she hurried out of the assembly hall.

Piecing the lilac chiffon of her blouse with her hand and covering her breast again, Sarah cursed inwardly. The school parties were a rare chance to hear modern music. But even in school, there was no peace because of the numerous idiots.

'Untouchable'

Sarah heard steps behind her in the deserted school corridor. Glancing back, she saw the longhaired blond.

"What do you want?" Sarah asked. Still agitated, she turned around abruptly to face the pursuer. Surprised, the fair-haired stripling grasped her forearms spontaneously while trying to avoid a collision.

They faced each other for several moments. Sarah inspected the boy's dark-brown eyes as if looking for something familiar in them.

Really, the blond was comely. Clean-limbed and perfectly built, he was nearly the same age as Sarah. Despite his efforts to look manly in his lounge suit, the boy was rendered girlish by flowing white curls and a sole golden earring, which Sarah only now noticed.

Being of opinion that the girl was attracted to him, the blond asked, "Wasn't that music you performed really about my eyes?"

Feeling an odd desire, caused by his strange looks and his hot breath on her cheek, Sarah tried to remove his hands from her forearms.

"You won't die with modesty," she whispered with a forced smile.

"Of course not! Only my unshared love for you will kill me!" The blond sensed Sarah's agitation under his magnetic look, but submissively released her forearms.

"Flourish ..." she answered wistfully, "though it's not as lyrical as foolish." Adding more coolness to her voice, Sarah said to the boy, who seemed to be making fun of her, "Sorry, I've got to go." And she went resolutely along the school corridor.

"Wait!" the importunate blond called as he blocked her way again. He seemed ready to grasp her once more, but held back. "I want you ..." he whispered in a deep voice. Sarah was bedeviled by the contrast between his dark eyes and white hair.

"Certainly! Right here and right now!" she said sarcastically, trying to stand firm against the strange power of his eyes.

"Stop!" the boy didn't let Sarah. "Do you want to get home today?" His voice was so emphatic that Sarah dropped the tips of her collar, which she was still holding with her hand. Her blouse, unpinned on her breast as before, slipped down over her shoulders. The boy caught up the flimsy chiffon and crossly tightened the silky gauze on Sarah's breast. Having taken off his earring, he used it to pin together the parts of her collar.

"Devilish touch-me-not ..." the boy uttered in a low, nervous voice, almost near Sarah's temple. "Why did you slap that fellow's face? Now he is waiting for you with all his friends in the schoolyard. Look through the window! Don't they want to take you home all together?" the blond needled. "It would be terribly nice of them!"

Sarah stared wordlessly at her unexpected guardian. She knew neither the boy nor his intentions, but she knew that painfully frustrated Andrew would go to every expedient for satisfaction, feeling the frenetic rancor of an offcast macho.

"Who are you?" Sarah asked as she collected herself at last. She had no choice but to put her trust in the boy's apparent amicability.

"I'm Serge," the stripling answered, happy to have engaged the girl at last. "And your name is Sarah," he uttered, faster than she opened her mouth. "Indeed, I know you quite well." He shocked Sarah with his conversance. "For example, I know you are still ... a virgin."

"What?" Sarah gasped. She was ablaze with anger, fighting an urge to slap Serge's face as well. "You can't know that!" she whispered through clenched teeth. Immediately, the boy's fingers wrapped nimbly around Sarah's wrist.

"It's a vicious habit." He smiled seductively, squeezing her hand. Serge glanced toward the schoolyard, where the herd of the smoking boys waited for Sarah. He whispered, as if testing her patience a little more, "So, my supposition was correct. My practiced eye didn't betray me." Providently not slackening his grasp and smiling in Sarah's face as before, he added, "But let's return to the dispute about your virginity later." Meanwhile, the crowd—with Andrew at the front—was returning to the school building to find Sarah.

"Come with me! I'll help you to get out before the arrival of all those rowdy well-wishers." Suddenly, Serge tugged at Sarah's wrist, carrying her along the faintly illuminated labyrinth of the long school corridors and staircases to the ground floor.

"Are you afraid of me?" Serge asked. He couldn't stop poking fun at the girl's steady poise.

"I'm afraid of nothing!" Sarah answered with childish self-confidence.

"By gad! But there's a reason why you have preferred me to the crowd of your impassioned admirers," Serge said sarcastically.

He glanced back and caught Sarah's stare. She cast down her eyes.

"It was a logical choice," the girl pronounced coldly. "If I'm to be raped, it will be done by only one ... and a quite attractive boy, at least."

"Rape. You say it so easily ..." Serge murmured in undertone, adding sharply, "What do you know about it? Unworldly girl from an unreal world!"

"How did you guess about the unreal world?" Sarah asked, puzzled.

Being at a loss, Serge fixed his look at her pale face again, as if he saw a ghost. "It's just a figure of speech ..."

He continued lugging Sarah away with him. "I think we'll come to accord." Suddenly, the boy pulled Sarah roughly into the dark, small anteroom of the school's back exit. Serge had known about its location all along ... He had used the entrance to get into tonight's disco. It was the only way for strangers, who were not admitted at school parties, to slip into the building undetected.

The fellow unexpectedly stopped in pitch darkness of the anteroom, and Sarah clashed with his chest. Again, she caught the scent of his hair spray near her face and stepped back in confusion. The girl realized that one of her comments might have seemed to be very provocative to the quaint fellow, who, patently, wasn't going to release her hand. The surrounding darkness was so deep that Sarah wasn't able to see even Serge's white hair, which could glint with the faintest light.

"At last. We've gotten rid of everybody ..." Sarah felt his hot whisper touching her cheek, "I want you."

"Please," she uttered, sensing Serge's fingers tenderly stroking her wrist. It was slightly awkward for her, but she couldn't get over her strong impression of the boy's showy appearance. "It's dark in here, like in hell," she said. "I need to see your eyes, at least."

Feeling her thrill, even in the darkness, Serge pronounced with wonder, "Huh ...I'd always thought that just my look affected people like that. But skip it ...Would you be so kind and let me finish what I have to say?" he added, being slightly irritated with the girl's habit of interrupting him.

"So, as I said," he whispered, almost enveloping Sarah with his hair in the darkness, "I want you ...to be my friend, the kind of friend I've never had before. I need you in my life. I have been shadowing you for almost a month, but you act as if you don't notice me. I know your everyday routine. I don't know why ... but I feel the strength to draw breath only near you."

Serge's words struck a chord in Sarah's heart. They brought to light his subtle spiritual orientation, which had been concealed under his overtly sexual manner.

The self-absorbed girl, who was always been preoccupied with her preternatural love for some phantasmal Stranger, memorized new faces badly—and Serge wasn't an exception. Sarah was convinced she had seen him for the first time at the disco. But then, unexpectedly, she remembered having seen the glaring white hair with its effeminate charm, and the golden earring that now connected the parts of her collar. Sarah had supposed those features had belonged to a girl. She saw that girl at different places recently.

Especially, Sarah had noticed the fair-haired person at the cafe, where the schoolgirl stopped on her way to the academy of music. Lacking the time and money to have a bite, Sarah usually ordered some slosh, a mere apology of juice. She drank it hastily at the counter, almost choking with each gulp of the beverage ... because she sensed, even with her back turned, the ogles of the strange, platinum blonde sitting at a table behind her. Usually, the fair-haired teenager was in a circle of some imposing men who were old enough to be her father. The blonde's companions familiarly cuddled the belle, constantly talking her into changing her seat for a more comfortable one. But ignoring the indignation of her mates, who disliked the miserable eatery, the fair-haired person had her eyes glued to Sarah. The seeming blonde girl was trying to catch just one of Sarah's curious, covert glances, by which the schoolgirl in the end scrutinized the belle's lonely earring. Sarah considered it a bold fashion for a girl in this conservative province—even for such a sexy one as the blonde was.

"Damned bisexual wear and all these hippy hair styles!" now Sarah inwardly cursed at the manner of dressing that made it impossible to distinguish a boy from a girl at first sight.

"May I hope to see you tomorrow?" Serge's gentle voice distracted Sarah from her intense thoughts. Feeling as before only his fingers locked over her wrist and his breath on her cheek, Sarah pronounced timidly, "If you want ...though I don't understand why we are talking in the darkness."

"I'm a sticker as well ... and you haven't answered me," Serge whispered with a quiver in his voice, as if also growing aroused by their nearness in so intimate a setting.

"OK," Sarah uttered silently, having abandoned her feigned Jewish habit of answering a question with another one. "I accept your friendship. In fact, I'm under obligation to you for tonight's escape."

"Well, let it go at that," Serge whispered, pining with lust. He ardently kissed her wrist, which had grown tired in his hand. Sarah's consent didn't seem quite right to him, but even so, the boy released her hand.

"As for talking in the darkness," Serge said as he grudgingly considered her question, "it's just the way to protect you against my spellbinding looks, which can force you to fulfill any of my desires." Sarah was surprised at his unusually bold manner.

Suddenly, Serge opened the squeaking wooden door of the back exit with his strong kick, easing Sarah out into the warm, sweet-scented May night.

"Sakes alive!" Sarah said sarcastically, passing by the boy and peeking playfully into his dark eyes, which she couldn't trace in the semi-darkness of the faintly illuminated street. Mocking his inexplicable self-control, she whispered, slightly touching Serge's lips and ignoring his nervous wince, "To force with a look? Funny ...two can play at that game."

School vacation came. Sarah and Serge spent long summer days together, relaxing on the beach of the river crossing their town or simply listening to the tape-recorder at Serge's home. The boy lived in the flat of a multi-storied building with his diseased mother, who needed her son's constant attention. Serge's deep attachment to his mother was very touching. Sarah knew that her new friend had lost an older brother, who had died violently. But Serge preferred to hold his tongue about their family tragedy. His mother, having mentioned the fate of her elder son, had burst into tears, frightening Serge gravely. He knew such hysterical fits were dangerous for her diseased heart.

Sarah had grown used to her boyfriend's inexplicable reservation: Serge was precocious and jaunty among his kith, allowing himself nothing more intimate than brushing over Sarah's wrist or a cursory glance at her eyes. Sarah hardly believed the boy's self-control was the result of his upbringing. Nevertheless, she tried not to take it to heart. In fact, the noncommittal, easy friendship satisfied her. She realized that the young boy couldn't supersede, in her mind, the desirable Stranger. It was the Stranger that Sarah loved, but she never stopped to doubt in his reality, as she had before.

The superhuman, fervent, dark eyes and extraordinarily graceful motions lured her more than all the handsome men on the earth. Sarah banished the incredibly strong feeling that had been inspired in her by the Stranger—whether he was a man or a phantom—who had burst in her life, without her ever knowing where from.

As for Serge, only one thing cast a shadow on their blameless friendship. Every evening, the boy brought Sarah home with enviable punctuality. He was motivated by his reluctance to engage in a clash of opinions with the girl's parents regarding her independence. This state of affairs greatly irritated Sarah. While most teenagers had been loitering about the town all night through, seeking adventures and sensations, she was made to stay at home, losing in vain the priceless time of her transient vacations.

It was such a night. Sarah was immersed in her thoughts; her writing table was faintly lit by a glimmering desk lamp. She was senselessly browsing a book lying on the table when the shrill ringing of the phone startled her out of half-drowsy meditation. Striking the wooden corners of beds and chairs with her knees, Sarah rattled to the hallway, where the phone was.

"Hello," she whispered with displeasure, pressing the receiver to her lips as close as possible, fearful of awakening anyone.

"Hi!" The sneering voice of Andrew, the neighbor who was so oddly partial to Sarah, jumped from the other end of the line. "How is it going? I can't imagine it's possible to have sex in your overcrowded flat! Isn't it suitable for your pretty *catamite*?"

"If you want to see a *catamite*, look in a mirror! Besides, I'm unwilling to discuss my intimate relations with you!"

"Naturally! Because there is nothing to discuss!" Andrew said. "In vain, I considered you to be ready-witted. But like the majority of females, you are not friends with your brain. Everybody except you knows that your sweetheart is a gay-boy!" The last phrase was a gloat.

"Scum ... I hate you!" Sarah sputtered into the receiver.

"I know, love," Andrew whispered with passion, "and that's the beauty of it. Don't get into a state! Give me at least a while to come to you."

"Come ... I'll suffocate you with my own hands!"

"Oh!" Andrew burst out laughing. "An alluring prospect to turn up in your hands at last." Suddenly, his libidinous voice reached Sarah's ear, making her heart palpitate with his infectious, Asiatic passion. "Believe me, your darling fag won't stop me from bedding you one day."

Sarah slammed down the receiver, realizing Andrew had delighted in her short temper, which was so similar to his own. She covered the constantly ringing phone with her pillow. The girl didn't wish to satisfy Andrew's desire even by phone. It was quite enough for him to mock the touching idyll of the loving couple.

Sarah rushed about the semi-darkness of her room like a tigress in a cage, regardless of the late time. She tried to forget Andrew's call and retraced the short story of her relations with her friend ...yet Andrew's claim explained Serge's physical coolness very persuasively. But in that case, her girlish boy-friend's ardent desire to be constantly near Sarah looked like some sheer nonsense. She so wanted to believe all that idle talk was no more than some unfounded rumors spread by envious boys like Andrew. But there wasn't another way to find out the truth, such as it was, except to ask Serge himself.

The next day, Sarah dropped in at Serge's place just about nightfall. His mother, still a nice-looking blonde in her middle forties, saw Sarah from the balcony of their flat. She opened the door silently, making the girl welcome, as usual.

"Serge's in the living-room. He's ironing," the woman pronounced with an inscrutable smile that expressed her pride in her industrious son, who helped her with everything. Certainly, there was nothing reprehensible in her pride; but the woman's words convulsed Sarah for some reason, reminding her of Andrew's call.

Sarah almost tiptoed into the living room to study the ironing boy. Standing at an ironing board with his back to her, Serge was pedantically checking the heat of an old iron without any temperature regulator on it. He tried to safeguard the delaine fabric of his mother's dress against burning. His snazzy blond curls hung down close to the hot iron each time he bent over the board. Having crept up to him inconspicuously from behind, Sarah gathered his hair, braiding it with a twine. Serge flinched. Reasonably believing that only his mother was in the flat, he said silently, "Thanks, mum, it doesn't hinder me. I've gotten used to it."

"And when did you have time?" Sarah whispered at last from behind of his shoulder, giving her intonation a deeper, intimate meaning. Having perceived the girl's presence, Serge turned around quickly, grasping Sarah's hands and kissing her wrists. "Sweety ... where have you been all day long? I have grown old ringing you constantly! I've missed you badly." Seeing that Serge had dissembled her suggestive words, Sarah didn't hurry to unclasp his hair, which he tried to pull out of her hand.

"Please, let me go," Serge whispered at last, realizing that Sarah needed a reminder.

"Sure," she answered softly, leading the boy toward an ottoman that stood at the wall of the room. "But right after our intimacy ... OK?"

"OK," Serge said, surprised, but trying to maintain her playful spirits. "You are in a very unusual mood today. Has anything happened?"

"There is nothing unusual in my desire to have sex with my boyfriend!" Sarah exclaimed crossly, pushing him down onto the ottoman. She was now irritated by his indifferent lack of resistance to her.

Having dropped among the cushions picturesquely, Serge gazed upon Sarah as if to absorb her fervor.

"Boyfriend?" he repeated, as if there were something novel for him in the girl's designation. "But you even don't love me?"

"That means nothing! You are my boyfriend, and I want you! Isn't it clear?"

Having lain down by Serge and avoiding his unbearable, dizzying look, Sarah pulled off his T-shirt and kissed his naked torso—even as she sensed his apathy. Her lips stole up over Serge's shoulder to his forearm. The forearm had a tattoo, which he had always concealed from Sarah, even on the beach. Noticing her intention to see the tattoo now, Serge struggled to endure Sarah's kisses, acting as if they were the most disgusting thing he had ever felt in his life. Suddenly, the boy grasped her shoulders strongly and said, "Don't touch me!"

"Why the mischief?" she raved, unable to resist him physically. "Is it because you are ..." Unexpectedly, Sarah stumbled, realizing she couldn't say more. In a blink, Serge's expression became the personification of breathless attention. Removing his hands from the girl, he helplessly sat beside her on the ottoman. But Sarah's resolution had vanished into thin air.

"Well ... in general ... how to say," she stumbled, now blushing, now paling under Serge's fixed look. "In a word," the girl said at last, "is it true what they say about you?"

Serge didn't bat an eye. Only the ghost of smile played over his lips. He pensively pulled the tape from his hair, which Sarah had bound too tightly. Tossing his lilac-white locks over his shoulders with a graceful motion of his head, Serge's posture suggested that Sarah's suspicions weren't groundless.

"In a sense." His answer was as cagey as Sarah's question. "It is better they backbite than shout about it from the top of the roof." Trying to ease the girl's perplexity, he whispered, "I haven't any intention to abuse you. My private life changes nothing in our relations."

A seemingly invisible force made Sarah jump up from the ottoman. "Good luck in your private life!" Her chill tone nearly choked with rising frenzy. Without turning back, the girl directed her steps toward the door, and she left the puzzled Serge alone in the room.

Wending her way along the evening streets of the town, Sarah thought indignantly, why she had to be so shamed. "He didn't even change his countenance!" Sarah visualized her ex-boy-friend's significant smile. Disgust and bitterness cast her down. But looking at it from another side, Sarah realized she had had affection for the effeminate boy, wh0 valued her friendship more than others did. But her too straightforward notion of good and evil didn't provide a choice. Sarah always disliked those who challenged "the high moral principles of civilized society" and found for their abominable sins exceptionally natural justifications. The girl adhered to her copybook maxims and prejudgments. Overpowering her best memories of Serge, Sarah marched home without any doubts about the rightness of her act.

Several days elapsed, and Sarah's home phone did not stop ringing. Serge begged her for a visit, but the girl refused him flatly, using specious pretexts or plain rudeness.

Once, coming back home, Sarah saw Serge squatting at the door of her flat in open daylight. Avoiding his hard stare, Sarah approached the door and got a key out of her pocket. She ignored Serge. The boy stood up as if allowing her to unlock the door, but suddenly, he grasped Sarah's wrists. He hustled her back to the wall of the landing, trying to touch to her as little as possible. Sarah dropped the key.

"I can't take this any more!" Serge whispered, staring at Sarah with the eyes of a dog yearning for his master. "My cursed life has lost its only sense without you."

The girl felt it was almost impossible to say "no" under his mesmeric look.

"I want to hear nothing!" she exclaimed, trying to sound firm as she struggled to free her wrists. Serge released Sarah's hands, but the next moment, he slipped down along her figure, kneeling at her feet and cuddling the girl's hips to his face. Shocked, Sarah couldn't budge.

"Stand up ... this instant," she whispered, dumbfounded.

"I won't get up until you'll hear me out at least," Serge pronounced. His theatrics confused the girl even more than his glaring curls pressed to her abdomen.

In the meantime, the lodgers upstairs descended the steps, watching with curiosity the scene unfolding before their eyes and noting the spicy idyll between a kneeling, fair-haired girl pressing her face to the hips of a brown-haired one.

Sarah was petrified. Fixing her eyes at the people's sneers, she longed for the earth to swallow her. She had grown up in this house. She was known as a very positive girl. But now the girlish hairstyle of the blackguard instantly destroyed her reputation!

When her neighbors departed, smiling and whispering, Sarah boiled with indignation. She grasped Serge's blond locks and yanked them, compelling the boy to stand.

Serge jumped up from the ground adroitly, without even flinching. But at the same moment, his eyes pierced Sarah with their fathomless darkness. That darkness spread over his eyes, alternating with some plasmic shadows. His fiery look, as if from the beyond, penetrated Sarah, and she shuddered.

"Angel's spawn ... You belong to hell," Serge whispered spitefully near her lips. Suddenly, his fingers enclosed Sarah's throat with a death grip. The girl struggled to breath, but he would not release her. Sarah lost consciousness without hearing the mad words of her demonic friend.

"What have I done?" Serge cradled Sarah's unconscious body, feeling the weak pulse on her wrist and vainly trying to revive her with his intense embrace. Having picked up Sarah's key from the floor, he struggled to carry the girl to her home. Serge unlocked the door with difficulty. After entering in the flat, he put Sarah in her bed. Losing his last nerve, he knelt beside the bed. Sarah seemed to torment him by so closely resembling death.

"My girl ...I'm so sorry... I didn't want this," Serge sobbed, kissing Sarah's wrist and washing her hand with his tears. Slowly opening her eyes and sensing weeping lips over her hand, Sarah drew a deep, spasmodic breath. She whispered, "Why do you always kiss only my wrist?"

Serge gave a start, releasing the girl's hand and mopping his tears in confusion.

Pondering whether Sarah would send him to hell right now or after the satisfying her curiosity, the boy remained silent for a moment. Then he began to speak, with a trace of fatality in his deep, strained voice.

"After I was first gang-raped, at the age of eleven ... when they set free me from handcuffs, a man kissed my wrists. That touch was embedded in my recollection as the best sexual sensation in my life." Folding Sarah's hand to his bosom, as if hoping to revive with it her broken, amicable attitude toward him, Serge went on. "After all, I hate any sex. Adding to everything, I have this awful, unpredictable, nervous reaction at any pang. Of course, all my lovers know about it, but they are men and can resist me. Sorry ... it was accidental ..."

Sarah was already sitting up in her bed, staring at Serge's tear-stained, dark eyes. She felt an inexplicable fever arise within her.

"What the blazes! So ... you can't lust after me?" she exclaimed, furiously removing her blouse and skirt and hurling them at the boy.

"I don't know yet," Serge whispered. "I have never been intimate with a girl." Sarah's clothes hung over his shoulder.

Being dressed only in her underwear, Sarah lay across the length of her bed. She closed her eyes and folded her arms, seeming ready to die.

"May I continue?" Serge asked cautiously, watching her reaction ... and her inability to grasp his humiliation.

"Blaze away!" Sarah answered with feigned indifference, still feeling Serge's finger-marks on her neck. "You have persuaded me to hear you out." She was all ears, although the boy's horrid story further agitated her.

As it emerged, some criminal gang in the provincial town, who had powerful backing in the corrupt municipal and state governments, used the showy boy as a prostitute and sexual slave for their own needs. It began when Serge's older brother, being unwise in the selection of friends, ran up a debt with bandits. Unable to pay back the debt in time, he had just departed from the town like the lowliest coward. The mobs made juvenile Serge pay off his brother's debt in this savage way. He had been doing it for several years.

Nevertheless, his brother's dead body had washed ashore during the spring overflow of the river that crossed the town. Either a deathbed repentance had finished him, or the mobs rid him of his guilty conscience once and forever—it remained unknown. Serge's mother had suffered a heart attack after the tragedy, so the boy feared revealing his troubles to her.

Nobody else was interested at Serge's dire plight, he said. They were afraid to clash with the merciless mafia.

"How is this possible in a humane society?" Sarah asked as she opened her eyes and stared at the ceiling. She was dumbfounded by Serge's narration. Mechanically having sat up again, she removed her clothing from Serge's shoulder, where it was still hanging.

"I like your use of the word 'humane,'" Serge uttered wistfully, assisting Sarah with her blouse, "but it's not about our criminal state. So, as you wanted, I have explained you the reason of my unnatural sexuality. I know it's nasty enough for any normal person. That is why people like you avoid my company, as if I were a leper. If you do the same, nobody will blame you. It seems I have dismayed you. Don't take it to heart. Maybe I'm just some unlucky exception from the rule."

Serge stood up, his head hanging down, and plodded toward the door.

"Wait." Sarah gazed contemplatively at the flaming rowan-berries hanging from the branches of a tree by her window. "I'll stay with you. Most people avoid me as well, and I don't even know why."

Serge glanced back, devouring every one of Sarah's word as if they were a source of some vital energy to his existence. Having rushed up to the girl, he kneeled slavishly at her bed again and hectically began kissing her wrist.

"Please," Sarah begged. "Forget your sadomasochistic manners concerning me. You wanted to find a friend, and not another lover. Same here."

Sarah and Serge's relations became even more confidential. But after the start of the school year, some salty rumors about the girl's love affairs with a filthy boy began to circulate among Sarah's schoolmates. Fortunately, her teachers paid little attention to the tattle-tales, considering as the rumors to be the wrongful accusations of reckless teenagers. The situation amused Sarah. It introduced into the matter-of–fact life of the excellent school-girl a fresh breath of intrigue.

Having noticed she was more interesting to her classmates as a "bad girl," who tested everything, Sarah skillfully imitated the corruption of her moral. She laughed up her sleeve at the stupid envy of her mates for her seeming independence from the conventions of societal morals. Remaining one of the best in the mastering of all school subjects, Sarah made up stories about love-making with her "depraved" boy-friend. As delicately as possible, she described her imaginary sex life to the dazed schoolgirls who surrounded Sarah in a compact circle during school breaks. The fabler had been screaming with laughter for several days, recollecting her mates' open-mouthed, stupid facial expressions. At the same time, Sarah's heart bled with bitter realization that the object of her true, eager passion—her unachievable, illusory Stranger—inhabited in some other world, very seldom crossing with her reality.

As for Serge, Sarah knew that her fables couldn't offend him or increase his notoriety more. In truth, when the girl's fanciful tales, exaggerated by her ingenious audience, reached Serge's ears, he just smiled sadly. Lackadaisically rolling his eyes and affectionately inhaling the aroma of Sarah's frizzy hair, the boy said reservedly, "Well then, you are well-read of sex. So...you attend school not without purpose. You've learned to read, at least."

Though their everyday relations were amicable, but it became unendurable for Sarah to see her sole friend looking crushed after his almost nightly orgies. They were destroying him. She didn't wish such a "love" even for an archenemy.

"Is it really impossible to change something?" Sarah once asked Serge cautiously, as he sat on the ottoman in his living room, swaying with the rhythm of the Scorpions. Squeezing his head in his hands and fixing his set eyes somewhere on the wall, Serge didn't even feel the tears trickling down his smooth cheeks. He was having a full nervous breakdown, and his life seemed to be unbearable for the sixteen-year old boy.

Realizing that Serge didn't hear her because he had lapsed into some kind of depressive shock, Sarah approached him guardedly and touched his forearm. Under the short sleeve of his T-shirt was his infamous tattoo. Now she knew it was some original stamp of a passive homosexual, a code invented by those who inhabited prisons. Serge's tormentors had applied the tattoo by force.

After belatedly recognizing Sarah's touch on his brand, Serge started. Sensing her finger slowly brushing over his forearm, outlining the depiction of devil cuddling a naked girl to his ghoulish flesh, he whispered crossly, "I have asked you many times, never touch me." Sarah's hand drooped.

"Moron! Have I done anything?" she asked, irritated and about to withdraw.

Suddenly feeling highly-strung, Serge jumped up, grabbed the girl's wrist harshly, and pulled Sarah to himself.

"To change something? It's really impossible!" He surprised Sarah with his ability to hear her even in his deep prostration. "I don't want to finish badly like my brother! My damnation takes him! The mobs will find me anywhere. It's the mafia. If I refuse to cooperate, they'll just clap me in prison, regardless of my age. You know our Soviet laws concerning amoral behavior, sodomy in particular. In prison, my life won't amount a row of beans, because of my reputation."

Sarah couldn't utter a word as she stood transfixed under his dark, lackluster eyes. Unexpectedly, some sleepiness and weakness mixed with her increasing desire. Serge's incredible blond curls, smoke-filled and disheveled by his male lovers, touched Sarah's face ever and anon.

"I warned you," he whispered, choking with passion and laying the girl on the ottoman because she had become weak in the knees. "I can make you do anything, but I want nothing without your love. I know I'm too filthy for your love ... and it drives me crazy!"

"What the hell?" Sarah whispered. She realized she could barely move or speak. But instead of understanding the reason for her condition, she now ached to fulfill any whims of the boy, who immediately took advantage of the situation ...

Having torn away the button on the cuff of Sarah's school uniform with his eager fling, Serge kneeled, as usual, near the prostrated girl. He dug with his ardent lips into her wrist, knowing for certain that she would tolerate his habit, although it usually disgusted Sarah. Obstinately covering Sarah's hand with his kisses and disregarding her strong desire for him, Serge whispered, as if in prayer: "My pure Angel ... don't make me to overpower you. I'm fed up with all this damned sex without love!"

Day after day, Sarah's physical attraction to Serge became stronger. It boiled in her veins, arousing her latent, Oriental blood. The boy hoped her hot nature would force Sarah to express her feelings to him at last. Serge naively believed the virgin's attachment might revive his soul, as if it were a Phoenix arising from the ash.

Sometimes Sarah seemed to be ready to do anything if only to have a one-night stand with Serge. But he mocked Sarah, trying to break the back of her haughtiness. When finally losing self-control, Sarah embraced the boy, at the risk of bringing on his nervous irritability, Serge just smiled indulgently. Casting an arch glance at Sarah's lustful lips approaching his own, he whispered feverishly, burning Sarah's face with his hot breath. "You know, I can't do it the natural way. Though ... maybe, if you'll say you love me." Then he retreated slyly from the girl's suggestive arms, leaving her to pout.

Sarah raged inwardly. Why did she have to love Serge? He demanded the impossible! It was quite enough her longing of their intimacy! In the end, she wasn't a god who could give love to everyone who was abject and hurt!

Serge's allurement sometimes distracted Sarah from her visionary love to the phantasmal Stranger, who seized her soul in some magic way. But the girl saw it was the same problem. She couldn't forget herself while in bed with that sensual, long-haired blond bedeviling her. It was as if he had inherited Sarah's habitual role of a touch-me-not.

Seeing Serge degrading physically as mentally by his forced prostitution, Sarah raged more. "You have to struggle somehow against your slavery."

But Serge just smiled sadly at her naivety, wearily brushing his marvelous locks, in which Sarah so longed to sink her hands. The declarations of love, which the boy longed to hear, seemed to Sarah a very high price for such impermanent pleasure.

Warrior

Sarah was determined to free Serge from the mafia. She had some hazy concept of the danger involved in confronting members of the criminal circles. However, she realized that she needed some physically strong support, but her teenage mates were too young and inexperienced. Suddenly, Sarah remembered the demobilized army officer who once had come in her school at a "lesson of courage" to give a lecture about his military service. He'd impressed the fifteen-year- old girl with his strength and charisma; he'd endured the horrors of war in Afghanistan, which were unimaginable to an average person. Sarah knew his address because, being the Komsomol monitor of her form, she was obliged to deliver invitation cards concerning any patriotic arrangements to the hands of their addressee, which she always did accurately.

Approaching the decent, one-storied brick house of the soldier, Sarah examined the high iron fence encircling the structure. The skill of a true master was evident in every part of the huge fence, as well as the wish of its creator to build a defense from the world's endless problems. Nevertheless, such a frank demonstration of hostility to the outside world, which was so familiar to her, convinced Sarah of the rightness of her choice.

After knocking lightly on the steel gate, she heard a dog's raging bark in the yard. Waiting for an opening, Sarah listened keenly to every sound behind the gate: unhurried steps and man's authoritative voice shouting at the dog. Then the gate opened.

A tall, broad shouldered man in creased jeans and mules stood before Sarah. His naked bosom and arms were covered densely with tattoos, which moved in accordance with the rippling motion of his muscles. It was Oleg. The man was in his middle twenties, ten years older than Sarah. Scrutinizing the girl's womanly stature, from her head to her fingertips, he waited for Sarah to explain her purpose.

The girl, who had already forgotten the man's substantial dimensions, became confused for a moment. "Hi ..." she said at last, mumbling irresolutely and moving back. "I might have some business for you ..."

"Really?" Oleg smirked, looking away from the curves of Sarah's tempting figure, accentuated by her tight-fitting blouse and skirt. "Welcome." He pointed to his house. But Sarah was suddenly embarrassed, realizing it was improper to go alone into a bachelor's dwelling.

Indeed, the former Soviet warrior-internationalist had lived alone for a long while. He was weary of girls, who invariably ran away from the ex-soldier, regardless of his attractiveness. They simply couldn't endure the man's constant depressions and nervousness; the echo of war in his mind was made louder by his habitual intemperance.

Oleg had his eye glued to Sarah, gazing at her the way a boa might look at a rabbit. The girl sensed his undressing leer with all her essence. *Idiot*, she thought as she studied the statuesque Oleg, ironically imitating the reverence of a doorkeeper. *Isn't it hard for such a stately man to find a girlfriend?*

"Why?" Sarah asked, smiling in response to his invitation. Simulating undue familiarity, she suspiciously examined the man's unshaven face, which was swollen with spirits. "Let's sit just here." She moved toward a wooden bench near the fence.

Oleg agreed with her, trying to hide his disappointment that he had alarmed the girl with his uncared-for appearance. After lighting a cigarette, he sat down on the bench not far from Sarah. He crossed his legs and leaned with his naked back against the steel fence, avoiding a direct stare at the young child who had unexpectedly dropped by.

The stink of his cheap cigarette immediately drove all ideas out of Sarah's head. Having dispersed the terrible smoke with her hand, she began her detailed narration about Serge and her wish to help him.

Oleg listened attentively without saying a word, sometimes flipping ashes from his cigarette. He sat peering at the earth before him, as if all answers to any questions could be found there.

Having finished her story, Sarah waited for his reaction, which, she was certain, should be affirmative. But Oleg was silent. Finally, looking at Sarah as if he were a man who longed for a woman's company, he stubbed out his cigarette against the bench.

"High-sounding nonsense," he said and exhaled the last smoke, irritating Sarah with it. "Listen here, baby. Are you not right in your head? Why do you meddle? If you want my advice, leave the rent-boy and find someone normal ... like me, for example." He moved closer to the girl, pressing down her tightly fitted skirt with his hip.

Sarah abruptly slipped off the bench and stood up. "I should have expected this," she muttered as if addressing herself. Then she hurried away with resolute steps, not offering a goodbye.

With several long strides, Oleg approached Sarah. "Sorry!" he uttered, confusing the girl again as he stood with his powerful torso blocking her way. "I don't want to hurt you ... but you are a grown-up girl and must understand that not everything can be changed at your pleasure."

"That's it!" Sarah said, interrupting Oleg. "There should be nothing more exchanged, if even such warriors as you would prefer indifference to injustice. My boyfriend extinguished his brother's debt long ago! Is it a miracle to give him a chance of a normal life?"

Oleg gazed at the girl with wonder. As an ex-bruiser, he usually argued with his fists, not with his words. Now he did not quite know how to talk to this remarkable girl, although her youthful enthusiasm excited him.

"Oh well," he said suddenly, making up his mind to play up to Sarah's naive aspiration to create justice in the cruel human herd. "Introduce me to your oddball boyfriend."

In a few minutes, after changing his mules for sneakers and putting on a black T-shirt, Oleg accompanied Sarah to the bar, where Serge now waited.

Having approached silently from behind, Sarah touched Serge's shoulder. The boy started nervously as usual and glanced back. He was playing with an earring he had removed from his lobe.

"At long last! One solid hour I've been wondering where you could be ..." Suddenly, the boy encountered Oleg's scathing eyes and fell silent.

"Let me introduce ..." Sarah began the procedure of acquaintance, overlooking the fellows' strange squints.

"Unnecessary!" Oleg snapped.

"What?" Sarah asked, not understanding.

"There's no need to introduce us!" Oleg repeated in the same icy tone.

"Hi, Relative!" Oleg now addressed Serge, coming up to him and clapping on his nape so strongly that the boy's blond hair flew to different sides.

"Oh!" Sarah sighed. She was bewildered.

"He's my second cousin," Serge said reproachfully, clenching his teeth and rubbing the back of his head with annoyance. "Where did you find him?" he whispered to Sarah. "It'll begin now ..."

Sarah sat down at the table in front of Serge while Oleg approached the bar and ordered vodka. Having drunk straight from the bottle, he returned to the table where the couple was sitting.

"You! Gangster's hot stuff!" he mocked Serge, piercing his second cousin with scornful look. "Have you got a taste for girls? The charm of novelty?"

Serge tried to ignore the big man's taunts, but Oleg had already fondled the boy's long locks with his powerful hand. Suddenly, he grabbed Serge's blond hair and yanked back his head.

"Dreamboat!" Oleg whispered maliciously near the boy's flinching lips. "Even I want you!" His fingers brushed Serge's face as if taking delight in touching the fine skin. "But where's your make-up? You have an unmarketable appearance!"

Everyone in the bar gazed at the entertaining conversation.

Resigned to the pain and mockery, Serge set his dark eyes with detachment. He seemed to shrink into himself, looking inward for some reprieve from reality. Suddenly Oleg yanked the boy's hair so harshly that Serge scarcely flopped from the chair. "Am I doing all this correctly? Does it start like this?"

Having lost his patience, Serge cast a leer at Oleg's eyes and answered sardonically. "Not nearly ... there's something more voluptuous for me ..." At the same moment, the boy jabbed the needle-sharp end of his golden earring into the arm that was squeezing his hair. Oleg ignored his hurt arm, but flung Serge, still in his chair, against a wall.

"Let him be!" Sarah exclaimed as she jumped up and rushed toward Oleg. She blocked his path to Serge, but Oleg continued approaching slowly and pertly, giving the boy a chance to get up before the next strike. Sneering and watching Sarah in front of him, Oleg said derisively, "That's rich! Will you defend this abominable creature? If you really consider 'it' as your boyfriend, let him to demonstrate his manhood, at least! Besides, I never fight with women. Your place is in the auditorium."

He suddenly picked up Sarah, who hardly reached the man's chin and seemed to weigh nothing, in his athletic arms. Having sat the girl like a big doll on an empty table, Oleg intended to return to his helpless cousin, who hadn't the strength even to stand up. But when the man moved from Sarah, he sensed her hand imperiously holding the belt of his jeans. Feeling Sarah's fingers on his muscular stomach through the thin fabric of his T-shirt, the drunken and excited Oleg clasped the girl to himself. He tried to kiss her, whispering, "Let's go to my cubby hole. I like inaccessible and mettled women."

"Really? All the more, it's incomprehensible. Why are you so intolerant?" Sarah demanded, not even attempting to avoid his powerful lips. "You like mettled women, but I prefer sensitive men."

"What?" Oleg shoved Sarah, who fell back onto the table. Devouring the girl with his insatiable eyes, he whispered, "Cursed lesbian!"

"You are a man of vision!" Sarah laughed at Oleg's frenzy blending with his lust. "Some of my ancestry really belonged to the mythical Amazons, who lived somewhere in the Southern Ukraine. They did without men in general!"

Finding no compromise between his wish to answer the girl's insolence and his strong desire for her, Oleg muttered, "In that case, it's not clear how you appeared in this devilish world ... without a man's participation." Having slapped Sarah's sharply delineated hip with vexation, he added, "Snooty girl. Thank God you're not a man!" Oleg wobbled out of the bar and slammed its door so harshly that windowpanes rattled.

Sarah approached Serge, who was still sitting on the floor near the wall and wiped his bloodstained face with his hand. "How are you?" she asked.

"Thanks. It's in the order of things ..." he replied crossly. Then he stood, suggestively grasping the waistband of her skirt.

"I had rather he killed me," Serge said. The boy pulled Sarah to himself by her waistband, sensing she was thrilled with his jealousy.

"I'll pay respect to it," Sarah whispered, licking her fingers and wiping the remaining blood on the boy's face. "But if you'll repeat each of my foolish acts so pleasantly, I'll do them exclusively for you."

Inspecting the boy's chiseled features and his incomparable white hair, Sarah uttered, "Funny. You're relatives, but so different. Your cousin is great fun in his own way ..."

Seeing that Sarah took delight in teasing him, Serge said, irritatingly, "There is nothing special about Oleg. He's just a senseless mass of muscles. In sex, he's an infant ..."

"How do you know that?" Sarah whispered, losing the logic of their conversation and pressing Serge with his back against the wall. Just as she was going to lick her finger and wipe Serge's face again, the boy caught it tenderly with his teeth. Licking her finger and seeing the girl became a hostage of her lust finally, Serge could no longer stand Sarah's hanging on his neck. "Quick ... say that you love me ..." the boy whispered hotly in her ear. But Sarah merely curled her lips, silently choking with desire and recollecting with difficulty the last phrase of their talking. "How do you know about Oleg?"

"I was intimate with him!" Serge pronounced crossly, realizing Sarah was defying his wiles. When he released the girl from his neck, she sat, disappointed, on a stool. Sarah was slightly sobered after her fit of lust, and now her spirits drooped, because of Serge's either crushing candor or filthy joke. After sitting on the floor near her feet and permitting her to rumple his divine hair, Serge bit his lips bitterly. He did not understand why Sarah tormented them both with her stubbornness ... as if it were really so hard for her to say the words of love to him.

'Friends in need ...'

It was already deep night when Sarah and Serge left the bar. Keeping silent, they approached a bridge across the river that divided the town into two vast districts. Youth gangs inhabiting each area were always at war with one another.

Sarah glanced at Serge, who seemed immersed in some meditation. She didn't want to break silence first, competing with the boy in contrariness. They reached the bridge, which was illuminated with numerous street lamps. However, just as they reached the middle of the bridge, Sarah and Serge saw a boisterous, free-and-easy company straggling from the opposite bank of the river. The crowd appeared so unexpectedly and was so near that the couple could contrive nothing to escape passing by them.

Spicing their language with expletives, the horde approached Sarah and Serge, blocking their way.

"Hi, girls! Isn't it boring without us?" An athletic broad-shouldered boy went ahead, moving close to Serge, whom he, as usual, had mistaken for a girl. Shielding Sarah with his body,

Serge stepped toward the boy.

"Be gone!" he whispered to Sarah over his shoulder. "I'll stay with them ..."

"I won't leave you!" Sarah answered just as quietly.

"I said, scram! Just as they get close to me ... I'll get their attention," Serge hissed crossly. He languidly smiled at the boys and shook his wonderful hair, which shone temptingly in the neon light.

"And what'll be next?" Sarah muttered, watching her friend's affectation. She seemed spellbound, either by his effeminacy or his artistry. But Serge did not answer; he was waiting until she could get away.

Nevertheless, Sarah stood still.

Suddenly the randy boy, who had first paid attention to Serge and constantly tried to kiss him, recoiled. "Devil! It's a fag!"

In a blink, his hand glanced to the hip pocket of his jeans and the blade of a barlow knife flashed in the light. Serge jumped back, but the other boys, who surrounded him, stopped his retreat.

Sarah saw her friend collapsed on asphalt, pressing his hands to his throat. She dashed up to him, ignoring the danger, and shouldering everybody out of her way. Sarah knelt beside her friend, who was sitting on asphalt and writhing with pain. She tried to help Serge stanch the flow of blood from the cut on his throat, but it was useless. The boy's snow-white hair was already bloodstained, as were Sarah's hands and clothes. Senselessly clasping Serge's head to her breast, Sarah sat frozen. She was in shock, as if time had stopped.

The rabble disbanded, and a militiaman, who appeared out of nowhere, asked Sarah something. But she heard only the pulse in her temples. She felt Serge's weakened hands releasing his cut throat slowly. He was already unconsciousness.

The militiaman called for an ambulance, and when it arrived at last, Serge was placed in it and taken to hospital. Sarah did not move a step from him.

While doctors were struggling to save the boy's life, the weeping Sarah sat on a shabby settee in the corridor of the municipal hospital, all night long. Just toward early morning, a tenderhearted nurse gave the girl some sleeping medication, which helped her to doze off and cease her self-reproaches.

Sarah awaked with a terrible headache and realized she could barely stand; her sore back had seemingly imitated the shape of the settee. She went to look for the doctor who had first treated Serge, and found him just around a corner.

"How is he, doc?"

"Lucky," the grey-haired man answered wearily. "A couple of millimeters deeper, and we could not have saved your friend. He is sleeping now. The doctor stared at Sarah's eyes, which were swollen with tears. "Deary, you have to look after yourself now. Don't worry. About nightfall, you'll be able to see your treasure."

Later, when Sarah entered Serge's ward, she saw the boy in bed with a bandaged neck. The cold scents of blood still streaked his hair. Serge was very pale, and his smile was ghastly.

"Nevermore will do it," he whispered. His breathing was labored. He closed eyes to savor the sensation of Sarah sitting near him on the bed. "I was scared stiff," he whispered. "Can you imagine if that boy hadn't had a knife? They might have had no reason to scatter ..." Serge nervously squeezed Sarah's wrist, smiling sadly at her weak attempt to free her hand.

"Well," Sarah managed, no longer trying to escape the boy's grip, "I'm obliged to you, after all ... but I don't know how to thank you." She wanted to explain her hesitation; Serge was always so nervous when she suggested intimacy. Besides, it seemed impossible in his weakened state. But suddenly, Serge pulled the girl to him. Having pressed Sarah under his body, he kissed her lips with a desire she had never felt from him before. Surprised, Sarah felt devilish fire flowing in her veins instead of blood, when their heated lips fused together.

"You know what kind of thanks I prefer," Serge whispered, fanning the flame with his unexpected passion. "I know that you love me ... but I want to hear it."

Sarah clenched her teeth, not opening her eyes after the dizzying kiss.

"You are a devil," she said, sensing Serge's inhuman efforts to quench his natural desire.

"Maybe," he whispered, baring Sarah's breast and gliding over her, intoxicated by the scent of the girl's flesh. "But it's not a strong argument for an atheist like you. Why couldn't you love me? You are an angel; I'm a devil. In any case, we are the gist of spiritual reality uniting our souls." The boy was overacting, obviously, trying to please Sarah's fervent idealism. Still, his words carried her away into the illusory world, where her beloved Stranger existed.

The Stranger embodied perfection and the harmony of the Universe to her mind. Only he was worthy of her frenetic love.

Realizing that Serge's sage reasoning had destroyed her animal passion, Sarah covered her breast and moved out from under his body.

"Why?" Serge asked in a whisper, surprised by her inexplicable inconsistency.

"You must rest," Sarah answered, casting down her eyes as if her friend should be able to see there something intelligible concerning her behavior.

"Wait!" Serge beseeched without releasing Sarah's hand, trying to keep her in bed. "That was my first kiss with a girl!"

"Mine as well," Sarah said reservedly. "My first ... with a gay-boy."

The next day, Oleg stood on the threshold of Sarah's flat. He had already inquired into the girl's name and address and had learned of her and Serge's night adventure. Shifting from one foot to another in the small hallway of Sarah's flat, Oleg appeared to be neatly dressed and smooth-shaven. It was as if, during the night, he had made up his mind to match the girl, regardless of her age. He began with an apology for his poor manners and drunken tricks in the bar. Sarah listened coldly, wearily examining his taut, muscular figure.

"If you took notice, it was your raff second cousin, who protected me from the danger on the bridge," Sarah said, interrupting Oleg without ceremony. "So he proved he is my boyfriend." She went in the parlor, leaving Oleg to stand at the door, showing him the highest degree of her contempt.

Sensing that the girl didn't understand the actual danger of Serge's presence in her life, Oleg had an irresistible impulse to remain with Sarah at any cost.

"I thought about your proposition to help Serge!" the man said, elevating his voice. He couldn't see Sarah and didn't venture to intrude into the home without her invitation. Therefore, he began speaking louder. "Of course, it'll be quite troublesome," Oleg continued with a concerned voice. "But ..." In a blink, Sarah stood before him. Her eyes sparkled with joy and a fervent faith in the inevitable triumph of justice; she seemed to be a naive child, believing in the happy end of fairy-tales.

"Jeez! Come in!" she exclaimed. "Why are you standing out there like a poor relative?!"

Serge slowly recovered. Meanwhile, Oleg patronized Sarah in the absence of her boyfriend. Sarah begged Oleg to allow Serge to eventually stay in his big house until they could free the boy from the tenacious claws of the mafia.

"Baby talk," Oleg grouched, listening to Sarah's suggestions, which bordered on foolishness. "It's impossible for a person to hide in our small town. Besides, it's dangerous enough. Serge is profitable for his *souteneurs*, and they won't allow his disappearance."

"Please ...he's so weak yet," Sarah entreated. She sat near the man on the bench at the fence of his house. She was, as usual, reluctant to enter the house. Absently listening to her, Oleg crossly rasped away at a plank that was necessary for some project in his household.

"Never," he mumbled.

Anxious to reconcile the cousins, Sarah pronounced with confidence, putting her hand on Oleg's muscle-bound haunch, "Do it. You'll see ... I can be grateful. I'll do what you want." Suddenly, she realized she had gone too far in her request.

Intrigued, Oleg scrutinized Sarah's hand on his leg and observed her embarrassment. "What's the use of promising what you'll never do?" he asked reservedly.

"So you're saying no!" Sarah fired back, removing her hand from Oleg's haunch. "Well, if it comes to that ..."

"I'm saying yes!" Oleg snapped. Suddenly, he grabbed Sarah's leg so painfully that she almost jumped up.

"Take into account, it's not so easy to slake me in bed," he whispered, touching the girl's ear with his lips. As if accidentally, he flipped up her skirt, even though they sat outside. "So spare yourself!" the man added crossly. He was tired of Sarah's getting on his nerves with empty promises.

Serge had been living in Oleg's house for two months after his discharge from hospital. The boy didn't believe Sarah's interference in his accustomed life would change anything, but he was afraid to betray her hopes that he might once again have a normal life. Serge fibbed to his mother, saying he would like to live in Oleg's house because it was close to the boy's school, which he almost didn't attend. He made use of his puissant patrons who rather preferred the boy in bed with them. At first, it really seemed that Sarah's simple plan had worked, and Serge had gotten out of sight of his mafia bosses.

Sarah constantly pressed Oleg, compelling him to look for a better outcome. Nevertheless, she always ran into his blunt response: Oleg explained that trying to save Serge was simply impossible.

One autumn night, Serge called on Sarah.

"What's up?" she muttered in the receiver after hearing the boy's soft voice. She had been nearly asleep.

"I've called a taxi for you. It's just at your porch," Serge said enigmatically.

"What for? Are you crazy?"

"I'm waiting."

Trying not to wake Oleg, who slept in a nearby room, Sarah entered Serge's quiet, dark room only a quarter of an hour after he called. She sat on the edge of his double bed, where Serge lay quietly scrutinizing Sarah through the semi-darkness.

"What do you want?" the girl asked wearily, wanting only to sleep.

Serge sat near her, and Sarah noticed his nakedness, despite the cool October night. He was dressed only in underwear. "Is it too hot here?" she asked drowsily.

"Not yet," Serge answered with some agitation. "But I hope that it will be ..." He squatted in front of Sarah and parted her knees with a light gesture. The girl woke up finally, trying to restrain her racing heart.

"Maybe," she said with quiver, "I should give you my jacket."

"The rest of your clothes as well," Serge whispered. He pushed Sarah back with gentle persistence. He undressed the girl with such a knack that Sarah's next awareness of herself was being naked under his hot body.

"What are you doing? Can you do this ... with girls?" Completely nonplussed, Sarah assailed him with questions.

"You're very inquisitive. But I really can't answer you right now ..." Serge slid along Sarah's body with burning lips and covered her with his long hair.

Sensing that the girl was unable to resist his fire and had sunk into the same, wild concupiscence, Serge brought his lips closer to hers.

"Please, stop tormenting me," he whispered. "I love you so lustily."

Sarah called his bluff. "I also ... want you."

Serge wilted, still hugging her in his arms, "What have you said? I probably misheard ..." the boy whispered, deeply agitated.

"The bane of my life! What else must I do to persuade you that it's your sole chance to prove that you are a male?" Sarah clutched Serge's naked forearms as if she were afraid he would disappear from her embrace.

"I'm going to prove nothing without your love!" Serge whispered, almost choking with his angry lust.

"I want you, and that is quite enough for any normal male," Sarah said, justifying herself while trying to stir up the boy. But

Serge suddenly was steeped in meditation, mechanically caressing her naked body.

"Well ..." he uttered sadly, "you make me do this. Unfortunately, I can't endure your endless mockery. If you are so ashamed of your attachment to me, I have no choice but to force you to say me about your love."

"Haven't you?" Sarah grinned with surprise, sensing Serge was freeing himself gently from her hands. "It's interesting. By which way?" she asked, watching the boy sitting in the bed and switching a lamp-bracket hanging on the wall.

"Easily." Having settled comfortably among the bedding they had thrown about, Serge closed his eyes and remained motionless for several moments. His long, blond hair covered his face, making him look a white-haired magus concentrating his magical powers.

Meantime, squinting in the lamp's light, Sarah slowly crept up on all fours to the boy. Her aim was to lay him back in bed. Suddenly, Serge shook his locks from his face and glanced at the approaching Sarah, giving her his entrancing, dark look. "Repeat after me," he said as Sarah paused not far from him. "I ... love ...you." She smirked, supposing it was a joke. But unexpectedly, Sarah felt unable to avert her eyes from Serge's look. She sat in the bed in front of him. Her usual self-control was falling away against the background of a drowsiness brought about by his low voice. Sarah's will became pliant under the boy's strange look. It seemed she really would do whatever he wanted.

Struggling to overcome the hypnotic trance, Sarah pronounced spitefully, "Do you think you have some power over me? Nothing of the kind! It's me who uses your love as a medicine for my exhausted soul. I need you, boy, but not so close ..."

Unexpectedly, she pushed away Serge. Being enmeshed in the bed linen, he lost his balance and struck his head against the backboard of the bed. Paying no more attention to him, Sarah looked for her clothes among the sheets and blankets. Having got out of the bed at last and beginning to dress herself, she ignored Serge until he appeared near her again.

"Vanish, downer!" Sarah growled, perceiving his closeness, but avoiding the boy's gaze. Nevertheless, Serge stood still near her. As if accidentally, Sarah glanced sideways at his face and nearly fainted with horror. The scleras of his eyes were black, and fiery shadows flashed in their hellish abyss. It seemed as if two empty holes yawned on his delicate face. At the same moment, Serge's hand grasped her throat and hoisted her from the floor. Sarah lost the sensation of footing.

"Angel's spawn ... you belong to hell," she heard the distinct, icy voice. It had no feeling, and sounded as if it came from out of the beyond.

Suffocating and fluttering in Serge's close grip, Sarah clutched at the boy's arm, trying to free her throat. She didn't sense her left palm become wet with blood from her cross-shaped scar. When Sarah's red hand touched Serge's arm, his incredible force vanished at once. He dropped the girl and crashed, unconscious, to the floor.

Barely able to get up, Sarah was in tears. She felt choked with hysterics as she backed away from Serge's body. Pressing her bloodstained hand to her throat, she whispered with deep horror, "Loony ...There isn't any hell! It may be just in your mind, because you are mental ... you have a split personality."

Sarah didn't realize, in her shocked state, that the heavy bleeding from her palm threatened her life now, no less than Serge did several minutes ago. Backing away, Sarah collided with someone standing behind her in the faintly illuminated room. Terrified, she cried out and jumped away.

The Stranger from her child's dream, who was branded on her heart, studied naked Sarah with his fascinating, dark eyes. The man's incredible attractiveness imbued her soul with inexplicable beatitude. The Stranger came up to Sarah resolutely and took her bloodstained hand, stanching the wound immediately. Feeling his elegant, tapered fingers interwoven with her own, staggering from fear and a considerable lost of blood, Sarah sensed an unbearable sinking in her body. Unexpectedly, she snuggled against the man's bosom, feeling the delicate touch of his hand against her naked back and his light breath on her shoulder.

Sarah was eager to kiss the ambrosial, deep-brown curls that were touching her cheek, but she couldn't pretend doing it. Sarah was losing consciousness with their physical contiguity, as she had at their first meeting. Nearly senseless with bliss, she just whispered, "Neither your incomparable eyes nor your unmercifully affectionate hands can convince me of your reality. Why do I long for you so much?"

After awaking in Serge's bed the next morning, Sarah was appalled. The room resembled a gas chamber. Looking over the small apartment through the turbid, pungent smoke-cloud that saturated it, Sarah at last noticed Oleg sitting on a chair. He had crossed his legs, and he was smoking right in the room, without opening a window.

"That beats everything! One more idiot!" Sarah exclaimed. Having forgotten her nakedness, she jumped out of bed and rushed to the window, opening it wide.

Oleg sullenly studied at vague figure of the girl, which was unclear in the smoke.

"Maybe I'm an idiot," he said crossly, glancing at Serge, who was still lying on the floor next to his bed. " But what are you doing here?" The man glanced at Sarah again, now devouring her nudity with jealous grey eyes.

"Exactly what you have thought about!" Sarah said, flinging the words at his teeth. She didn't wish to justify herself and reveal that Oleg's lustful look really confused her.

Oleg got up quickly and approached her. "Well, children ..." he pronounced with the same irritated tone. "So, you have a pastime. Now I understand why you talked me into taking him into my house." Oleg nodded toward the motionless Serge, who was dressed only in underwear. The man pulled deeply at his cigarette and contemptuously exhaled the puffs of disgusting smoke out of his powerful lungs at Sarah's face.

Coughing and angry, Sarah burst out, "Unbelievable! When I don't love men, you are angry! When I try to make a man of your cousin, you are angry, too!"

"Indeed," Oleg smirked, realizing she was just scoffing at his attraction to her. He turned back and approached Serge.

"Stand up, Romeo!" the man demanded in a military tone. He toed Serge slightly, and the boy stirred.

Oleg once more evaluated Sarah's naked body with such a penetrating look that she wanted all the clothes of the world to cover her. Sarah grabbed a sheet from the bed and draped it around her body like the tunic of a Roman patrician. At last, Oleg left the room.

Slowly rising and squeezing his head with his hands, Serge asked Sarah perplexedly, "What's the matter with me? Why am I here?"

"You fell off of the bed!" Sarah replayed him sarcastically.

"Maybe you forgot also that you called me here in the midst of the night?"

"No, I remember it," the boy answered, bewildered. "But my mind is completely blank concerning our possible intimacy."

Sarah laughed. "Perfect! Always say so! It sounds very manlike!" She was examining Serge aimlessly loitering about the room with his bad headache and partial amnesia. The girl expected to find some of her blood in the room, but she discovered nothing. Seeing silent Serge standing next to the open window and wrapping up his naked torso in his long hair, Sarah addressed him reflectively. "Funny ... it seems we both have to cure our heads."

One autumn evening, Sarah and Oleg walked along the street downtown. Since Serge had been living in the man's house, Oleg always escorted the girl in such crowded places. Walking with a bodyguard seemed to Sarah very amusing, but Oleg insisted that he knew more about criminals than the reckless young girl did.

Oleg smoked too much, and Sarah almost choked. Changing from the left to the right side of her companion every time the wind shifted, the girl walked along the curb near a busy road. As the cars' exhausts were no better than Oleg's smoking, Sarah was about to ask him to step away from the road. But at the same moment, a passer-by asked Oleg to light a cigarette.

The man seemed on the alert for something. But gazing around, he noticed nothing unusual ... just scurrying people and the cars of rush hour. Besides, the plaintive voice of the young boy awoke in Oleg's mind complete understanding and compassion. Searching for his lighter, Oleg lost sight of Sarah for a moment. In a flash, a screech sounded behind the girl and strong arms enfolded her, pulling Sarah inside a car. Before she could collect herself, her head struck the frame of the vehicle, and the same hands roughly covered her mouth.

Then the car was gone.

Shocked, Sarah sat between two men on the rear seat of the car. Two men sat in the front. All kept silent. Having driven nearly two blocks from downtown, the vehicle stopped and Sarah was pushed out of it.

She was in a deserted park located near a small, but deep, lake. She noticed that another car drove behind the first, and now eight huge men got out of both vehicles. They looked much older than Sarah. Their leers were beastly. Squeezing their brass knuckles and clinking with the joints of their formidable fingers, they approached the terrified girl. Sarah's fearful look was fixed upon the holsters visible under their leather jackets. *No*, she thought fearfully. *They'll simply drown me, not shoot ... after all ...*

Suddenly, the men stopped. Only one of the advancing flounced about Sarah as if wishing to grasp her.

"Where is he?" the mob asked. He didn't leave Sarah in peace.

"Who?" she simpered with false concern, avoiding the man's touch.

"Serge!"

"I don't know," Sarah replied, feigning naivety.

At the same moment, she ducked, instinctively dodging the brass knuckles that whistled past her temple. Sarah's short stature had served her well. But the kick in her solar plexus drove her to the brink of the lake. After rolling down a slope into the cold October water, she jumped up, feeling no pain in the rush of adrenaline.

I must swim, was the only thought in Sarah's head. But instead, she plopped without consciousness into the lake, which numbed her with unbearable autumn cold.

As she opened her eyes, Sarah saw Oleg. She rested with her head in the man's lap. Having stationed themselves on the rear seat of a taxi, the couple was on their way to the nearest hospital.

Trying to gently wipe the girl's face, Oleg merely spread more dirt over Sarah's cheeks. Taking his hand and inspecting the man's bloody phalanges, Sarah asked weakly, "Was it necessary to fight?" Oleg smiled, neatly freeing his hand from Sarah's.

"Are you jeering?" he asked with wonder. "Maybe I look brave enough, but battling eight gunmen is too much even for me."

Studying Oleg's bare bosom, Sarah belatedly realized she was dressed in his pullover and jerkin, whereas her legs were naked and icy.

"What's this?" she exclaimed, indignantly inspecting Oleg's clothing on her. "How can we go to the hospital like this?"

"Don't be so worried. Who will be interested in your appearance in hospital? Besides, your clothes are soaked."

The man sustained a conversation, discussing Sarah's decorum with such zeal that she again fixed her suspicious eyes on his powerful hands.

"Well ..." Sarah whispered. Her stomach throbbed from the kick. "Tell me, how could I escape those degenerates?"

Oleg was carefully wrapping the girl in his jerkin. "Isn't it the topmost?" he replied unwillingly. "You got off easy, and that's the main thing. The end justifies the means."

But Sarah stood her ground, staring down the man and lost in wild conjectures.

"They looked like scoundrels. How could you stop them? I want the truth! How long will you play the fool with me?!" Combating the pain in her solar plexus, Sarah was ready to claw at Oleg's naked chest. His furtiveness was insulting.

Realizing it was impossible to hide his deception, Oleg uttered with annoyance, "Damn, why do you always complicate everything?

I know them! Not long ago, I earned my living by the same trading in prostitution ... is that what you wanted to clarify?"

Sarah stared with astonishment.

"You? With them?" She almost jumped up, instinctively pressing with her hand the painful area on her stomach, but Oleg's steely hands suppressed her. "But why?"

Keeping Sarah from unnecessary motions, Oleg glanced at her, as if he saw an extraterrestrial. "Nothing personal with this world. It was all for the sake of making money. Besides, battlecraft is the sole occupation, which I use skillfully. In the upshot, I killed nobody here without counting a couple dozen broken noses and ribs. But it's incomparable with my service in Afghanistan ..."

Listening to Oleg's unconvincing self-justifications, incredible revulsion suddenly seized Sarah. In spite of her rescue by Oleg, the girl saw him as unprincipled and venal.

"So," she said, unable to restrain her resentment, "you were not going to help Serge ..."

"Of course not!" Oleg snapped, losing his temper. "Nobody could do that! But I was able to save you from Serge's lot after your inevitable encounter with his patrons. Do you ever think about the consequences of messing with my unlucky cousin?"

"Don't speak his name!" Sarah exclaimed, as if it were some sacrilege in Oleg's words. "You may not hold him up to shame! You are much worse! Serge is just a victim of brute force, but you ..."

Suddenly she pressed her face to Oleg's hairy bosom, which was covered with tattoos. Tears washed over her dirty face and the man's chest.

"There," Oleg whispered, pecking Sarah's wet hair. "It's too much water for tonight. I didn't create this world with all of its cruelty." But Sarah wept bitterly, disregarding his heartfelt whisper.

"My tattoos will be dissolved by your tears," the man joked feebly. At the same time, he carefully touched Sarah's icy legs, preoccupied with her immediate warming, which he knew was so necessary to the girl after her chill.

Suddenly, Oleg glanced archly at the crying Sarah.

At the same moment, she stopped sobbing and stared at the man, her sparkling eyes even greener from the tears. "What are you doing?" she hissed, feeling Oleg's hand sliding along her hip.

Hardly restraining his laugh at Sarah's quizzical reaction, Oleg pronounced, "I'll warm you at last." The man's hot hand squeezed Sarah's cold buttock.

"What?" She darted from Oleg's hands, having cried out so loudly that the cabdriver hit the brakes and skidded to a stop near the ditch. "Not for the world!"

"Oh yeah? Isn't your pretty-pretty rent-boy much better?" Oleg scoffed. At the same time, he was surprised by Sarah's strong resistance.

Oleg embraced her tightly, twisting her arms behind her back. He whispered, taking sexual delight at Sarah's pluck in his arms, "Good girl ...you can warm yourself, if you don't want me doing it. Or you'll really regret wasting your time with your gay boyfriend."

At last, Sarah and Oleg burst into the room of a doctor on duty of a hospital. Hardly restraining the quarrelsome girl, who constantly tried to scratch him, Oleg pulled up Sarah time and again "Enough! Behave yourself!" he reworded again and again. But at the same time, Oleg was roaring with laughter. He found no strength to avoid the temptation of touching Sarah's naked legs.

A young physician, who had been peacefully slumbering near a writing table in the spacious room, awoke to the unexpected noise. The doctor dropped his head, which he propped up with his fist. He could barely see the strange, half-dressed couple cuddling each other in his room in the nighttime. Fixing his drowsy eyes on a barelegged girl dressed in a man's hard jerkin and attacking a strapping man, who relished her aggressiveness, the doctor said, "Young people! Are you drunk?"

Dying with laughter and exhausted from fighting with Sarah, who flew into rage after his attempts to play with her like a toy, Oleg replied, "Nothing of the kind! I can't imagine her drunk!"

The physician gathered himself and said, as authoritatively as he could, "Out! This isn't a brothel!"

"What a pity!" Oleg laughed, playfully defending himself from Sarah's strikes. "The matter is, a brothel isn't suitable for us." Now he bantered, seizing Sarah and clasping her to his muscular body. "You see, my girl reacts badly to the opinion of people about her moral image. So, doc, I'd be very obliged to you if, making use of your authority, you would pick out a small room for us." Oleg's eloquent gesture of a man feeling for cash in the breast pocket of his jerkin awoke the doctor finally. But instead of pulling out money, the hint at which the physician perceived so literally, Oleg squeezed Sarah's nipple.

"I'm fed up!" Sarah cried, pushing off from the man so strongly that she plopped to the floor. After jumping up, the girl threw anything she could find at Oleg. In her rage, she hardly appreciated the value of medical supplies appearing in her hands. Hot-water bottles, plastic syringes, and packs of cotton wool turned the room into chaos. Watching the outrage, the doctor leapt up and exclaimed, "Pack it in! Or I'll call militia!"

Oleg laughed, "Militia ... so, soon we'll see the same men who abducted you not long ago. Except they'll be dressed in their regular militia uniform. Do you like men in uniform?"

"I hate all of you!" Sarah hissed, rushing about the doctor's table and avoiding Oleg's attempts to catch her.

"Come here, man-hater, I won't touch you," Oleg whispered, beckoning the girl. But seeing that Sarah had worn herself out at last, he sat on a couch.

The doctor took his place at his table as well. He was upset, squeezing his temples with his fingers. "Idiots! Indeed, a bedlam exactly for you."

"Sorry, doc," Oleg said, still ironically. "I'll tidy up. It's just my non-traditional way of warming her up." He nodded toward Sarah and squinted at the girl, who was almost falling down with fatigue. Cautiously sidling up to the couch, she craved only rest. Suddenly Oleg rushed to Sarah, scooping her up. He sensed with satisfaction that her legs had grown blood hot.

Putting the girl on the couch and mopping the drops of sweat from her face, Oleg wrapped her in a coverlet. Exhausted, but breathing too excitedly, Sarah sank into a daze. Oleg squatted at the couch, wearily keeping her wrist in his hand. His fingers were still quivering with lust, which always accompanied his nervous irritability after his shell-shock in Afghanistan. He tried to inhibit his desire by concentrating on the girl's pulse.

At last, the doctor came up to Oleg and cast a leer at Sarah's heaving breast. "What passion ..." he whispered. But being engaged with the counting of Sarah's pulse, Oleg paid no attention to his words.

"And what about a separate room?" the physician said more loudly, addressing the motionless Oleg. "Were you serious?"

Oleg glanced vacantly up at him.

"Yes, indeed." He had not cooled down after flirting with Sarah. Now he scrutinized the doctor, who was nearly the same age as him. "Is it possible?"

"There is nothing impossible in principle," the doctor replied, without apprehending Oleg's facetious tone. "It should be even free of charge," he added with some confusion.

"Curiously enough!" Oleg said as he slowly rose. His countenance became stern. "What's behind it all?" He approached the retreating doctor, who cast glances at Sarah. "I think true men always come to accord," the physician muttered. He realized belatedly that the good-for-nothing girl wasn't worth his standing in awe of Oleg's formidable fists.

Having been driven into the wall by Oleg's punch, the physician collapsed in a heap of the medical supplies that had been hurled by Sarah. After lifting the doctor by the scruff of his neck, Oleg pronounced, with deep contempt, "You 'porno-star.' You ought to be proud of your noble occupation of a healer. But you travel along the same beaten path."

He threw the doctor toward the dazed Sarah so crudely that he was within an inch of falling on the girl. Nevertheless, he tried to avoid clashing with Sarah, with acrobatic virtuosity.

"Examine her! Now! In my presence!" Oleg ordered, squeezing habitually a cool knuckle in the hip pocket of his jeans. "Just one unnecessary touch, and I'll fix you up with a taste of your hoped-for Soviet arms of law. You'll never forget it!"

"It was just misunderstanding," the doctor muttered with a strained voice, carefully undressing Sarah with trembling hands.

Sarah was in the hospital for three days. Fortunately, the after-effects of her encounter with Serge's patrons were not life-threatening.

Both Serge and Oleg visited Sarah. Their silent tolerance of each other in her presence moved the girl until Oleg appeared in Sarah's ward alone on the day she was to be discharged.

"Where's Serge?"

"Ask me another question! I don't know where the devil took him!" Oleg replied with asperity.

"But ..."

"You make too much of him!" Oleg shouted. "He is a big enough boy to care for himself! Have a good head on your shoulders! You can't give him what he's used to."

"I hoped we were friends with you," Sarah uttered pensively, enduring the cross fire.

"Friendship with a female?!" the man raged. "It's just an abnormality!"

"What? Is it a hint?" Sarah was losing her self-possession, as if imbibing upon Oleg's spite. "Don't protect me any more! It's better to die than be obliged to you!"

"You are obliged!" he interrupted maliciously.

Sarah stumbled as a word faded on her lips. "Well ..." she pronounced silently, after a short pause, "I'll think over my gratitude to you."

"Will you?" Oleg didn't calm down. "It's just guff! Once I heard something like that from you! Cool it! You haven't quite enough health for the gratitude I prefer!"

His disparagement struck home. Suddenly Sarah ran up to the man, grasping his powerful forearms and sensing his steely biceps, even through his leather jerkin.

"You'll never win my dependence on your sinews!" she whispered perkily, shivering inwardly with Oleg's feverish breathing over her hair. "As I said, I prefer to settle my debts!"

"Really?" Oleg asked nervously as he clasped Sarah. "Here goes! If you are so thankful ..." Kissing the girl violently, he squeezed Sarah so strongly that her clothes bulged at the seams. But Sarah didn't resist. In spite of her silly self-conceit, she was aware that kisses were the most she could allow Oleg. But now she realized that she couldn't limit the man's urges, because of his incredible strength. However, Oleg's arms inexplicably slackened, releasing the girl.

"Why are you not opposing me?" he asked, gazing at Sarah, his big gray eyes intoxicated with lust.

"What for?" Sarah asked sadly, maintaining her composure. "It's in vain ..."

Still holding the girl's arms, Oleg whispered with vexation, "What are you doing? I can't so ..."

Suddenly, Sarah realized it was her indomitable temper that so aroused Oleg. Kissing Sarah time and again, the man tried to breathe into her the passion. But in response, he felt only her serenity.

"Unbelievable," he whispered in disappointment, setting her free again. "What's happened with you?"

Sarah just smiled enigmatically.

"So, we'll remain friends ... and your sole foible will remain a secret between us," she whispered derisively.

"What?" the man realized that Sarah had found out his Achilles' heel. "It's indecent for a female to be so acute!" He again grabbed her.

Enduring his painful caress and embracing with pleasure the man's broad shoulders, which gave Sarah the sensation of sheer protection, she replied, "I'm always at your beck and call. But I know a soldier will never harm a child." She nestled to Oleg's bosom trustfully, as if he were her father.

Standing still and looking sideways at Sarah clinging to him, Oleg pronounced perplexedly, "Damn it ... just sloppy sentimentality. Forget it. You owe me nothing."

Neither the next day nor the following ones did Serge come to

Oleg's place. Sarah phoned the boy's mother to ask after him. The woman replied that her son lived at a relative's house and hadn't been home in a long time. Otherwise, she knew nothing about him.

"What's become of him?" Sarah asked Oleg. "It's necessary to find the boy."

"I have no intention of looking for anybody!" the man snorted. "You've got very short memory." Oleg pressed upon her solar plexus, watching Sarah wince with residual pain.

"That was just the mobs' warning."

A half a year elapsed after Serge's disappearance. Sarah called on Oleg sometimes. She still cherished the hope that the man would help her to find Serge.

One fragrant May night, Sarah dropped in at Oleg's house. She entered the gate by stealth, intending to surprise him. The watchdog in the forecourt had grown accustomed to Sarah long ago. It wagged its tail, playfully tearing about the girl. After briefly playing with the dog, Sarah entered the large anteroom of Oleg's house. The girl paused. She could hear a muffled conversation in the distant living-room. Sarah identified Oleg's interlocutor soon. It was Serge.

"Why the hell you are here?" Oleg's voice rang with irritation. "You promised never come to me! Or have forgotten my phone number? You know, she looks for you here constantly. Do you want her to be involved in the same mess you're in?"

"I want to see her so badly," Serge said. His voice quivered with his repressed tears. "I die without her. It's as if we are chained together!"

"Why, of course! Chains. You've always had some fixation on them!" Oleg said with derision.

"You understand nothing about love!" Serge replied heatedly.

"But you, moll, know too much about it! Do you suppose I'll be able to withstand the criminals when their dirty claws get your love? I'm not the Lord, if you haven't noticed! I ask you in a friendly way, leave her. Play the man at least in this way."

Sarah listened with a heavy heart. Serge's touching love was a balm for her soul, which was exhausted with her senseless attachment to the illusory Stranger. An unconquerable, selfish desire gripped the girl: she wanted Serge always staying near her and being satisfied only with her lenience to his depravity.

Having approached the open door of the living-room, Sarah's eyes clashed with Oleg's apathetic gaze.

Sitting in a chair with its back to Sarah, Serge also turned around. He was impressed with his cousin's drawn face, which reflected unconcealed annoyance.

Realizing Sarah had overheard their talk, Oleg stood silently. He loathed to collide with her and walked to the door, where the girl stood. Oleg was ready to go out, but he glanced at his effeminate cousin. Trying to ignore Oleg's gaze, Serge looked at the approaching Sarah, who seemed shocked by her boyfriend's exhausted appearance.

Serge's face was emaciated, with enormous, deep-blue circles beneath his sunken eyes. His blond hair was dirty and seemed to have been either crudely trimmed or just torn off.

"You are a beauty," Sarah whispered, touching his once-divine curls. Breathless, Serge stood up slowly, as if fearing Sarah's touch. His nostrils quivered at the aroma of her rich hair; its redolent scent reminded him of the May night two years ago, when they had met at the school disco. Sarah struggled against her lust, which was kindled by Serge's hypnotic eyes.

"Once I promised to stay with you, and I will! Even if somebody doesn't like it!" She stared with ill will at Oleg, who devoured the couple with his hard look.

Serge took Sarah's face in his hands with heat, as if to kiss her. Only now, she noticed bruises over the veins of his arms. The girl belatedly recognized the drugged-out look in his eyes.

"Why do you never come to me, even in hallucinations? It's unfair," Serge whispered, again drinking in the scent of Sarah's hair.

But Sarah's heart was ready to break with wild despair. She grabbed Serge's arms. "What's this?"

Half-heartedly shifting his gaze from Sarah's eyes to his pricked veins, Serge uttered indifferently, emerging from his post-drug euphoria, "This ... a mere nothing. My masters just use it to keep me from running away." The boy's voice was quiet and plain, as if he were ready for all circles of hell.

Suddenly, Serge pressed his lips to her, madly whispering, "Don't be afraid. Just one kiss, and I'll go. I don't need your pity."

Now the boy's dark look, the expression of both sinfulness and saintliness, reminded Sarah of her astral love. She would have to do something peculiar to retain Serge in her life. Realizing her direct, fleshy pretensions would only exasperate the boy, Sarah acted upon instinct: she grasped Serge's hand, franticly kissing his wrist. The boy flinched and withdrew his hand, as if he had been scorched, but Sarah held firmly. A sarcastic smile played upon the face of mixed-up Serge.

"Promising beginning ..." he said. His bleary eyes now languidly closed and then re-opened with difficulty. He moved closer to

Sarah, still trying to free his hand and whispering near her hair, "There is only one way to keep me. Say you love me."

But Sarah kept silent, affectionately stroking his slight wrist and watching the boy growing faint with desire.

"I don't get anything," Serge whispered near Sarah's ear, trying to interpret her eloquent silence. "If I hear you correctly, you still think that I must be content just with our intimacy, and no more."

Refusing to speak, Sarah drew Serge close. Her eager fingers, squeezing his wrist, made the boy lose his self-control. Brushing over her breast with his chest, Serge unzipped Sarah's skirt with his free hand and uttered with some impish vehemence, "Why do you always harass me with your humiliating pity? Eventually, I gain revenge ..."

With those words, he went his knees, stripping the girl's skirt and enfolding Sarah's hips with his free hand. Bemused by the boy's persistent lips upon her panties, Sarah said, "Come to bed, or I'll fall now."

Meanwhile, Oleg, whose presence in the room seemed to be indifferent for both lovers, stood at the door as before. As if he were transfixed, he couldn't find the strength to avert his gaze. Sordid desires, beginning with wild jealousy and ending with the urge to participate, reflected in his gray eyes. The emotions took turns there as if they were in a devilish kaleidoscope.

Clasping Sarah's hips in his free arm, Serge suddenly stopped to remove her panties with his teeth and moved over her body, then cast a wicked glance at the woozy Oleg.

"Will you make a move?" Serge uttered crossly, even more arousing the man with his eloquent, dark eyes and his quivering, deep voice. "Or I'll never leave her ...even if we'll be damned all together!"

In a blink, Oleg appeared behind Sarah. He locked the girl in his bear hug and pressed her back to his body so strongly that Sarah, nearly choking, released Serge's wrist.

Aroused by the petting of the boy, who was still kneeling at her feet, Sarah also sensed Oleg's rapid heartbeat. She whispered sneeringly, trying to suppress her misgivings, "Oh ... both at once? Funny. Well, let's have a go at it," she said and coolly tossed back her head upon Oleg's shoulder. Closing her eyes and feeling the man's lips over her neck, she felt certain Serge wouldn't leave now.

Seeing Sarah had overrated her ability to withstand temptations, Serge grudgingly stood.

"Yeah, it should be funny, if it wasn't so deplorable." He straightened Sarah's dark-brown frizz extending over Oleg's shoulder. The girl seemed to have forgotten herself in Oleg's compelling arms. Kissing her neck, the man hugged her breast tightly, as if wishing to stifle her.

"Hi!" Serge said, clapping Oleg on his back offhandedly. "You are too immersed by the process. It's high time to stop!"

"Shut up!" Oleg snarled. "If I'm absorbed, you won't stop me! It's you who can't cope with a girl alone!"

Having lifted Sarah's head from Oleg's shoulder, Serge peered at her half-opened eyes. Having found some sign of good sense there, he pronounced lovingly, "Is it OK? Sorry, but you started this ..."

Suddenly, Sarah's naked legs entwined Serge's hips strongly. "You will be mine, one way or another," she whispered. Making use of Oleg's physical support, Sarah refused to surrender her mad resolve to become intimate with Serge.

"Of course!" the boy said, jauntily smiling at her face and gratified by her preference for him. "Right after your amorous outpouring with me! By the way, don't hurry. Half the pleasure lies in anticipation."

At the same moment, Sarah felt Serge's hand insinuated into her underwear. The boy's heady touch forced her to recline on Oleg's shoulder again, freeing Serge's hips from the captivity of her legs. But the boy was then imprisoned by her emotions. Heeding Sarah's urging, he merged with her in organic whole, involuntary holding his breath and biting his lips as well as Sarah did. Serge seemed nearly ready to abandon his longing for the words of Sarah's love in favor of their immediate sexual delight.

"No!" Serge whispered desperately, his love suddenly sunk in deep, unruly orgasm, convulsively pressing her head against Oleg's shoulder. "Don't keep silent! I need your power of speech ..." But Sarah didn't hear him.

"Damn! What are you doing?" Oleg's defiant voice was so near that Serge almost sobered, having clashed with the man's bloodshot eyes.

"I'll be the first and the only! And you'll have nothing to do with it!" Oleg whispered, baring Sarah's bust. He was angry that Serge's bosom was too close to the girl.

"Oh! How lovely!" Serge replied with feigned rapture. Oleg's hand was clutched between the juvenile lovers at Sarah's breast. "You're a fount of compliments! I haven't heard for a long while anybody who wanted me to be exclusively for him. But if you so insist ..."

"I haven't meant you, driveller!" Oleg snapped out, dismissing Serge's foolish attempt to seduce the man.

"Botheration! Nevertheless, I still have flashbacks of my one-night stand with you," Serge said, while maintaining Sarah's ecstasy with his petting. Taken aback with the exposure of their long-ago incident, Oleg flinched, staring maliciously at the dove-eyed dastard, who   abased him before the girl.

"Famously, molly!" Oleg snapped at him, wishing his cousin to be torn to pieces with all his ill-placed recollections. "It was only once." Oleg whispered, keeping an eye on Sarah's quivering eyelashes. He could not determine whether she could hear their talking. He added in hateful whisper, "I warned you! Make yourself scarce with all your girlish appearance, when I'm blink drunk!"

"It's a typical excuse," Serge said, continuing to flout his discouraged relative. "Had you been so drunk, there should be nothing to reminisce."

"Chippie!" Oleg hissed. "Take your hands from her! I abhor you!"

"It's only measurable," Serge replied leniently, not stopping his tender indecency concerning Sarah. "Of course, one could say you have no special liking for me ... but so many times, you get me out of different scrapes. Indeed, you roughed me up afterwards, and gave me back to my bosses on their demand. But that was just your job. In other respects, only our kinship dampens your attraction to me."

"Don't kick against the prick!" Oleg warned, squinting at the boy. At the same time, he seemed placated with his cousin's apologetic tone and magnetic, dark look.

"But this bout," Serge said suddenly, challenging the man, "I'll show you it costs me nothing to take you abed without any drink!"

Seething, Oleg studied the smart aleck's face. "It's over your head, scum!" he whispered contemptuously, yanking free his hand from Serge and Sarah.

But Serge's counter of the man's left hand surprised the ex-bruiser. Sarah was lying with her head on Oleg's right shoulder, which hampered the man, limiting his motions. But in a blink, Oleg seemingly forgot her. He couldn't overcome his morbid desire for the source of reciprocal aggression in the person of Serge.

"Damned hermaphrodite!" Oleg whispered, unexpectedly stroking Serge's buttock. The boy's dark stare redoubled his inadequate, nervous rut.

Observing his cousin's ignominious lust, Serge fleered, "I know what you want. Isn't it clear, she won't endure you for a long while ... in contrast to me?" The boy glanced at Sarah, who still seemed to be in a trance. "So, nothing less than your apprehension of my ability to satisfy you ... I don't matter in this connection," Serge added, scornfully returning the brusque kisses of his infatuated cousin.

"Well," Oleg whispered, yet feeling his self-control slowly returning. Maintaining the tempter's delusion about his attraction to Serge, the man pronounced, "You may have persuaded me. Leave the girl and let's continue in some other place."

Serge glanced at him with a cunning smile. Like a hunted animal, he sensed a dirty trick. "No ...as I see you can't reconcile your mind to my male physiology. I won't leave her until I obtain what I want. Don't interfere!"

Oleg suddenly grasped the boy's blond hair.

Serge winced.

"Don't twitch! My reaction to it is unpredictable. I'll just ruin the girl right now ... with my fingers. Ouch! And this cutie pie will never belong to you. You don't know her racy blood of the Saracenic scions. Her love is for the man who will break her arrogance. After me, you'll have lost any chance with her."

"How you talk!" Oleg hissed. "There isn't such self-devotion as well as such women! I saw bags of them!" In a blink, Oleg yanked Serge's hair, making him feel the man's superior strength.

Sarah also flinched tensely in Oleg's arm.

"Stop!" Oleg exclaimed, seeing Serge's words were not bluster.

He released the boy's hair. "Do what you want, but don't infatuate her, or it'll be really impossible to drive out of her this inexplicable bias toward your depravity."

"Excellent! I knew we'd come to understanding!" Serge said, removing his hand from Sarah's panties.

Approaching her ear, he whispered, emphatically articulating each of his word "Lassie ... haven't I earned your love?"

Slowly coming back and moving in Oleg's arms, stretching, Sarah whispered disappointedly, "No. You have done nothing."

"Naturally," Serge answered, slightly kissing her lips. "I need your purity, until I clarify our relations."

"You're irritated with my compassion for you, and now you want me to debase you with my lie."

"Yes!" Serge said as he hotly clasped Sarah, almost denting her into Oleg's nervously heaving chest. "I'll accept any humiliation! I want to be deceived by you! But I need your love, not just your lust!"

Struggling against her strong desire of the boy, Sarah gaped at him. Now Serge really seemed to be going to entice her. But the fact that he was playing upon her innermost feelings and friendly attitude toward him offended Sarah.

She was growing angry, avoiding Serge's mesmeric stare. "I can't love you. My heart belongs to someone else."

Sarah's unexpected openness shocked Serge. He moved over the girl.

"Behold!" suddenly Serge exclaimed at his ease, clasping Oleg's back. "She's rebuffed me! For the first time in my life, someone is refusing me!"

Ignoring the man's bemused glance, Serge unexpectedly wended his way to the exit.

"What?" Sarah could not believe her boyfriend's apparent indifference. "How could you demean me? I've considered you to be my best friend!" Serge glanced at the girl shrinking into Oleg's powerful arms. The man still lightly kissed Sarah's neck, as if to accustom her to his harsh lips.

"I think he'll more than equal your hopes," Serge said, and nodded sadly toward Oleg, who waved away the boy and delighted with Sarah's nakedness in his hands.

"Remember me," Serge whispered. "It's easier to part this way."

Annoyed by Oleg's kisses, Sarah realized Serge was smitten with his unfounded jealousy. He was sure that Oleg was Sarah's love, thinking she had referred to him decently as "someone else."

Before Serge turned to go, Sarah unexpectedly rested her head on her naked breast, unconscious. The boy rushed up to Oleg, snatching Sarah from his arms.

"What's up?" Serge asked Oleg as he laid the fainted girl on a sofa. "What have you done with her?" He tried to revive Sarah with slight pats over her cheeks.

"Me?" asked the surprised Oleg. "It's *you!* Besides, it's an ordinary swoon," the man said casually, leaving the room to find some restorative in his house.

Meantime, Serge leaned over Sarah, kissing her and whispering, "Sorry, girlie." But just his lips touched hers; Sarah gripped Serge's wrists, upsetting his unstable pose. The boy draped himself across Sarah, who twisted his hands behind his body.

After the hard clash with Sarah, Serge studied her green eyes in amazement. There wasn't a sign of her recent unconsciousness.

"You wanted me to gull you. I have done it," the impassioned Sarah whispered, hugging him, "Now it's your turn to fulfill your unwary promise. Deflower me!"

"Naughty baggage," Serge smiled wryly, burning Sarah's lips with his whisper. "I have misjudged you. You are a quick learner!"

"No, you are a versed mentor," Sarah replied, still stroking his wrists.

"Oh! I forgot, you prefer to be passive," she said, as if being an adept in such matters. Having offhandedly pushed Serge onto his back, Sarah made herself comfortable on his hips. She adroitly intercepted his wrists in their new position. Confusedly sensing the boy's tense genitals through his jeans, now Sarah realized her own complete inexperience. Serge whispered with soft-hearted laughter, "Well, and what next? You have to set free my hands or we'll stay like this until doomsday."

"I can't do it. I distrust you." Sarah squeezed his wrists more tightly.

Suddenly, Oleg came in the room with the vial of liquid ammonia in his hand. Scrutinizing with surprise the half-dressed Sarah perched over Serge, the man nervously squeezed the vial. "Oh, I see! You've found a restorative without me!"

"Yes!" Sarah shot back. "If you want me, you'll be next!" She was playing with fire, but she felt certain that Oleg would never accept her proposition.

Angered, the man tossed the medicine through the open window. Hearing the vial shatter upon the pavement outside, Sarah was relieved that Oleg didn't smash it right in the room.

"Remember! What you are doing is not of your own accord. He tricks you!" Oleg nodded toward Serge. "You really don't understand this demonic pest. He's an *afreet* in flesh!"

"Sorry, I don't believe in *afreets*!" Sarah said, smirking.

Being tired with the girl's whimsical tricks, Oleg hurried out, the door slamming behind him.

Slyly struggling while she wrangled with Oleg, Serge had freed his wrists at last, forcing the girl to switch places with him. Sitting over her hips, now he nervously strapped together Sarah's hands with his jeans belt.

"Seeing that my sensitive wrists give no rest to you ..." Serge said as he checked the belt to be sure it wasn't too tight. "It's just until I'll endear myself with you."

"Nonsense!" Sarah pronounced, closing her eyes with desire. "I want you as nobody else in this world."

"Really?" Serge uttered discontentedly in a deep, low voice that was unusual for him. Lustily inspecting Sarah, he continued with the same mellifluent voice, warming her heart. "That sounds great, but what about the 'someone else' you love? Why are you not with him now?"

Memories of her illusory Stranger overwhelmed Sarah. "I don't want talk about it! It doesn't concern our relations."

"Even so ..." Serge insisted in the same, deep voice, which was more appropriate for a virile man than a young boy. "Tell me about him. You won't regret it."

The image of Sarah's inaccessible love recurred in her mind, stronger than mere reality. Twitching under Serge, as he sat over her hips, Sarah tried, but couldn't get away from him.

"Please, let me go," she whispered without opening her eyes. "You are right. All this love-making is unnecessary..."

"At last," Serge sighed with passion, tenderly brushing her chiseled waist and ignoring her request. "You have fallen into a trap. Open your eyes and I'll untie you."

But Sarah shook her head negatively, as if afraid of even glancing at the boy, whom she had pursued so persistently not long ago.

"Look at me!" Serge repeated, quietly but emphatically.

Sarah opened her eyes, sensing that they were becoming wide with dazed fixation at the appearance of the person astride her hips. Perplexedly pawing over the sofa and feeling the man's Hessian boots squeezing her hips, Sarah couldn't utter a sound. She realized that she perceived an unexpected avatar of her beloved Stranger.

"The power above ..." she could only say, sensing her heart was ready to break away from her breast. "How are you doing this?" the girl asked weakly, trying to find in the midst of this hallucination the signs of Serge's mind.

"It's just your high sensitivity to my innate mesmerism," the Stranger replied in Serge's stead, with his deep voice. Sensing Sarah's desire to brush over her true love's dark-brown locks, the man inclined to her, freeing her hands from the belt with his elegant fingers. The Stranger pronounced in a quiet tone, as if afraid to dispel Sarah's illusion, "I don't know what you see now, but you can't resist your fancies, which are within my grasp. Sorry, I had no choice ...you are my everything, and I want you, up to the last drop of your seraphic integrity."

His fathomless look whirled Sarah into the boundless Astral Universe. Even realizing that her love was just a deceitful projection of her subconscious in corporeality, Sarah could not withstand the might of those magic eyes. The Stranger had mastered her soul, once and forever.

After fully divesting Sarah of her clothing, Serge undressed himself without stopping to magnetize the girl, who was deep in a hypnotic trance.

"That's great," he said, silently maintaining her erotic delirium.

Still escaping her kisses, Serge permitted Sarah to take a delight in her delusion. "I remember," he said at last with the plain voice of a hypnotist, "you had something to say to me ..."

"I love you," Sarah whispered heatedly, interweaving with her fingers in the boy's dirty-white hair, which she imagined to be dark.

"Now you are talking! Say more, my pure angel," Serge whispered madly near Sarah's lips. "You love me, only me. Your immaterial lover doesn't need your attachment. He's a saint without it. It's me who needs the affection of a virgin. Only your love can save my soul." Serge whispered with wild passion, although he bitterly feared he was losing his power over Sarah's mind.

Hoping she was still apperceiving his hypnotic suggestion, the boy whispered right into her ear. "As ever I'll kiss you, you'll come back. I have heard what I wanted. Now it's my turn to fulfill my promise." But Sarah didn't hear him. Suddenly, her hands clawed at the bedspread of the sofa, as if she wished to shred it.

"Oh, no!" Serge groaned, clasping her body as it convulsively shuddered with orgasm. "I've overdone it again."

His blond hair spread over Sarah's face: he couldn't return her elusive mind to reality. Deliriously parroting the same declaration of love for her illusory lover, Sarah was sunk in some inexplicable, ecstatic trance. Perplexedly arming the girl, who didn't need his skill of a perfect seducer, Serge whispered amazedly, "Orgasm ... with a look? It's too unnatural, even for me!"

He bit Sarah's lips effusively, solacing himself with the study of her passions. "Indeed ... I felt a strong desire to break my own oath to never pervert virgins. But you have rid me of this temptation. I am not worthy of your love. But maybe withstanding your mindless lust for me will extenuate my soul on the Last Judgment."

The next morning, Sarah awoke alone in Oleg's living room. After getting up from the sofa, she looked for her clothing. Suddenly, she saw her reflection in a mirror on the wall and cried out with surprise. Her naked body was painted with some red free designs: words, pretentiously scribbled with a ruby lipstick by Serge's hand, spread across her bust and stomach: "Adieu! Thanks for your empyrean love."

Sarah burst out sobbing and fell to the floor.

"Devilish daubster!" she wept in her hysterics, crossly spreading over her breast the lipstick paint and mixing it with her tears. "Did you invent a tin god? But in what will I, your paltry idol, believe without your ecstatic love?"

Sarah felt with all her essence, even worshipping her chastity, in fact, Serge had seduced her. Sarah was impassioned with unconquerable attraction to the unordinary boy, who sensed her soul as his own. Only he could externalize Sarah's inmost mare's-nest, for which she was ready to sell her soul to Devil -- not speaking of Serge's harmless wish to hear the girl's blarney about her nonexistent love for him.

'Hero, I don't love you!'
(from A. S. Pushkin's 'Ruslan and Ludmila')

Summer 1987 was stressful for seventeen-year-old Sarah. After graduating with distinction from her high school, she left her native town for Moscow, wishing to further her education at the University. But the provincial girl's erudition and vague ambitions were not quite enough to beat the hard competition of thousands of pretenders, who were coming to the metropolis from all ends of the enormous Soviet nation.

Having failed her entrance exams, Sarah was obliged to go back home. Nevertheless, she was inwardly glad to return, for it fostered hope that she would find Serge. Sarah hadn't seen him since his disappearance from Oleg's house, and she was resolved to rehabilitate their friendship at any cost. She believed that Serge's mesmeric abilities, redoubled by his natural sex appeal, might heal her heart from the surreal love for a nonexistent illusion.

The day after she returned, Sarah called on Oleg. The man was distracted and met her coldly.

"You must help me to find Serge," Sarah began, just having stepped over the threshold of his house. "I can't be without him. I know you see him sometimes. Tell him that I'll do anything he wants, and any of his conditions are acceptable to me," Sarah continued. She noted upon Oleg's sulky face all the signs of hard drinking. He seemed to look through the girl, not truly hearing her. Having taken a bottle of vodka from a table, the man tossed off the rest of the drink.

"Why do you say nothing?" Sarah asked. She was indignant with Oleg's disregard for her person, although she had turned up without invitation. Having paused a while, she watched the haggard Oleg moving about his living room. Avoiding the girl's look, he pointlessly rearranged things. Realizing at last that he apparently had real problems, Sarah approached the man, embracing his muscular torso and confidentially studying his sad, drunken eyes.

Sarah whispered, "Please, help me find Serge. If it's necessary, I'll spend a night with you ...but only a one-night stand ... after Serge."

The man flashed a rabid glance at Sarah. "Don't talk rot!"

He sat on a sofa with his face in his hands and whispered through clenched teeth, "Leave me alone."

"What?"

"I said, be gone!" Oleg shouted, burning Sarah with a look full of despair.

Scared and puzzled, Sarah trudged toward the exit. Shrugging her shoulders, the girl concluded that she had insulted the man with her lewd proposition.

Passing by a cupboard, Sarah unexpectedly recognized a photo placed on the lower shelf of the furniture. It was Serge's portrait. Sarah was surprised that Oleg would display a photo of his cousin, whom he disdained. Not finding strength to remove her eyes from Serge's tender portrait, Sarah stopped. Suddenly, she realized that, if she could fully dye Serge's hair, he would be the exact image of her beloved Stranger. Then she noticed that the lower right corner of the photo was crossed with a drooping, sable crepe.

A glass of vodka, with the piece of rye bread over it, stood before the photo, in accordance with the tradition of an Orthodox funeral.

Her boyfriend's image faded before Sarah's eyes. Slowly turning back and gazing at Oleg with her glazed eyes, she groaned in a dreadful, tuneless whisper, "Why didn't you tell me?"

Oleg studied Sarah with the same inexpressible despair in his eyes. Being immersed in melancholy, he had forgotten to hide the photo from Sarah, who had come so unexpectedly.

"I couldn't. You ached for him so much."

Sarah swayed. Supposing the girl would lose consciousness now, Oleg rushed to catch her collapsing body. But instead of fainting, Sarah pounced at the man's face with her fingernails, scratching him and shouting, "It can't be true! You are lying! You are always jealous of him!"

She accused him wildly while clawing Oleg's cheeks. "No! The photo...you can't be so blasphemous. It's you who killed him! You gave my boy to those monsters! Nobody asked you to protect me from his seduction! How did he die? I have to know!"

Oleg even didn't try to defend himself. His cheeks were bleeding slowly, but he easily withstood the pain. Nevertheless, his war-worn nervous system, aggravated by the influence of alcohol, couldn't endure the girl's hysterics. Oleg shouted as he grabbed her forearms, "You want to know how he was killed? By a pitchfork, in the back country!"

But Sarah did not faint even after hearing it. Instead, she became more enraged. "And you are crowing now! You stayed without an adversary!" With her last ounce of fading energy, she pushed away Oleg's hands from her shoulders. The last drop of Sarah's aggression was challenging the man's morbid desire.

Oleg couldn't restrain himself any longer, suffocating with surged lust. "My adversary wasn't born yet! Leave death alone!" he whispered spitefully, snatching Sarah like a kitten and hurling her against the table near the empty bottle. In a blink, having shredded her light clothes, Oleg appeared between Sarah's legs without hindrance, pawing over her naked flesh. Pressing her hands to the table, the man hissed through his clenched teeth, "Relax ... or I'll tear you more than I must."

"I hate you!" Sarah shouted in Oleg's face, pointlessly trying to escape his steely arms. The empty bottle was nearby, but Sarah could not grab it. However, after freeing her right hand at last, she upset the bottle, trying to break it and to slash her vein with its fragments. Oleg pushed the bottle off the table. "One martyr of love is quite enough," he whispered as the girl choked under his body.

Then he saw it: beneath Sarah's hand was a growing pool of bright, red blood. It trickled from her palm. Oleg squeezed Sarah's wrist so strongly that she cried out, but the bleeding only increased.

"You are a queer mortal," he said wistfully, squinting at her bleeding palm and regaining his temper.

Weakening from the bleeding and feeling the cold metal clasp of the man's belt on her naked stomach, Sarah smirked crossly, "What's wrong? Is my blood green?"

"No." Oleg didn't appreciate her joke. "Serge said about you ... you are like chains for a soul. God forbid falling in love with you!"

"Be ashamed!" Sarah replied theatrically. "You're a warrior! And you're afraid of a feeble girl."

"True power often looks worthless at first sight." Oleg squeezed his head with his hands as if trying to pacify a bad headache.

"Maybe," Sarah said, sustaining their conversation. She was glad that some extravagant philosophizing had distracted him from assault. "In any case, we're all prisoners of hell on the earth," the girl said cautiously, attempting to free herself. But whether in response on her words or motions, Oleg grasped Sarah again and jammed her tightly against the bloody table.

"You're crazy," the girl whispered.

Slowly opening her eyes, she involuntarily made a wry face. Oleg's eyes became completely dark up to their scleras. Two empty holes yawned balefully on his face. Fire shadows, like the conglomerations of cosmic plasma separating from Sun, flashed in the hellish abyss of the empty eye-sockets. The man's body seemed red-hot, burning Sarah.

"Angel's spawn ..." he hissed. Sarah heard the same icy voice, sounding as if it were out of Abaddon.

"I know!" she interrupted the entity. Sarah sensed her authority of the creatures intruding into the mind of the men attached to her. "I belong to hell. But why?" she whispered. The entity was silent. Sarah was dying, bleeding from the cross-shaped scar on her palm. Doubts enveloped her soul, but she was ready to die. Nobody in the sublunary world attracted her more than the celestial Stranger. But his spiritual nature also ignored Sarah's frenetic attachment. She so wanted to escape her physical body, which hindered her fusion with that longing, spiritual world that held out promises of some Empyrean Love.

Feeling her tattered clothes soaking with blood, Sarah felt her strength wane. "Let it ride," she thought in her death agony. "It doesn't matter ... paradise or hell ... his eyes are the only Elysium! I agree to be his shadow anywhere."

Sudden light dazzled Sarah. In a blink, Oleg crushed on the girl with all his weight. Groaning under his insensible, huge body, Sarah was losing her consciousness, too.

Tapered fingers with their usual styptic effect touched her bleeding palm. Sarah hadn't the strength even to glance at the Stranger, answering her slight handclasp with his ardent one. The only unspeakable beatitude flowed in her veins.

After the incident in Oleg's house, Sarah eschewed the man. She believed he wouldn't abandon his longing for her, which exasperated the girl even more after Serge's death. But contrary to her expectation, Oleg didn't trouble her, never ringing up or coming around.

At first, Sarah had thought of death as the objective reality of her earthly existence. Only her perished friend, Serge, had sensed Sarah's inwardness and mollified some of the absurd torments of her heart with true human love, which could not help but find response in her lofty soul. After Serge's death, Sarah could feel only hatred for the world, with all its cruelty.

Once, while sitting in the kitchen of her flat, when all her relatives were absent, Sarah stared sadly straight ahead. An unbearable aversion to materiality enveloped her mind. As never before, she hated the earthy reality. It demanded so much strength for adaptation to its Procrustean conventionalism, but returned nothing to her sensitive soul.

Sarah got up and mechanically approached the gas cooker of her kitchen. After turning on all its gas rings, she apathetically settled into the chair and, flattening her arms against the table, rested her head. The girl listened indifferently to the sinister hissing of the gas, which filled the small kitchen with the stink of rancid garlic.

Sarah was on the floor.

Somebody lashed her cheeks without remorse, savagely

enough to wake the dead. Feeling a man's lips pressed against her own, Sarah felt pain in her lungs and opened her eyes, barely aware of Oleg kissing her. The man hoisted her from the floor with a single, strong arm.

"What are you doing?" Sarah whispered. Oleg's unshaven face was too close to hers. Her head ached from the kitchen gas.

"Just artificial respiration!" Oleg snapped, squeezing the girl's body. "Bitch! Are you looking for euthanasia? I'll kill you personally and find some more sophisticated way to do it!" he whispered maliciously, pressing his face to Sarah's disheveled tresses, which were reeking with methane.

"I'll be much obliged to you ..." she whispered sarcastically, not understanding how Oleg had appeared in her flat at the wrong time.

Made angrier by her ingratitude, he pressed Sarah to the floor again and attacked her with brutish kisses. The girl struggled for breath, and Oleg set her free at last, watching her gasp for air like a stranded fish.

Suddenly, he hugged Sarah. "Goosey," he said. She sobbed silently, wiping her tears against his broad shoulder. Sarah hated her inability to love the man, who drove her to madness with his restraining affection: an adamant warrior, he was too proud to express his sentimentality, for which Sarah so longed.

Even after Oleg had saved Sarah through a fluke, their relations didn't become warmer. Having seen his car moving along a city road parallel as she walked, Sarah ignored the man until he parked his car and impatiently approached her. But Sarah's eyes were cold and apathetic, as usual.

Half a year elapsed after Serge's death, but Sarah still couldn't recover from her first taste of death and the loss of her intimate.

After her failed suicide attempt, she seemed barely able to save herself from inexplicable folly.

Once, in early spring, on the eve of her eighteenth birthday, Sarah came across her neighbor, Andrew. The boy was familiar with Serge's death and had observed Sarah's crestfallen state. The vengeful Asian was still obsessed with desire for revenge. Sarah had disparaged him, but had been intimate with two other young men; the feverish boy grew more agitated. Andrew saw it was the best moment to break Sarah's haughtiness at last. As if by chance, he offered the girl to visit one of his mates living in an outlying district -- to cheer Sarah up. Andrew claimed that there would be a birthday party for a friend, which coincided with Sarah's own birthday. The girl heard a trick in his words. But at the same time, she couldn't shake off the desire to attend. After all, they had been neighbors for many years, and their conflict was long in the past. Andrew was stunned when Sarah, always cautious and circumspect, suddenly accepted his invitation.

Making herself at home in the overcrowded, large living room of the house of Andrew's mate, Sarah tried to accustom herself to its semi-darkness and noise. As usual, she took a seat in a far corner of the room. As she sat in an armchair, the girl's hands lingered upon the old-fashioned, carved armrests, making her feel like a visitor sitting on a museum piece. Andrew nestled down on the armrest of Sarah's queenly armchair. Promising to introduce her at last to the host of the festivity, Andrew detected solicitude in Sarah's manner.

Scrutinizing the room's dark interior, Sarah was absently watching smooching couples rhythmically dancing to the sound of a powerful stereo. However, the girl felt she did not belong to the encirclement. She was preoccupied with an incident in her own flat recently.

After coming back home from work the day before, Sarah had found the contents of her writing table strewn over the floor of her bedroom, as if after a search.

Having suspected her younger brothers' pranks, Sarah went for the boys with her reproaches and threats. But seeing only fear in their childish eyes, she realized they had been out of the flat all day, just as she was. At last, she noticed the wide-open window over her table. They were on the ground floor. Had someone entered her room through the window? But who, and what for? Everybody knew about the poorness of her family. Besides, it was funny to look for something compromising in her table among journals with rhapsodic love verses and old school copybooks.

Sarah didn't notice Andrew's unexpected disappearance. As if rooted to her comfortable armchair, she wasn't dejected that nobody paid attention at her. Suddenly, Andrew reappeared. The boy held in his hands two tumblers, offering one of them to Sarah as a true gallant. Not wishing to drink, Sarah unwillingly took a tumbler from Andrew's hand. She was trying to discourage his importunate courting. She put the glass to her lips, considering its content was some juice. But the taste of the beverage was very unusual ...

"Is anything wrong?" Andrew asked. He had already drained his tumbler. In the semi-darkness, Sarah inspected the contents of hers. The feigned concern in the boy's voice made Sarah glance at him. Almond-eyed Andrew watched her. His moist lips shuddered in the variegated highlights of music. Feeling his hand upon her forearm, as if anticipating her impulse to spring to her feet, Sarah got up with the tumbler in her hand. Andrew copied her motion defiantly.

"What's this?" she whispered crossly. Escaping Andrew's gesture to embrace her shoulders, Sarah tossed the drink into his face.

"Go to blazes!" she pronounced, ignoring Andrew's embarrassed attempts to wipe the liquid off his face. While Andrew tried to clean himself up, Sarah left the dark living room for the lobby. She sensed a faint scent of ether. The girl couldn't get rid of the sensation that she was in the apartments of medics. Then her legs gave way, and everything misted before her eyes.

"Where are you going?" Andrew's voice rose from behind Sarah's shoulder again. She about-faced, trying to conceal her disorientation. Sarah hoped she had not drunk much of the intoxicant from the tumbler, so that her dizzied state would be noticed.

"Home!" she snapped.

"But it's too far from here!" Andrew said with feigned reflection, imitating Sarah's manner to muse. "Besides, it's an unfriendly gesture of disrespect for my hospitable friend, to leave him without the most desired gift for his birthday."

"Where do I come in?" Sarah answered coldly, trying unsuccessfully to get into her boot with her foot. "You can wish joy to your friend without me."

"But I can't!" Andrew answered in the same mocking manner. "Because you are the gift for him! He has been dreaming of picking you up for a couple of years!"

"What? Will you set me up as a match for someone? I always knew you were a cretin, but not to such an extent."

Suddenly Sarah's dizziness compelled her to kneel. Her body did not submit to her mind. Enjoying the sight of Sarah so weakened, Andrew sighed ardently. "Oh! A pretty pass! It's pleasant to see you so docile!"

Squatting near Sarah, who was now definitely high on the drugged juice, Andrew whispered, unbuttoning her blouse, "It's not matching. There are too many fiancés for you here. I'll be the first, by your leave." He gripped Sarah's weakened body, feverishly licking her neck. Sensing her distaste and hearing her gnashing, the boy whispered lustfully, "How long will you impersonate a virgin? It begins to irritate ... remember, you agreed to come here."

Lifting Sarah, who was rolling drunk with her flagging head constantly falling on her breast, Andrew lugged her into the darkness of one of the numerous rooms. "At long last, you are not a virgin. That's great! To tell the truth, I hate virgins."

"Why so?" Sarah asked, sobering from his words.

Andrew glanced at her askew and added, with unconcealed aversion, "I hate blood."

"Even your own?"

"Enough on that chapter!" Andrew snapped.

"In that case, we are quits!" Sarah said, barely overcoming her intoxication. "Your lickings are as disgusting for me as my virginity for you."

"What?" Andrew exclaimed, dropping Sarah on the floor near the door of the dark room. His Asiatic eyes opened wide, but in a blink, he screwed them up again. "You are lying! Everybody backbit about your living in fornication with two fellows! As if I didn't know that bisexual pervert and the other one, the shell-shocked, sottish ..." Sarah struggled up onto all fours in her intoxication.

Suddenly, she burst into drunken laughter.

"Have you said, pervert ... and sottish? So, you can imagine our inimitable love-making, you-know-what. Besides, if you prefer our intimacy to be done naturally, it will be too gory!" Shrieking with impish laughter, Sarah realized that even her arms and legs together couldn't withstand the earth's gravity.

"Shut up!" Andrew's pathological phobia mixed in his mind with aversion and fury. The boy's face became pale and maculated with red, nervous spots.

"If so," he whispered crossly, "my friend will be only more satisfied with your sophistication! As for our relations ...they'll be postponed."

Andrew lugged her into the other half-lit room. Blacking out from time to time in his arms, Sarah couldn't move. At last, Andrew prostrated her on a rug in the same chic room, which was as stylish as the bedchamber of a Turkish pasha. Only an enormous, console mirror in the corner of the room clashed with the Oriental color of the numerous hand-woven carpets on the walls. The carpets featured the archetypes of some ancient Turkish arms, which awakened Sarah's latent blood of Polovtsians' khans intermarried with Slavs, many centuries ago.

There were several doped boys in the room. Sitting on a broad ottoman, they smoked and laughed.

"Here she is, Aesculapius! As I promised!" Andrew said. He harshly turned Sarah onto her back, addressing one of the boys in the smoking company.

The boy Andrew had called "Aesculapius," being the only sober person in the relaxing company, glanced at Sarah's flat figure, which was dressed in jeans and a silk blouse. The cold look coming through his elegant, gold-rimmed spectacles involuntary fixed at her breast, which was unbuttoned. Aesculapius flashed his gray look at Andrew again.

"It happened accidentally. She resisted," Sarah's neighbor mumbled, dropping his almond eyes and sensing the discontent of his domineering friend.

"Really? After my cocktail?" Aesculapius smirked, scornfully squinting at the salacious Asian.

Other drug-addicted boys, sitting on a spread divan, also

watched Sarah with interest. But they didn't express desire without permission of their mastermind.

"I said," Andrew tried to explain, "she had been living in fornication with two fellas. It speaks for itself!"

"So what? Now it means nothing!" Aesculapius snapped at Andrew. The grey-eyed, bespectacled boy jumped off the divan and approached Sarah. "I wanted her to be untouched exactly for tonight! It's important!" Aesculapius hissed in the face of Andrew, who was afraid even to move in the presence of his patronizing friend. Suddenly, Aesculapius left Andrew and approached an antique bureau. After searching through in its top-drawer, he withdrew a small card.

Meantime, Sarah perceived her surroundings fuzzily. Her giddiness, alternating with blacking out, suddenly assumed the similitude of some unbearable lust. Lying on the floor, she hardly saw Andrew through her misted look.

"You are sunk," Andrew said under his breath, devouring the girl with his vindictive gaze. "If you are modest, then behave modestly!" Andrew's malicious words echoed in Sarah's dulled mind as if he had roared them from the mountain tops.

Card in his hand, Aesculapius knelt near Sarah. His scathing look compelled Andrew to move away. Having taken the hint, the boy plodded obediently toward the drug addicts, who were making some vulgar remarks concerning Sarah.

Trying to overcome her exhaustion, Sarah barely traced the boy kneeling by her. She just guessed he was the same one who celebrated his birthday that night and wished to hook her as a gift.

In fact, Aesculapius was the sole son of outstanding parents, hereditary physicians. After finishing high school *summa cum laude*, the boy became a medic, having equaled completely the expectations of his parents. His image was too far from the appearance of a hot pasha or a feverish khan. He was an ordinary Slav fellow with big gray eyes and a titian haircut. Being quite handsome, he would be the dream of any girl, except for his awful, piercing look and icy voice. His eyes and voice seemed to belong to a soulless robot that had learned some pure logic and utterly realistic intellect at his mother's knees.

"Don't be afraid," he said to Sarah. "The mixture you drank is safe for your health." Aesculapius's soft voice sounded in Sarah's mind like thunder.

Sarah was startled. The voice was familiar. She heard that cold, imperturbable intonation. Sarah made an effort to glance at the kneeling boy, but it was useless. His face blurred before her eyes, as did the rest of his appearance. Nevertheless, she contrived to catch Aesculapius's unfeeling gray stare, which was examining her through elliptic specs in golden rim.

That gelid look belonged to a boy Sarah had seen only once. It was a couple of years earlier, when she was still a schoolgirl. The boy had been sitting at a desk near Sarah during one of the city contests in chemistry, where he and Sarah represented different schools. The girl didn't know the contestant's name, but his inimitable, rational look and his voice that had no hint of emotion impressed Sarah. Even at first blush, she was convinced such features should belong exclusively to a congenital researcher, who would be able to dissect anything in the cause of pure science. Feeling like the focus of such an experiment now, she lay in a drugged delirium on the floor of his house.

During the contest, the boy had been asking Sarah for an insignificant kindness: he wanted her to pull up the skirt of her uniform, where right on her legs had been written the chemical formulas that seemed for Sarah to be the most complicated. Sarah just permitted the contestant to shift her skirt by himself, when it was necessary to crib a formula.

A while after the competition, Sarah found out it was that boy who had won the contents. She wasn't interested in the winner's name, being satisfied with knowing of the number of his school, although it seemed very unjust that, thanks to her assistance, the boy had outmatched Sarah as well as other contestants. Eventually, she'd arrived at the conclusion that her underclothes cribs, for some reason, didn't help her to achieve the same great result as that boy did. It was clear that he had some other basis to win: more solid knowledge, or some outstanding talent in that branch, at least.

The bespectacled boy knelt by Sarah, prostrate on the floor of his house. It was so disgusting for Sarah to meet that master-spirit in this den of drug addicts.

"Do you remember me?" he asked.

"No!" Sarah replied crossly, turning aside her vacant look and surmising that her humiliating state now was the boy's performance. Andrew was too inept for such refined tricks.

Disregarding her irritated tone, the "experimenter" continued. "I'm very thankful to you for your assistance at that competition. Besides, I solved your tasks by the method you had chosen! Indeed, it was quite complicatedly, but brilliant in its singularity! Of course, you couldn't do it during the limited period of the contest." He seemed to be excited.

Having closed her eyes and trying to sting the boy's outstanding intellect, Sarah whispered through clenched teeth, addressing the character as if he had become mad with his constant learning. "Egghead ... are you given in chemistry? But you couldn't even dose your devilish mixture correctly! I apprehend everything! So, all are apt to trip ..."

"It had to be!" Aesculapius replied with concern. "Otherwise, it might have some negative influence on the embryo of our progeny!"

"What?" Sarah's hair stood on end.

"Yes," the boy continued his unimaginable flirtations. "You are brainy and tough. It's the reason I chose you for the extension of my genus. Could you imagine our future children's versatile and capacious minds, if we'll join my logic and your irrational intuition?"

"Indeed! It's awful to imagine! Just some neutralization reaction, or full annihilation! What's more reasonable for you?" Sarah exclaimed. In her drugged despair, the boy appeared to be a Frankenstein, who wanted to create the race of some perfect monsters by combining, in their essence, his dry rationalism and Sarah's inability to love people.

"Only over my dead body," the girl muttered, battling her mind's fearful hallucinations. "Besides, even if we copulate, it doesn't mean I'll become pregnant immediately."

"I took that into consideration," Aesculapius answered reservedly. "I ciphered out the day of your ovulation, using the calendar of your menses, which Andrew got for me." He was nervously shredding Sarah's small calendar in his hands.

"Mamma Mia," Sarah groaned, uselessly exerting every effort to move away from the boy, who seemed prepared to drive her crazy with his sophisticated cynicism. She realized, at last, who had turned upside-down the contents of her writing table, and why.

"You are maniac!" Sarah whispered helplessly. The boy seemed shocked by her reaction, which was unfamiliar to his restrained nature. "It's unlikely there is a woman who could fall in love with such a moral deformity as you are ...let alone desire to have your children." Sarah's words were like a cold shower on Aesculapius, benumbing his body.

"Andrew!" Sarah suddenly called. She asked her neighbor for quarter, looking for some warm feelings in her heart toward Andrew, whose lickings now seemed a true delight compared with his frenetic friend. Andrew, as her playmate, seemed to Sarah now as the only salvation from the pretensions of this terrible "chemist."

Andrew came back to the couple, ascertaining with wonder that nothing had changed during his absence: Sarah was still lying on the floor in delirium, and Aesculapius was still kneeling at her side in the posture of a samurai preparing to commit hara-kiri.

"Sakes alive!" Andrew stopped near Sarah and addressed Aesculapius. "My dear, isn't it possible to test a girl's patience only so long?" But his spectacled friend was motionless and sullen.

At last Aesculapius lifted his cold eyes at Andrew and whispered, with an unfeeling voice that sounded as if it came from beyond the grave, "I need your help with her."

Andrew stared at him with his wet, sensual, dark eyes. His lips quivered in a sarcastic smile. "Well," he said languidly, taking off his sweater, which was still damp with Sarah's beverage, "I'll help you. But only on the condition that the other boys won't touch her. I think we both will be enough for her."

"What?" Aesculapius shouted, losing his control. "Dare you impose conditions to me? As for the other boy's ... they'll bonk you next because of your mulishness! You know that they'll do anything to get their fix! Come on, pet her!"

In a blink, Andrew, dressed only in jeans, appeared over Sarah without lying on her body. He just rested on his palms, as if preparing for a push up. He tongued her lips, making Sarah half-open her eyes, returning from the drugged dreamland to reality.

"You," Sarah whispered. She breathed easily, being friendly to him as never before. Trying to answer him with the same passion, she hoped he would take her away from this place, which was as ghoulish as its inhabitants. Sarah tried to recollect something pleasant about Andrew. Really, with his jetty, eloquent, Asiatic eyes and the same-colored, quite long hair ... and considering his well-made stature ... he was handsome in his own way. In Sarah's mind, he was imagined an outré resemblance to a brave from James Fennimore Cooper's novels. Feeling his skillful kisses, the girl involuntary memorized their first kiss, which had been on a landing of their five-story building.

Back then, they had been children pretending to be adults. Andrew could in no way cope with the subtlety of a French kiss, and he irritated Sarah with his clumsiness. At last, the boy had tired of her constant disappointment and simply licked Sarah's face, as if he were a playful puppy, making her laugh until she wept with his awkwardness.

Andrew had always remembered her malevolent laugh.

"What the dickens did you want in my flat?" Sarah whispered, becoming turned on by Andrew's fervid lips as they dug into her neck and slowly descended to her breast. The boy's lips quivered with a smile in return. "In your flat? Nothing ... I just explored the way to get you through the window one night."

"Idiot!" Sarah whispered, nervously fumbling his hair in her hands and trying to face his lips again. She struggled with the unbearable lust flowing in her blood after Aesculapius' drug mixture. "You are a miracle of acumen, as usual! At long last you found windows in our building!"

Realizing she would need his help, Sarah tried to nestle to her breast the boy, who hovered over her. "Listen," she whispered as hotly as she could, "let's come to accord." Sarah pondered what kind of sexual satisfaction she could offer, taking into account Andrew's phobia, if only he wouldn't leave her with that maniacal four-eyes who was still kneeling and studying the prelude of their love-making.

"What?" Andrew stopped to kiss the girl and burned her with his leer, angered by Sarah's deathbed repentance. "It's too late! Now I can do nothing! You'll come to accord with every one of them ..." Andrew crossly pointed with his look toward the group of drug-addicted boys, who were laughing at the ad-lib lovers weltering in pleasure on the floor.

But then, unexpectedly, all Andrew's touches disappeared. It was as if an unknown force flung him from Sarah. An awful shriek destroyed the ease of the room. Sarah's bleary eyes saw that Andrew writhed upon the fragments of the broken console-mirror. His naked chest and arms were freely bleeding. Kneeling somehow on the floor among the smashed glass, Andrew bellowed and cursed, uselessly picking at the smithereens of mirror embedded in his bleeding flesh. Stunned by the awesome sight, Sarah fought to remain conscious.

"Phobia," she thought. "Why does it always happen, what is the most frightful for us?"

The surroundings became unclear again. Sarah's mind traced only some abstracted sounds of rough-and-tumble around her, until somebody's strong arms picked up her from the floor. The scent of smoke-filled fabric seemed to her so pleasant now; Sarah instinctively kissed the sweater of the man clasping her to his bosom. She couldn't govern her lust, which tingled in her flesh with new strength as her consciousness slowly recovered.

Lying on the rear seat of a car, Sarah glanced heavily toward an inside, rear-view mirror and saw the reflection of driver's eyes. Oleg.

While motoring along a byroad next to a snowy plain, Sarah's clarity and desire both increased.

"Stop the car," she said to Oleg at last.

He parked his car at a roadside and glanced nervously at Sarah over his shoulder. "What's up?"

"I want you," she whispered, writhing with desire on the rear seat.

Having clutched at the steering wheel and setting his forehead against his hands, Oleg tried to restrain the same lust, which Sarah always aroused in him.

"The tiptop muck they hocused you," he whispered as she climbed toward the front seat. Squeezing between Oleg's body and the wheel, Sarah settled herself in his lap, brushing her hands under the man's sweater and over his brawny chest.

"Don't be afraid. I've come of age today. Lay with me and let's have done with it," she whispered, kissing Oleg's lips. Sarah vainly struggled to penetrate his tight jeans with her fingers.

"What for? To earn even more your contempt, having used your lunacy at a weak moment?"

"Where did you pick up such rubbish?" Sarah replied. "You want me. That's why you are always on my trail. Besides, I may not be in eternal debt of gratitude for your rescue services." She tried to pique the man's self-respect by any way.

"You'll outlive such debts somehow," Oleg said with tension, helping Sarah down from his lap and sitting her on the front passenger seat. She had strongly excited him. Nevertheless, wishing to answer some stinging remark in response, he added, "I said, you can't pleasure me in bed with your rawness. Besides, I can afford a prostitute ..."

Sarah grinned, seeing he had fallen for her bait.

"You are a dull beggar!" she said with feigned sympathy. "You can delude yourself, but I won't buy that. I see you're ready to raze to the ground anyone who touches me. And your aim is to win my favor. But to me, you'll always be an unscrupulous procurer and fratricide!"

Thunderstruck by her insult, Oleg became pale with frenzy. "Bitch! You are not drunk!" He pushed Sarah with such strength that she fell out of the car and onto the field in the drafty, open countryside. Staggering and leaning against the ice-cold car, Sarah stood. Without a coat or boots, she was now standing in calf-length dirty March snow. The strong wind penetrated her body to the bone through her thin silky blouse.

Having jumped out of the car after her, Oleg grasped Sarah's chin with his powerful fingers. Looking intently at her still-bleary eyes, he asked furiously, "What about it? Have you sobered up finally? Well, let's resume. So, it's exactly you, who is a consistent bitter-ender ... especially tonight, among that ragtag..."

Shifting from one soaked foot to another in the wet snow, Sarah continued to flout Oleg, just quizzing at his wrathful eyes. "Strike me ... Oh, sorry! I have forgotten that you never beat women! It's your sole principle ...because it's more common for you to trade them up!"

Oleg ached to give a bashing to the girl. But his sexual appetite was much too powerful now.

"Indeed," he hissed in Sarah's chilled face. "I won't strike you."

He ripped her blouse so roughly that its buttons flew asunder over the snowy field.

"A shade better," Sarah whispered mockingly, feeling the man's hand nervously unzipping her jeans. Adrenalin warmed her body, and new strength joined with the hormone storm raging in Sarah's blood, which was caused by Aesculapius' devilish drink. She exulted that her violent abandon was so voluptuous for the man.

Slowly removing his hand from Sarah's unzipped jeans, which now hung loosely at her waist, Oleg tried to control his rising lust. "You won't make me rape you, as you once tried. Serge would never forgive me ..."

Sarah started at the mention of her perished friend. Oleg seemed to make up his mind to fight back against Sarah's madness using her own method, touching the right chords of her soul.

"Very nice!" Sarah whispered. Her skin was bluish with cold as she stood, wrapping herself up with her torn blouse. "Only don't say you'll never touch me! Indeed, you very nearly abused me just after Serge's death! What's happened now? Maybe you vowed celibacy in commemoration of never-to-be-forgotten Serge? It's funny, taking into account that you hated him the most of all."

Sarah found within herself the strength to restrain the poignant reminiscences about Serge. The pain of her heart came with a lump in her throat.

"How can you say so?" Oleg was susceptible to her violent cynicism. "Don't you remember how you longed to liberate him from the filth and people's indignity? I'm so antipathetic to you, but you loved him."

"Who, me?" Sarah exclaimed as if scalded. "I can't fall in love with anyone on the Earth!" She spoke as if her heart were broken fully. "Yes! He was my best friend, who could ease the pain of my heart, and I tried to give him the same. Indeed, it became unbearable ... to love without him ... someone else."

Oleg stared at the girl.

"You contradict yourself," he said at last. "Who is your sweetheart in such a case, if you can't love anyone on the Earth?"

Studying the dark, beclouded sky, Sarah whispered wistfully, "He … it's a being … an entity from some other world. But I can't contain its All-Embracing Love in my heart without feeling certain of its real existence, somewhere in the Universe."

"What?" Oleg glanced at her incredulously. He tried to comprehend some possible meaning of the words "being" and "entity," which Sarah had used to accentuate the sky-born nature of her desired Stranger. Only after her revelations, the man noticed at last that Sarah was barely standing on her almost-frostbitten feet.

"Indeed …you're drunk!" Oleg said with vexation, sitting her on the rear seat of his car again.

After switching on a water-controlled heater to full power, Oleg nestled down near the shivering girl. Enwrapping Sarah in his hard leather jerkin and strongly chafing her feet with his powerful hands -- after removing her sopped jeans and socks -- Oleg was bemused by her unexpected confession. He muttered to himself, "It's delirium tremens or some coma vigil, or maybe both of them."

He asked Sarah at last, "Why aren't you a man, if you can bear such pain? If you were, you'd serve in Afghanistan, like I did."

"Thanks!" the girl said, still chattering with cold. "But I hate the desert heat!"

"Rather!" Oleg agreed sarcastically. "Without it, you have

parched in the hell of your arrogance!" He razed over Sarah's naked hip jokingly, as if brushing off some ashes.

His touch was so pleasant that Sarah sank into her recent, wild lust again. Throwing her arms around Oleg's neck, she tried to lay him on her frozen body, whispering, "Do you think you have gotten rid of me so easy? Like hell!" Searching with her lips for the sensitive areas on his face and neck, she prickled her lips with Oleg's bristly cheeks.

Realizing that Sarah would settle down for no particular reason, the man resisted no more. Obeying all her actions, he whispered, "Oh, well. Have it your own way."

"No, do it the way you like," Sarah replied, taking delight in contradicting him.

"Anything you say," Oleg agreed with her, not wanting to be brutalized by the girl again when he would lose control of his lust.

Petting Sarah and trying to convince her of his full resolution, he, as if accidentally, brushed his hand over her tender neck and whispered, "It'll be a little painful ..."

"I don't need lessons in sexology!" Sarah said, smiling with self-assurance and lapsing into ecstasy with Oleg's loutish endearment.

"Are you sure?" he retorted mockingly.

At the same moment, he pressed the area of carotid on Sarah's neck with the flick of his thumb. In a blink, the girl lost her consciousness without crying out.

"She-devil ... tired me stiff," Oleg whispered madly, still caressing Sarah's insensible body and not finding the strength to stop. He was filled with the sole desire to remain in that ice-covered car with that self-contradictory girl, just being gone astray in the middle of the snowbound plain, holding itself aloof from the wild world with all its ignominy.

Some unpleasant sensation in her cramped chest, impeding her breathing, made Sarah awaken. Murky March dawn lit up Oleg's bedroom with pale sunlight. Sleeping in the bed near Sarah, the man involuntary enfolded the girl, locking her breast strongly and pressing into her naked body with his muscles. Despite the pressure of his heavy embrace, Sarah felt a giddy languor flowing in her flesh with the sensation of unconditional protection in his arms. She realized with wonder that even the smell of cigarettes tincturing Oleg's body, as well as his dwelling, didn't bother her now. But suddenly, Sarah felt some aversion—to herself. It grew into an almost physical qualmishness.

Having forgotten the sleeping Oleg, whom she might awaken with her harsh motions, she tumbled out of the bed. Sarah nearly fell all her length as she stumbled against two empty vodka bottles that were scattered on the floor next to the bed.

Glancing with astonishment at the bottles, and then at Oleg, the girl thought sadly, "It's true. There aren't undesirable women; it may be just the deficiency of vodka for love-making with anyone ..."

Sarah tried to remember the evening's events.

"It's awful," she thought, becoming rattled. "I remember nothing! Devilish 'chemist' with his philter! It's me who needs some vodka for the quenching of the abhorrent sensation after spending the night with an unloved man. Though ... I remember nothing."

Having composed herself, and realizing Oleg would not recover soon, Sarah didn't burn with the desire to converse with him, after all. She directed her steps to a radiator, where her clothes, accurately laid out by Oleg, were drying. Smiling ironically at her blouse, which had been reduced to rags by Oleg, she indifferently put on her jeans and coat over her naked body. Feeling the unpleasant cold of the silk lining, Sarah was glad the man didn't have quite enough strength to destroy the coat, which she'd bought with difficulty on a mere pittance, her hard-earned wages from the garment factory.

Pausing by the door of Oleg's bedroom, Sarah cast a glance at the peacefully sleeping man. Waves of gratitude flowed across her heart. After all, without his timely interference, that March morning would have been much duller for her in the blackguard hang-out.

As usual, assured Oleg would exact the continuation of their close relations, Sarah persuaded her parents and ordered her brothers to not invite her to the phone if the caller was a man.

Several days elapsed, and some distressing thoughts about a possible pregnancy troubled Sarah's mind. The words of the terrible "chemist" about her too-high chance of pregnancy on the night she had spent with Oleg stayed with her. Vaguely imagining the signs of the physical state that was so worrying her, the girl's anxiety rose. Sarah was aware that she should stay with Oleg in the case of her pregnancy. She would never deprive her child of his father, whoever he might be. She was ready to abase her pride and live with an unloved man to assure the happiness and prosperity of her child. These thoughts depressed Sarah, because it was easy to imagine her own altruism, but difficult to act upon it.

Once, having forgotten about her caution, Sarah answered a phone call and heard Oleg's voice.

"Your parents and brothers are very nice people, but they

can't lie about you. They need to say something more plausible," the man began indifferently, trying to restrain his malice at Sarah, who didn't wish even to talk to him.

"What in the world do you want?" the girl bristled. "To refresh my flashbacks about our intimacy?"

Oleg kept silent for a moment.

"I just wanted to hear a human voice," he muttered at last.

"Put aside your drink and go out," Sarah said in a moralizing manner. "There you'll find people and hear their voices."

"I hoped we were friends." Imitating Sarah's parlance, Oleg repeated the phrase she had once said to him.

"Hoity-toity!" Sarah blew up, her anxiety rising at the thought of being pregnant. "Friendship between man and woman is abnormality!" she said, quoting Oleg's reply. "Isn't that your attitude? I've adopted it as well, thanks to our far-reaching relations! If it turns out that I'm pregnant, it can only end with an abortion!" Sarah shouted.

Oleg didn't utter a word. It was as if he were trying to apprehend the girl's full antipathy toward him.

Sarah paused and struggled to speak with less melodrama. "No," she said more calmly, "I couldn't do that. I'll give birth. But you'll never be my 'lord and master.' Don't think that night was the avenue to retain me in your bed!"

Only Oleg's feverish breathing disturbed the silence. Although he realized that Sarah was in hysterics, he couldn't find the strength to penetrate her emotional state. "Just settle down and visit a gynecologist," Oleg said listlessly. After he spoke, only neutral, short beeps reached Sarah's ear from the other end of line.

A woman gynecologist was writing down something in Sarah's

medical record, disapprovingly squinting at the girl who was dressing herself behind a folding screen. After she had taken a seat, Sarah was waiting for the doctor's verdict. The physician glanced with strict eyes at Sarah.

"Dear, do you understand how impregnation takes place?" The doctor studied Sarah as if the girl were playing a trick.

"What?"

"How old are you?" the doctor asked Sarah, suspiciously watching a smile playing over the girl's face. The doctor, obviously, imagined herself as a psychiatrist, comparing Sarah's answers with data in her medical documents.

"Eighteen," Sarah said softly, without changing her resigned air of a pregnant woman reconciled to her lot.

"Well ..." the physician drawled, "Maybe now it's unusual, at your age, but that's not important. Actually, you can't be pregnant because you ...have never had intimacy with a man. Is that clear? Be so kind," she added crossly, "as to not drive me crazy with your foolish misgivings! I have a plenty of work to do."

Sarah madly gawked at the doctor. Not understanding the cause of the patient's shock, the woman tried to reduce her tension. She began tell Sarah some facts about safe sex, advising her to read more on that burning subject.

Dropping her eyes and nervously smiling, Sarah stood up. She removed her medical papers from the doctor's table, but then suddenly exploded with such hysterical convulsions that the physician winced. Sarah grasped now that Oleg had demonstrated his true friendship by exercising his self-control. But that act seemed unbelievable, as his nerves had been destroyed in the war.

Nevertheless, Sarah could never forgive how the man had injured her vanity. Now she squirmed as never before, sensing her complete inadaptability and helplessness in human world. But she refused to admit that fact.

"Angel's spawn," she whispered now, choking with her hysterical laughter, as she wended along the hospital corridor. "Is it really so difficult to get rid of my own chastity? I'd never have believed it!"

Having made certain there was nothing physical connecting her with Oleg, Sarah returned to her usual habit of giving a wide berth to the man. She didn't talk to him, even when, having lost his temper, Oleg grasped Sarah's shoulders, shaking her like a pear tree. But the girl's wintry smile and willful silence were just Sarah's refined revenge for her downtrodden pride.

Sewing machines rumbled from both sides of a long, worn-out conveyer belt that slowly moved through the enormous workshop of a garment factory. Almost gasping in the hot, dusty air of the old shop, where the summer temperatures reached 45 degrees Celsius, Sarah earnestly tried to concentrate on the buttons of soldiers' greatcoats. Miserable in the heat, and sweating, she struggled with the old, obsolete sewing machine.

Suddenly the needle pierced Sarah's thumb.

"Damn!" she whispered as she turned off the machine with her other hand. The pain traveled like waves from her thumb to her backbone.

Extracting the fragment of the broken needle from her bleeding flesh, Sarah involuntary felt some disgraceful pity for her hands. They were the hands of an ex-musician, who had betrayed her own vocation. It was awful to imagine that her hands, which once created music, would be reduced to such dull, menial labor.

Struggling still with the malicious fragment of needle, Sarah suddenly visualized Andrew trying to free his cut body from the smithereens of the mirror in that hellish hang-out. After the accident, the boy's torso and arms were covered with scars. Now Andrew sidestepped Sarah , but he continued spreading some absurd rumors about her unbelievable survivability, saying Sarah was a witch living under the auspice of hell. The vicious words didn't dispirit the girl. Long ago, she had grown used to the unconquerable distance between her and the majority of people, and she no longer sought their approval.

"Of course, it was very cruel on Oleg's part," Sarah thought, taking compassion on the miserable Andrew for losing some of his refined Asian beauty. "It's true that Oleg controls himself badly in such situations. Maybe that's the reason why the mobs refused his services as a prize-fighter. He can kill and he won't notice it," the girl thought, tensely bandaging her injured thumb with a greasy rag.

Unexpectedly, Sarah's heartbeat became faster. The memory of Oleg immersed her in the same heated state that she had felt in his arms on that unforgettable night. Oleg's almost fatherly protection of Sarah brought on memories of her early childhood. She had felt that same protection in the strong and tender embrace of her grandfather, who also had been an army officer. He'd died when Sarah was six, but his love warmed her heart forever.

Sarah's unexpected longing the love of a kindred spirit mixed in her mind with her surge of desire and pricks of conscience.

"Indeed, Oleg is a true friend," she thought. She re-collected Oleg's bluff passion. "He did for me more than any other man in this damned world. I must be sorry. He didn't want to hurt me; it was just my own foolish suspicion. He was right. I couldn't exist in this world without the support of a strong, experienced man.

I'll make myself love him, because he deserves a little happiness in his terrible destiny!"

Suddenly, Sarah jumped up.

A forewoman had been angrily watching the girl daydream for some time. She shouted over the deafening metallic rumble of machinery: "Where are you going?"

"Couldn't be better!" snapped Sarah.

The chief roughly grasped Sarah's sweaty arm, which was covered with prickly nap of army cloth. "Don't stop the conveyer!" she shouted. "You'll forfeit of your wages!"

"Hands off!" Sarah cried as she yanked herself free from the woman's sweaty grip. "You can keep this mere pittance for yourself!" And she ran to an exit at the farthest end of the workshop. Sarah ran past the rattling sewing machines, which were indifferent to the curses of the women who struggled with their work.

"He'll forgive me, because he loves me," Sarah assured herself as she rode the bus to the district where Oleg lived. She paid no attention to the glances of other passengers, who were scrutinizing her overalls blotched with oil. The girl cared nothing for their judgments. She concentrated on her thoughts about Oleg's generosity and strength of spirit, which he usually demonstrated without being fully aware of it.

In fifteen minutes, Sarah was pounding upon the locked steel gate of Oleg's house, but nobody responded.

Where is he? the girl thought perplexedly. She hadn't seen her friend in nearly a month.

Sarah's pounding upon the door forced Oleg's neighbor to go out. It was a wizened old woman. She doddered along the dusty road running by the houses, and glanced suspiciously at Sarah, who resembled a beggar with her slovenly aspect.

"Where's Oleg?" Sarah rushed to ask the old lady.

"Who are you?" The lady asked. She scrutinized Sarah closely.

"I'm ... I'm his fiancée!"

The girl struggled to explain her relations with Oleg in a way that would satisfy the old woman's Puritanism.

Suddenly, the woman's wrinkled face frightened Sarah, for now the lady resembled a mummy. She grasped Sarah's arms, squeezing them painfully with her gaunt fingers. Gazing at Sarah with sad, sunken eyes, the woman began quivering and sobbing, "Dear ... where have you been? You are so nice. If you'd been near him, he would never have done it."

"What's happened?" Sarah exclaimed, wanting to strangle the crone who kept her in suspense.

"Oleg is no more," the old lady whispered sorrowfully. "He was buried yesterday. He shot himself." In the next moment, the woman's eyes expressed fear rather than suffering. "Wait ... I'll bring some water," she muttered. She could barely hold up Sarah's body. Struggling to bring the girl to the gate of the house, the woman sat her on the bench, which Sarah and Oleg had shared so many times.

Lacking the strength even to move, Sarah couldn't comprehend her own thoughts. She had just begun to fear that her disregard of Oleg might somehow lead to his self-destruction.

"Scoundrel!" Sarah whispered, cursing her "fiancé" inwardly, "You protected me so many times. You saved me from suicide. Was it only so you could drive me crazy by doing the same, after I fell in love with you? I so believed in your strength. Why must I stay in this goddamned world, if you—a *warrior*—could not?"

Sarah stood from the bench and shambled slowly. Suddenly she paused, staring blankly at the abysmal summer-blue sky.

"Grim, inane ..." she whispered, on the brink of madness. "Inscrutable blend of cold order and senseless chaos. You can't warm anybody with some Almighty Love. You just take away the last flashes of it from this accursed Earth. Only hell is real."

Sarah abruptly collapsed on the dusty road near Oleg's house. She didn't hear the groaning of the old woman who had returned with a cup of water. Helplessly rushing about the girl's body, the woman lamented, pleading with other neighbors to call an ambulance.

'Everywhere is a desert to the lonely man.'
(inscription engraved on a finger ring worn by A.P. Chekhov)

"We come to love not by finding a perfect
person, but by learning to see an
imperfect person perfectly."
(American philosopher Sam Keen)

Boundless astral cosmos whirled through Sarah's consciousness. Falling into the swirls of gigantic galaxies and myriad stars, Sarah's soul perceived the reality of Omnipotent Spirit. It transfused every quark of materiality with the power of divine love ... its empyrean charm and beauty, truth and strangeness.

The fathomless, dark eyes of Sarah's illusory love watched her soul wandering in a reality as inhospitable as the sublunary one. His gaze, attracting the girl like a magnetic trap, protected her from being lost, once and forever, in an unknown dimension. Melting in the dark-eyed profundity of her unrealizable love, Sarah felt despair for being unable to stay in that otherworldly reality.

Suddenly, she was dazzled. Lying upon some firm base, Sarah jumped up, recognizing immediately the shining hemisphere that was so familiar to her from her childhood.

The Stranger squatted, half-turned toward Sarah in the middle of the shining room. He wore the long frock-coat of a medieval lord, which touched the fulgent floor with its friezed lap. Broad wristbands accentuated the grace of his tapered fingers, plotting some invisible sings on the floor with a walking stick. The man's dark-brown locks hung down over his shoulders, concealing his face.

Breathless, Sarah moved toward the Stranger. She pulled down her overall, which was dusty after her fall on the road near Oleg's house. Without looking at the girl, as if just sensing her approach, the Stranger rose. Having dropped his walking stick and flicking his silky locks from his face, the man stood half-facing Sarah, but he continued ignoring her as before. However, his splendid, dark eyelashes quivered languidly. Stunned by his appearance, Sarah brushed over the man's shoulder. In return, she suddenly sensed his long fingers tangled in her own rich hair. The Stranger's dark eyes, which reflected the saintliness of Paradise and the passions of hell, struck Sarah like a thunderbolt. They compelled her to understand that she was the same stranger in the spiritual world as she was the odd girl in her material reality. She was a wanderer of the Universe, fated to flounce in pursuit of a nonexistent, empyrean love.

Sarah's legs, as usual, weakened at the Stranger's touch, pervading her body with approaching fainting-fit. She grasped the man's hand with her last strength, kissing it ecstatically and whispering, "For pity's sake! Let my soul go, or stay in my human world. I can't love an illusion."

The Stranger's long eyelashes were still quivering; his

celestial soul was touched by the attachment of this true-hearted human being.

After coming back, Sarah glanced at the white walls and ceiling of an apartment, which looked like the continuation of her alarming hallucinations.

"Where am I?" she asked silently, as if addressing herself and not waiting for answer.

"At hospital," a girl's heartfelt voice answered immediately. Sarah looked toward the speaker: a pretty nurse, maybe the same age with Sarah or even younger. She was dressed in an immaculate, snow-white coat. Preparing an injection for the patient, the girl carefully measured off the necessary quantity of medicines with a syringe. Her manner expressed satisfaction with the patient's long-awaited recovery.

Still scrutinizing the girl, Sarah asked, "Is it the mental hospital?"

"Why on earth would it be? No, this is a general, municipal hospital, the neurological department. An ambulance brought you here."

Having filled the syringe, the girl, who resembled a guardian angel with her pure, snow-white image, approached Sarah. She addressed the patient with the same tender voice. "Let me give you an injection ..."

"What's this?" Sarah looked askance at the syringe.

The nurse answered with beaming smile. "It's just some drug. For all I know, it's some variety of a weak tranquillizer. The doctors ordered it for you!" She pointed with her porcelain finger to Sarah's case-record on a bedside table.

Having heard the words "drug" and "tranquillizer," Sarah

seemed to be finally running mad. Unexpectedly she remembered one of the last times with Oleg, when he remarked that some drastic tranquillizers were prescribed to him by doctors. Against the background of his alcohol abuse, such a cure, indeed, looked like murder. It was the last, very vague, excuse for Sarah's pining conscience, which sorely needed self-justification.

"What? Drugs? For me?" she tumbled out of her bed, grasping the nurse's coat just on her bosom. As if wishing to shake the girl out of her clothes, Sarah squeezed the coat with her still-dusty hands, which had grown much stronger from her work at the factory. "I don't need your damned tranquillizer!" raged Sarah. "I live in unreal world without your drugs! Which kind of human nerve should endure this, existing in different realities?"

Sarah's eyes flashed with such madness that the shocked nurse recoiled. But the distraught patient clenched her uniform, advancing on the girl and making her to move back again and again. "Drugs, tranquillizers ... all this muck! It killed my friends!" Sarah hissed, almost stifling the nurse with her coat. Suddenly, Sarah's hands grew weak. "No," she whispered, finding no more strength to restrain her mourning and search for self-justification. "It's me who killed them with my inability to love ...although they were the salt of the earth, and deserving of my deep attachment."

Having become contrite just as unexpectedly, Sarah embraced the nurse, who was scared of the patient's erratic emotions. Clasping the girl, Sarah wept like a child. She smeared the nurse's snow-white coat with her dusty overalls.

Nerves shredded, Sarah didn't notice a man leaning against the door and watching the scene in the ward with curiosity. Seeing the nurse couldn't withstand Sarah's clutching, the man entered. Running an eye over the nurse's graceful figure in Sarah's arms, he took the syringe from her numbed hand, still keeping it in readiness.

"What does it all add up to?" the man asked, as Sarah's hug prevented the nurse from moving.

Sarah glanced at him through the mist of her tears. She identified him immediately as the doctor into whose room she and Oleg had burst that night, after Sarah's encounter with Serge's *souteneurs*. Suddenly, she felt inexplicable reliance on the man. He seemingly had appeared from her past, when she knew nothing about death, when she had considered it as something abstract that could happen to anyone, but never to her intimate associates.

Having left the nurse in peace, Sarah turned to the doctor. She grasped the man's hands. Ignoring his nervous flinch, Sarah peeked into the doctor's eyes, as if looking for some sympathy there. "Doc, do you remember me? Once I had recourse to your medical skill," she whispered.

"Maybe ..." the doctor muttered with a strained voice, avoiding Sarah's doleful look. "I have a lot of patients. I can't remember them all ..."

"Do tell!" Sarah exclaimed in amazement. "You were going to call the militia for my pacification. I was with my boyfriend, such a formidable fellow."

"Oh ... so, it's you," the physician interrupted, realizing she would never let him alone until he recalled everything up to Oleg's hard blow. "If I'm not mistaken, you're the cutie who trashed the duty doctor's room." He seemed barely able to withstand Sarah's hot clutches.

Nodding nervously, Sarah didn't grasp the meaning of the doctor's stare, which was fixed at the deep V neck of her unbuttoned overall. Almost losing her voice, Sarah squeezed the man's hands. "That fellow ... my boyfriend ... he is dead", the girl said. Her voice quivered as she realized she couldn't even say that Oleg had done away with himself.

"It's a pity, but it can't be helped. He seemed so lively," the physician said, still inspecting Sarah's slightly uncovered breast. "Indeed, there is nothing to be done. But he isn't the only pebble on the beach."

Being lost in her tears, Sarah didn't comprehend the doctor's hint.

Tipping the wink to the nurse, who still stood in the middle of the room, the doctor whispered, "Come alive! You get back to work. I'll treat this patient personally."

The ward was deserted because it was the dinner hour. Sarah felt the doctor's hands upon her own. Squeezing her fingers as ardently as Sarah had, in her hysteric fit, the man whispered, "Listen here! I know being so close to death is hard. But it's objective reality, not depending on us. I see you're too dispirited with your insubstantial perception of the actuality. Nonsense! You must be happy with your ability to escape this despicable human world! Most people are ready to give everything for some induced delusion of pleasure! But you ..." The physician pulled Sarah toward him, still whispering, "So ease off and enjoy your life! Leave the spiritual for your soul, but give material to your flesh."

In a blink, the tears dried in the girl's eyes. Endeavoring to move back from the young man, who was holding her strongly, Sarah whispered, "Be careful! I'll spoil your white coat with my dusty rags!"

"Little silly." The physician tried to overcome Sarah's resistance. "It's not that kind of filth that makes one become dirty ..."

Suddenly, a patient came in, and the doctor released Sarah immediately.

"Well," he said, renewing his double-talk, as if he'd been interrupted by the new patient. "Medical inspection will be administered to you," the doctor continued coldly, avoiding Sarah's stare. She was still wiping her tear-stained face. "If your morbid mental condition reveals itself, it might be too problematic for you to exist even in one, material reality." He continued sarcastically, "I can help you cope with these troubles. But I prefer to consult with my patients in my office."

The doctor stopped in front of Sarah and pierced her with his gaze. The girl couldn't trust her misgivings, thinking it might be just her sick imagination.

"OK," she whispered, trying to restrain her indecision. It was absurd to fear an ordinary doctor's consultation! "How can I make an appointment with you?"

The man gave his business card to Sarah. She glanced at its inscription, and her face grew green with frenzy. In the context of their conversation, the doctor's specialty seemed to be a dirty innuendo.

"What?" Sarah whispered maliciously, "A gynecologist? You undertake too much, trying to cure my brain with gynecological ways!"

She threw the card in the doctor's face.

Frustrated, the doctor whispered, answering her insolence, "Psychopath! You'll rot in a nuthouse!"

"Really?" Sarah sneered, approaching too close and tantalizing the man with the possibility of a kiss in front of the other inpatient. "Living among blessed idiots would be better for me than vegetating among such sham gynecologists who imagine themselves as great tempters."

She left the ward and saw the young nurse in the hospital corridor. After taking notice of the girl in the white coat, who was trifling with some test tubes, Sarah hailed her. When the nurse approached, Sarah said to her with apologetic tone, "You said something had been prescribed to me. Give me your devilish injection. I'll endure it somehow."

Spending long, blank days in hospital, Sarah existed with the memories of Serge and Oleg. Nobody could substitute for them. At 18, the girl's life seemed to have become the endless train of self-reproach about her friends' deaths.

Staying alone in the ward during the hot summer days, a dejected Sarah sat at an open window. She meaninglessly covered the white sheets of a copybook with the names of her perished friends, as if to suppress the pang of her heart. After hearing nearby the footfall of her portly female doctor, which was easy to recognize, Sarah jumped into her bed. She feigned sleep, avoiding the tedious discussion about the state of her health.

Scrutinizing the girl, the doctor smiled leniently at Sarah's childish disinclination to talk. Without troubling the patient, she inspected Sarah's copybook, which, in her rush, she had left on the windowsill. The doctor knew nothing about the fellows whose names appeared in the book. But she was convinced that only generous natures deserved the love of that pure-minded girl, who, nevertheless, seemed fated to perish in the hell of her pride...

'Take your cross ...'
(Holy Bible, Matthew 10:38)

Having suffered through her hardest depression, Sarah was discharged from hospital at last. As she slowly recovered the sensation of everyday reality, she perceived only despair and loneliness, which had become her damnation. This sublunary actuality, which had always seemed unfriendly and alien to the girl, became even more senseless now that her friends were gone.

Wandering aimlessly about the evening streets, Sarah sometimes stopped beside the Orthodox churches, which were plentiful in her town. Their spiritual majesty always impressed her.

Sarah especially adored a stately cathedral located downtown that was built in the 18th century. The architecture of the church combined the virtuosity of Baroque with the strictness of Classicism. The sky-high belfry of the church reached with its huge golden cross toward heaven. The golden dome of the belfry was surrounded with four bronze sculptures of evangelists, looking toward the four corners of the earth.

From her early childhood, Sarah had seen two golden domes of the cathedral dominating her town. She called that church "Italian." On a sunny, summer day, against the background of sky-blue, the brilliant domes awakened Sarah's fancies about Italy, whose architecture the structure had assimilated. But the girl never went inside the church. She was an atheist, as were the majority of Soviet people. She knew it was almost a crime to visit a church. But now, in the end of 80[th.] when the Soviet country had disintegrated, Sarah was free to enter any church without fear.

Once, passing by the cathedral, Sarah couldn't resist the temptation. After mount the steep steps, she passed inside through the huge, arched gates of the entrance. The gates were miraculously woven with inflexible metal rods as delicate as lace.

Sarah eyed ancient icons and frescos depicting angels and holy men. Gazing at the icons, she felt like a person first seeing the portraits of his eminent primogenitors. Now she knew: it was precisely the place between the earth and the heavens created for a lost soul like her.

Sarah breathed with pleasure the intoxicating incense. But suddenly, the polyphony of a choral destroyed the blessed silence. Having sounded stunningly from the loft and echoed from the majestic dome, the music flabbergasted the girl. Her soul always thrived in the harmony of sounds, which reconciled her exalted mind maybe a little with the vulgar actuality. Sarah's legs weakened. The high, painted dome with its arched, stained-glass windows faded before her misting eyes. Mental exhaustion made Sarah kneel. She longed to pray, even though she knew no orison and didn't understand the Slavonic language of mass. That divine, cosmic music seemed created a cure for her despair.

Kneeling on the mosaic floor of the cathedral, among its marble and malachite pillars, Sarah sobbed. She sensed strange energies, as if the building had absorbed the faith of the previous generations of the Christian living and dead, with their steadfast belief in the triumph of the All-Conquering Love of God to All Being. Their faith throughout the centuries had supported the warped souls of their reckless posterity, saving them from collapse in the underworld of hopelessness.

In two years, Sarah couldn't imagine how she had lived without those altruistic ideas of Christianity before. Her favorite cathedral became a second home. As usual, finding nobody in her human surroundings worth her exalted love, Sarah tried to control her distaste for people with Christian compassion. And so, the twenty-year-old girl considered life in a convent. It seemed to her that it might be the only way to escape the world's imperfection, which was always depressing her with the senselessness of her own existence.

Occasionally, she memorized the fathomless, dark eyes and fascinating look that was burning down her soul. Banishing the chain of flashbacks about the Stranger's deep-brown locks, his elegant hands and tender lips, Sarah sensed the same unconquerable attraction to the phantom. Waves of love for that mirage enveloped her as before. She uselessly argued with herself that it was just some profane obsession, demanding from her the years of praying and penance.

At the same time, she never forgot her dead friends. Their unblessed souls had left the world in torment, as if invoked by Sarah's innate ability to intuit God's verity. Nevertheless, she couldn't gain absolution for sodomy and suicide. Only their true love for her was justification for her late friends before the eyes of the merciful Maker.

At last, Sarah pretended to herself that the only hope for her life was full devotion to God.

The local eparchy of her town directed the novice to one of the most ancient Orthodox convents, which was located on the board between Ukraine and Russia.

The door of an old, shabby bus opened with a disgusting squeak. Being among the passengers of the bus, Sarah forced her way through the tight opening of the door. Having stepped off with difficulty, she appeared not far from the enormous, arched, oak gate of the convent.

After dropping her traveling bag on the thick grass at her feet and tossing a small handbag across her shoulders, Sarah looked about. A golden ocean of ripening wheat spread across the region from the foot of the hill, where the convent was. The girl inhaled the scent of endless Ukrainian fields along with the aroma of wet stubbles and cornflowers that showed blue, like tiny stars.

Contemplating the timeless, massive walls dominating the plane, Sarah realized the convent was one of the oldest strongholds of Holy Russia. It reminded her of the onslaughts of the hordes of her ancestors, Tatar tribes, tormenting Slavs over the centuries. But the conquerors, who were accustomed to winning by force, couldn't have imagined that their half-bread offspring would become hostages of the local religion. That profound belief in God's Mercy couldn't be destroyed by sword and fire.

The sluggish summer sun slowly slipped downward beyond the forest, which darkened in the distant west. Suddenly a ringing bell filled the surrounding space, heralding the beginning of Mass. Sarah's heart sank. Having studied the green, wooden domes of the minster, topped with a simple, silver cross, she felt an almost instinctive wish to cross herself. Now a flock of tourists crowded with impatience at the cloistral gates. They waited for their carriage. The people seemed eager to leave this place, which they saw as dull and depressing, marked with a hermit's asceticism.

The tourists exchanged glances, confusing Sarah. The girl suppressed her impulse to cross herself, despite her two years of professing Orthodoxy. With vexation, Sarah thought that, if she were dressed in a monastic cassock, she could be an essential of that oppressive exotic, which didn't depend on the opinion of the people. Their snide narrow-mindedness now pricked her self-esteem.

"Did you arrive to stay with us?"

Surprised, Sarah glanced back at a man who had approached silently.

He was elderly, but still a hale clergyman. The skirt of his baggy black vestment touched the dusty road and enshrouded his stooped posture. His sunken, blue eyes suggested a unique world outlook. The man's long grey hair, matting with his thick beard, made him looking like a scripture anchorite.

"Yes, father," Sarah answered. She bowed and kissed his hand in response to his silent blessing.

Regarding the girl with his fatherly stare and habitually adjusting the big, silver cross on his bosom, the cleric uttered wistfully, "Well ...But you are so young ..."

Sensing his irresolution, Sarah countered reasonably, "Father, youth is a temporary shortcoming."

"It's true," the man agreed sadly. "In fact, I haven't held your age against you. But your undue haste and fervor put me on my guard ..."

Sarah grew nervous. Hadn't she endured the long route? Hadn't she chosen her fate long ago?

"Father, excuse my impatience." The girl fumbled with her hand-bag. "But I have all necessary papers with me. Besides, I listened to the same edification in my local archdiocese before arriving here."

Having found his glasses in a secret pocket of his vestment, the cleric put them over his straight nose and attentively scanned Sarah's letters, which she also had discovered in her handbag at last.

"Well, for that matter ..." He seemed vexed, unable to pick a hole in the girl's reputation at first glance. Neatly straightening the sheets of paper, which Sarah had folded in half, the clergyman added, more indifferently, "Just here ... there is some formality." He pointed with his calloused forefinger at Sarah's papers. "It behooves you to sign them."

Unexpectedly, the man picked up Sarah's heavy traveling bag and directed his steps toward the cloistral gate. He carried Sarah's simple things with the knack of an industrious peasant. Running after him, the perplexed girl kept looking for some occasion to retrieve her baggage from the hands of the old man. His unexpected etiquette confused Sarah.

They passed across a spacious yard with numerous farming implements, which were needed to maintain the semi-natural economy of the convent. Farming provided the modest needs of its hard-working inhabitants.

The clergyman and Sarah came upon the imposing wall of the fortress. Having ascended a steep stone stage, they stepped into a dark, arched ambulatory of the convent through an embrasure that served as an entrance. In a trace, Sarah was blinded with the low rays of the setting sun, which permeated the inside through the wall's small embrasures. Slowly passing by the range of heavy wooden doors, which were set an equal distance from one another along one side of the ambulatory, Sarah sensed the heroic past of that gloomy place.

At last, the cleric and the girl stopped before a door. Jingling keys deep in his pocket, the man found the necessary one, as if through a miracle. He unlocked the door, letting Sarah into a small, dark cell. After placing the girl's bag on the stone floor, the cleric tabled her documents somewhere in the deep semi-darkness. He groped for matches and began to light tapers and icon-lamps, mysteriously illuminating the icons on the walls. The cell overlooked the east with its sole window, which failed to let in enough of the sunset's afterglow to illuminate the small room.

"Doesn't such austerity depress a young girl?" the cleric asked provocatively, glancing askance at Sarah, who was fascinated by the images of Christ and all the hosts of heaven. From the walls, they seemed alive with the fire's gleaming.

Sarah shrugged her shoulders in silent response. At last, she could look around. Excepting for a handcrafted, wooden table by the window and two clumsy stools, there was just a steel bed. It was covered with modest, but clean, white linen.

"Well ..." the clergyman pronounced, trying to fill the awkward silence. "Whatever the appearances, this place is really sacred!" He continued in a fluster, as if bragging about his proximity to saintliness. "Churches and convents were always built in such peculiar confluxes of different worlds. People always seek spiritual support from the powers above. And the heavens reciprocated everyone who longed for their divine love..."

"What?" Sarah asked, as if stirring from a stupor. "Reciprocated? Heavens? Huh ..." She tried to hide her sarcasm, not wanting to offend the old man. However, she couldn't black out the pangs of her friends' death, which those "heavens" hadn't prevented.

"And whereby do they reciprocate? It would be interesting to see."

The man ignored her poor temper. With his masterful hand scraping beeswax that had dripped onto a candlestick, he uttered wistfully, "Our Maker's Epiphany is said to have condescended on some nuns here."

"Really?" Sarah asked with the same affected curiosity as she cleaned the candlestick with her fingers, but from its other side. "And what the kind of Epiphany it was? None other than some angel's appearance?"

"Yes," the man answered calmly. "I never saw the beings with my own eyes, but they supposedly don't differ from us." The clergyman almost whispered, as if he were afraid the angels would overhear. "There is only one distinctive feature they have: their incredible look. The superhuman eyes can exalt you to Paradise or precipitate you into the abyss of hell, in accordance with your perception of the creature's essence. Their nature is very unstable. It's necessary to be careful with one's emotions in the case of visual contact with them. Besides, angels never converse with people ..."

"Oh!" Sarah exclaimed, having scorched her fingers with the candlestick. Squeezing her cool earlobe with her burned fingers, she whispered in imitation of the cleric's cryptic tone. "It beats all! They don't converse with us? Quotha! Isn't it Our Lord's grace? Just some cosmic dig!"

"I don't know why they are so stern with us," the cleric said, watching the girl wrinkle up with pain. "Maybe we just have to reach some higher level of spirituality to understand the celestials without any words."

He wasn't afraid of looking ludicrous in front of Sarah.

"It's scandalous!" she whipped out at last. "How can you, the man whose mission is to serve to Our Maker selflessly, believe in some gathering of nonexistent pagan's idols with human visages and some absurd bird's wings, depicted in fabulous icons? You are so defying your human nature as a top of perfection that you are ready to see such features even in the empyreal world! The Spirit of the Universe doesn't need any physical avatar! There is only one way to perceive God's verity: sense His Love as an integral part of human soul."

The ecclesiastic stopped to abrade wax and stared at the young theologian. He sat down upon a stool, nervously mopping his sweaty forehead with the broad sleeve of his vestment.

"It's unbelievable!" the man whispered at last as he fixed his blue eyes on Sarah's papers, which were lying on the table. "So ... you are not a devotee of Orthodoxy. You are a Gnostic." Meanwhile, Sarah feverishly revolved the words in her mind, as if they had escaped her lips by themselves. That ominous designation, "Gnostic," which had sounded in the man's utterance as if it were an affront, suddenly erected a wall of misunderstanding between the two.

"That's not so!" Sarah excused herself, regretting her hasty remark concerning icons, which she knew were one of the most significant material attributes of faith for any Trinitarian. "Gnostic? It means nothing to me." She tried to iron out the vexing effect of her gaffe. Sarah realized she was within a hairbreadth of conflict with the clergyman, who seemed ready to send her home at any moment.

"Gnostics were such heretics, who had justified even Judas." The man explained, patiently and dogmatically, his interpretation of the word, which suddenly had become the seed of discord.

"But Jesus himself absolved Judas!" Sarah blurted out. "Why may not we, being good Christians, do the same?" The girl surprised herself. She couldn't suppress the strange voice in her mind, as if it were making her contradict the cleric and undermine all her efforts to stay in the convent.

"What?" the graybeard exclaimed, starting up from his place and rushing about the small room. "There is a great difference between Christ's All-forgiving and our meager justification of our fellow creatures. In fact, we can't forgive each other for even little nothings of life! True Absolution is in Our Redeemer's authority! "

"There is nothing impossible in forgiving ..." Sarah muttered perkily, restraining the tears of fear that were coming with the lump in her throat. "Satan could be justified with the imperfection of this world!"

"God Almighty!" The cleric sighed deeply, realizing that the arch enemy had sent this girl. "It's over my head! Overcome your hellish pride, and you'll do the great service for the imperfect world!"

He didn't pause to be surprised by Sarah's audacity. The cleric was ready to defend his creed against the backslider's attack, even if it meant expelling Sarah from those dignified walls, in contradiction of the traditions of Christian mercy.

The man stopped before Sarah, who stood as if rooted to her place, shivering with nervous energy. "Why? Why do you come into this Orthodox convent? You don't follow the dogmas of our faith!"

Seeing his implacability and finding no strength to withstand the man's devotion, Sarah sensed that he could not grasp her arguments. They were at the end of all logical and verbal resources of human understanding. Nothing but the cleric's goodness remained at her disposal.

Suddenly, drowning in tears, Sarah collapsed. Her skirt barely covered her naked knees. She grasped the hem of the cleric's cassock, kissing it. "Father, forgive me! Have a heart! Let me stay here! I can do nothing with my critical nature, finding imperfections everywhere. But I'll never reject the religion and the blessings that protected my mind against madness. Even day after day, finding new contradictions in the doctrine, I cannot disown the choice of my soul."

Staring at the kneeling girl, the cleric sensed her sincerity. He realized it was her way to believe, although it appalled him. "What?" he whispered, nearly overtaken by terror at Sarah's words. For the first time in his long life, he saw someone ready to reside between these walls without any frenetic religiosity, but because of some abstract choice of her soul, which would never be appreciated.

The cleric argued against Sarah spending the bloom of her life in the convent's burdensome routine. He noted that living away from civilization was far from her idealistic notion about the exclusively spiritual existence of the cloistral inhabitants, who seemed to be surviving almost immaterially with only the bliss of the Holy Spirit.

"Your beauty is not for a nun," the cleric whispered, trying to appeal to the vanity of youth. "I'm sure you have a boyfriend. He loves and waits for you."

"Two boy friends," Sarah sobbed, as before. "They loved me as nobody will again. They're waiting for me, but somewhere in eternity. I can't live without them in a constantly deceitful world, where even the mirage of love slips away from my hands."

The cleric's hands flinched. As before, he felt thunderstruck by Sarah's irrational devotion to the religion, the dogmas of which she could not accept. But at the same time, he realized that a person with such a potential for love was self-defeating in the world, which someday would catch her illusory mind in its sophisticated mesh. He began to understand Sarah's longing to stay in the convent. Her longing was the impulse of the pure soul to save its integrity.

"There, there," the man uttered, lifting Sarah from the cold floor and sitting her on a stool. Mopping dry her face with his calloused hand, he whispered peacefully, "In the end, I'm just an ordinary cleric. I won't dare question the decision of His Grace Archbishop, who signed your letter of credence." The man motioned with his head toward Sarah's papers. He gave her to understand that he wouldn't interfere with her zeal to stay in the convent, regardless of the differences of their gospel and the girl's heretical attitude of mind.

Having left Sarah sitting on the stool by the table, the cleric turned to icons. Crossing himself, he muttered, "Good God! Absolve me, sinner, praying to You! Make her to listen to Your reason. So far, You have led her to Your cell …"

Standing by Sarah, the man lapsed into mute praying. Meanwhile, gloomily looking at her papers, Sarah fumbled in her handbag for a fountain pen. But it was in vain. Suddenly, her attention was attracted to an antique ink stand. It was darkened with time and stood at the farthest end of the table. Writing with a true feathery pen seemed to Sarah very alluring. She moved to the ink stand and took the corny, scratchy pen in her hand. Being under the spell of a viscid, dark liquid dropping in the ink-port from the sharp tip of the pen, Sarah lingered.

Suddenly, some light breath touched her curls, and the girl turned around. At the same moment, her eyes clashed with the penetrating, dark look of the Stranger, whose stare pinned her in place. The man was slightly inclined over Sarah's head from behind. She sensed his hot breath reaching her tresses, again and again. Sarah couldn't long endure these temptations, which had seemingly dropped from the clouds at such a painful moment. She suddenly leaped up, forgetting about the pen in her hand. Sarah accidentally touched the man's dark-brown lock, and his lips nearly brushed over her cheek. Immediately, thrilling weakness flowed in her blood. Sarah swayed and clumsily overturned the ink-port. Lacking the strength to look away from her beloved, the girl sensed how the spilled ink was covering the table and destroying her papers.

"You!" she whispered, indignant with her inability to withstand the Stranger's inexplicable power. "Devil incarnate! I thought so! You would do anything to keep me from God!"

After regaining consciousness, Sarah found herself in bed. She set her eyes involuntary on an icon hanging just over the door of the cell: an angel with fathomless, black eyes and long, dark-brown locks that contrasted with his draped, pastel vestment and enormous, snow-white wings.

Sarah closed her eyes at the amazing image. Dark color was not suitable for a Light celestial; he was traditionally depicted as having blond hair and blue eyes.

The door of the cell opened, and the old clergyman came in with a cup of hot tea. Having put it on the table near Sarah, the man took a seat on a stool near her bed. Seeing the girl's opened eyes, he breathed freely. "Thank God, you have recovered. I was going to send for a doctor. You scared me badly ... and all because of our senseless discussion. Never start it again! There is nothing more foolish than enmity because of some abstract philosophy. We are human beings, and it's quite enough to understand each other, regardless of our outlook."

Sarah barely heard the man. She thought sadly about her spoiled documents, which were still lying on the table. Not wishing even to glance at them, she recollected with a pang in her heart the difficulties she'd had to overcome to obtain them. Sarah knew it would be impossible to explain her negligence to the clerics of her town. Having suspected the young girl's frivolity, they wouldn't give her another chance.

"Father, what will it be, after all?" Sarah asked. She nervously crumpled in her hand the tip of the blanket with which the man had covered her.

"What do you mean?" the dumbfounded ecclesiastic asked.

"My documents …"

"Papers?" The cleric was surprised at her sorrowful tone. "They are just paper …" He took the snow-white sheets of paper in a perfunctory manner from the table. The text of the letter was impeccable, including all necessary signatures. The man folded the sheets half to half before Sarah's widening eyes. "I'll just bring them to our Mother Superior tomorrow. It's too late tonight. Welcome to our big, united family!"

Shocked, Sarah involuntary shifted her eyes from her ink-stained hands to the ink-covered table, contrasting them with whiteness of her papers in the cleric's hands.

"Unbelievable!" Involuntary, she fastened her abstracted look at the image of the dark-eyed angel over the door.

The angel stared back.

Having snuffed out most of the tapers, the cleric remained the only one illuminating the cell, enigmatically and faintly. After wishing good night to the girl, he went out, carrying Sarah's ill-fated documents.

Watching the flickering flame of the sole taper, Sarah couldn't sleep, re-collecting time and again her Stranger. Why did he appear in that sacred place after more than two years of absence? Trying to escape these thoughts, the girl rolled over onto her other side.

Suddenly, she jumped up and cried out. Sarah's back had pressed against the cold, stone wall.

She barely saw the silhouette of a man sitting on a stool not far from her bed in the nearly blackened room. Fervently crossing herself, Sarah recited her prayers. After the first sounds of her praying, a shining halo shrouded the graceful form and features of her celestial affection.

The melancholic dark look of the Stranger invited Sarah into the abyss of temptation and threatened to vanquish her mind— and her very sense of reality.

Suddenly, absolute silence and peace reigned everywhere. Feeling neither fear nor surprise, Sarah found herself standing in the middle of an infinite, snow-white field of flowers. The breast-high plants, resembling poppies with large, cool petals, brushed the girl's naked body. Mist spread over the field, veiling the strange, grey sky as if the sun didn't exist here ... or anywhere.

From behind, long fingers brushed against Sarah's naked forearms, bringing to mind a ghost's brushing. Only tall flowers obscured her nudity, as the Stranger's hands squeezed her arms tenderly, but more and more palpably. Sarah spun around and found herself in the arms of the man devouring her with his dark, magnetic look, but always keeping silent. His graceful motions seemed to defy gravity. The Stranger's kisses were ethereal and almost indifferent, as if they were just his unskillful attempt to condescend to Sarah's human nature. However, the celestial's engrossing gaze was the true source of ecstasy that freed Sarah's soul from materiality. No earthy temptation could compare with that divine sensation of her full dissolution in All-absorbing Love of his eyes.

Trying to warm the reserved celestial with her ardent desire, Sarah couldn't overcome his spiritual nature. She was just losing her heat to stimulate the man's kisses with her own. She drank in the Stranger's breath over her lips. At the same time, Sarah was surprised, inwardly, that she hadn't fallen unconscious with their closeness, as she was used to.

"What are we doing?" Sarah whispered, still kissing the man's cool lips. "Some immaculate intimacy? In any case, it's the perfidy of my faith in the convent ..." Having unbuttoned the Stranger's medieval-style, bag-sleeved shirt, Sarah couldn't slip it from his shoulders. Squeezing with ardor, his forearms became naked; she whispered madly, "So, this is the place where we can touch each other, somehow. Is that the reason you helped me stay in the convent? " The Stranger kept silent. As usual, he didn't interrupt the girl's monologue, leniently permitting her to caress his body, which was cool to carnality.

"A pity you aren't an ordinary man. You are so cold ..." Sarah mumbled deliriously, wearying of her struggle with the man's shirt.

Suddenly, the Stranger shucked off his shirt with one light, graceful motion. At the same moment, some incredible power tossed Sarah away, and she landed on the ground.

Trying to rise among the flowers, which were now tossed about as if by a sudden hurricane, Sarah covered her eyes. She struggled to see something in that dazzling light that spread overall. At last, the light dimmed a bit, and she again saw the Stranger. The formless outpouring of some incandescent gas escaped beyond his shoulders. In fact, it resembled a pair of unprecedented, cosmic wings. With the barest fluctuation of irradiation, all surrounding space transformed: the flower field became a dark plain covered with the shimmering stars of a gigantic, traversing galaxy. The next moment, the space turned to the overflowing of the blending colors of the spectrum, wrapping everything with colossal patches of aurora Polaris.

Naked, Sarah appeared in the man's arms again. His fiery eyes and disheveled, dark locks made the Stranger appear fiendish. His scalding flesh burned Sarah's like some hellish fire. She whispered, with a thrill, "It couldn't take my breath away. Now it's too hot. So ... there is nothing human in you as before."

The Stranger's body became unfeelingly cold again. The profundity of his dark look returned, dissolving Sarah's mind in the superhuman nature of the celestial again.

Losing the strength to withstand his gaze, Sarah drooped along his body. She tugged the man away to the carpet of flowers, which was stamped flat and turned now to the starred universe, and now to dispersed iridescence.

Angels' enormous wings spread over the ground with luminous stream. They covered the bodies of two alien creatures, who were embracing one another. The Spirit of Empyrean Love attracted them more than their different physical natures.

After regaining her consciousness, Sarah stared at the old cleric, who was nodding on a stool at her bed. It was an early summer morning, and dazzling sunlight burst into the cell through its sole window.

"Am I ill?" Sarah whispered, thinking the man couldn't hear her. She was surprised at how quickly her mind exchanged one reality for another.

The cleric awoke immediately at the sound of her voice.

"No," he said, carefully touching Sarah's forehead with his

palm. "The doctor who examined you three days ago said you were just sleeping."

"What?" Sarah whispered, horrified by the man's words. She perplexedly inspected the clock face of her wristwatch. "Dear me ..." The girl hardly moved, feeling an unpleasant weakness in her muscles from such a long quiescence. She still wore the clothes she'd worn for her arrival, three days earlier.

"I'll go out," the cleric said tactfully, giving Sarah opportunity to recover from the shocking discovery and restore her appearance.

Eventually, Sarah got up, with difficulty. Her body ached as if after some exotic massage. Suddenly, a long black cassock hanging over the footboard of her bed attracted the girl's attention. She grasped the dark vestment and pressed it to her face. Inhaling the scent of aniline dye that still penetrated the new fabric, Sarah felt such happiness—as if any girl would dream of such a dress. But for Sarah, it symbolized new life, free from the ambitious and callous world.

Clasping the dress to her breast, Sarah noticed two large, white petals had fallen on it from her disheveled hair. The girl glanced at the flower petals, as if hesitating to touch to them. All her experiences in that strange stupor, during three long Earth days and nights, floated through her mind. At last, she picked up the petals, carefully hiding them in a secret pocket of her new cassock. They were the irrefutable evidence of Sarah's unearthly contact with her illusory love.

Unexpectedly, Sarah began to sink into her three-day lethargy. Every time, after coming to herself, she was blissful and slightly absent-minded. Taking the white flower petals from her dark-brown curls and putting them into the pocket of her monastic vestment, Sarah smiled to herself. "Everything as usual ..." she thought confusedly. She ignored the faint stings of her seared conscience.

Now the girl seldom thought about her past. Her former life seemed a distant nightmare. Instead of her previous despair, now an almost unceasing euphoria lived in Sarah's heart. Her suffering soul was regenerated just by the angelic look of her celestial lover. For the young novice, there was no place on the Earth closer to the Lord than the obscure convent.

Sarah's inexplicable fits of lethargy made her seem nearly an elect in the eyes of the other nuns, who cared touchingly about the strange novice. They spared Sarah from the hard work and inevitable discomforts of their common existence. Their sincere care confused the girl to the very roots of her being.

The cleric also became attached to Sarah with whole-hearted love. The girl seemed to him a unique combination of integrity and intuitive wisdom.

Having found some spare time in his compact daily timetable, the man tried to hide Sarah away from the sight of the censorious Mother Superior, who demanded the rigorous fulfillment of duties by everyone. Unafraid of provoking the abbess' wrath—now by species of cunning, now by insistency—the cleric seized Sarah's time and carried her off to his homely hut, huddling to the minster.

Regaling the girl with scalding tea and freshly baked cloistral mince pies, the man fervently tormented Sarah for an hour, reasoning out of her idealism, which cast away everything material. Having handled all philosophers from Plato up to Kant, not having left behind the all-honored Christ with his scriptural wisdom, Sarah at last escaped from the hole of the wily man. Such talks were the only way for the cleric to satisfy his only sinful predilection, which was the indulging in philosophic discussions. It was almost impossible for him otherwise, as he lived among very kind nuns whose rustic minds were immersed solely with dogmatic prayer and natural worries about daily bread.

Once, the clergyman was invited to one of the nearest hamlets for the christening of a sickly infant. The man again endeavored to call Sarah away from her duties. Grown bolder, he declared his intention to take Sarah with him. Ignoring the suspicious stare of the Mother Superior, who had noticed long ago his interest in the novice, the cleric just laughed off the abbess' grumbling about Sarah's constantly shirking her duties. The puzzled girl overheard the ecclesiastic's wrangle. Suddenly, the cleric stopped to altercate with the abbess and turned to Sarah. He scooped her up resolutely and set in the bottom of a hay-covered cart. Having felt for a moment the man's strong hands as they threw her into that odorous sheaf, Sarah immediately sank into the usual bliss with the recollection of her lethargic dreams.

Resting on the bottom of the jerky cart, Sarah studied the azure sky and drifting summer clouds. Smiling absent-mindedly to herself, she answered the cleric's captious questions purposing to reveal her ignorance of the main postulates of apologetics. Annoyed by Sarah's indifference to his inquisitiveness, the cleric sluggishly flogged along a sorrel. Meanwhile, Sarah basked in the sun with unspeakable placidity. She didn't wish to shine with her useless erudition, which never made her feel as happy as did that bottomless sky, where her love lived.

Lost in reverie, Sarah paid no attention to other travelers

passing by the monastic cart. Bumpkins perched on their horses goggled at the strange girl in the long, dark vest, lying in the cart. Sarah's dark-brown curls spread over the hay attracted the men's prurient stares, making the cleric nervous.

"Hold your horse!" he shouted at the curious drivers, who approached the monastic vehicle so closely they seemed to want to clash with it.

Having apprehended the cleric's jealous, sidelong glances as they neared their destination, Sarah covered her head with the same dark sheet that was fastened to the back of her head with a dark silk tape. The sullen pall hid her posh hair and high cheekbones, and made the girl slightly moon-faced, suggesting kinship with Asian berserks. Now Sarah looked very peaceful. With her drooping, big eyes, slightly *retrousse* nose and neatly outlined, small lips—accentuated with her dark head scarf—she resembled a sentimental Slav beauty.

Having arrived at the village and climbed out of the cart, Sarah obediently trailed behind the cleric. He blessed local peasants right and left, taking into account that they met the ecclesiastic as if he were the True Lord. Crossing herself and staring at the earth, Sarah entered a peasant's beggarly hovel, which smelled of cheap liquor. Looking about at the squalid dwelling, she wasn't surprised at the sickliness of the infant, whom the cleric had been invited to christen. Preparing for the christening with the help of the infant's relatives, Sarah sensed the leers of the rustic men gathering in the house. The religious rite was, obviously, an infrequent entertainment here. Sarah ignored the provocative squints of the filthy fellows, who looked dark with dipsomania. She willfully pierced the floor with her languid look, revealing her latent, hot nature.

In a singing voice, the cleric began the ritual. Without knowing all its fine points, Sarah studied the man's eloquent glances, which indicated the assistance he needed.

Suddenly, some whisper reached the novice's keen ear. It was the quiet gossip of women talking about Sarah. Hearing the women's grievous sighs for the unenviable destiny of the future nun, who would never feel the happiness of motherhood, Sarah became furious. Even her garment of a novice—which indicated she still might leave the convent at her convenience, at any time—couldn't moderate the disparaging compassion of these people!

Sarah, shocked with the obtuse lip right behind her back, looked aside from the cleric for a moment. But the man relied on her continuing assistance, as before. After taking the christened baby out of an extemporary font, the ecclesiastic turned unexpectedly to Sarah. He held up the sickly infant in his powerful hands; the cleric was assured his deft assistant was ready to wrap the baby in a christening towel. But Sarah stood still with the opened towel in her hands. She looked perplexedly at the helpless creature in the man's powerful hands and hesitated. The infant wrinkled up his face, seemingly ready to bawl: regardless of Sarah's nervous lingering, he wanted immediate drying and warmth.

The girl at last grasped the meaning of the cleric's stern look. In a blink, she wrapped the baby in the towel, clasping him to her breast, as if wishing to warm the child with the heat of her heart.

The tiny tot quieted in Sarah's arms. Suddenly, she felt an overpowering desire to clasp the dumb creature to her body forever.

When the cleric allowed the child's return to his relatives, Sarah felt a pang in her heart as if she were losing the sense of her existence.

Reluctantly giving the infant to his mother—a young woman

who showed signs of premature aging on her face, exhausted with hard work and monotonous life in back country—Sarah shifted her eyes to the baby's father. He seemed to be mummified by spirits, unable to comprehend the happiness of having a family.

En route to the convent, Sarah no longer lay on the bottom of the cart. She sat on the end of the vehicle, wistfully watching the boundless Ukrainian plains alternating with broad belts of forest. Vague doubts about her decision to domicile in the convent treacherously wormed into her heart, like the old Serpent.

But regardless of her sudden longing for family life, Sarah couldn't accept any man, as before. Her soul desired only those superhuman eyes.

The cart rounded a small grove. Moving out onto a plain again, Sarah shuddered. The incredible sight of a far-flung, flowery field opened before her eyes ... large, white poppies ...

"What's this?" Sarah asked softly, staring at the flowers billowing by her feet.

"Ah! This ..." the cleric bucked up, lightly whipping the horse, which slowly made its way along a country-track by the flowery paradise. Since leaving the hamlet, the man had hesitated to talk to Sarah, who had sunk into a deep melancholy. Now he was relieved that the girl spoke.

"What ineffable beauty!" the cleric said, shaking his grey head and pointing toward the snow-white blooms that spread up to the skyline. "Incomparable sight! Moreover, you can't even imagine this plain on a warm summer night!" he said with intense feeling. With his back to Sarah, he couldn't see the girl's pale face. "Thousands of shining fireflies alight on these calyxes just as it grows dark. Then it seems the starry universe spread at your feet, inviting you with its mysterious eternity. But toward the predawn hours, some matutinal brume shrouds the Earth, and the first shy rays of the day-star refract in the mist. They overflow the field with the iridescent waves of rainbow, the symbol of the Old Covenant between God and Man."

Sarah stared at the field as if it contained a flying saucer. Her hand dipped into the secret pocket of her cassock and pulled out the dry petals.

"What fragrance! Inexpressible aroma!" Despite the cleric's efforts to cheer her, Sarah's anxiety increased. "Our Mother Superior, let Our Maker extend her days," the man smiled slightly at his mention of the strict battle-axe, "she allows our nuns to strew the bed-linen with these petals for more freshness after laundering. You know our old-way of hand-washing. So, after getting out of your bed, you have been shaking off these petals from your good head of hair all day long."

Sarah was exhausted. The wrinkled petals dropped from her weakened hands. After short sailing, they laid resignedly on the dusty road forming a dotted white track after the lumbering cart as it moved away.

"My God," she thought, burying her face in her hands. "I invented everything. My illusory love is just the ejection of my morbid imagination. Obviously, I saw the flower field through the window of the bus on my way to the convent, but I didn't pay due attention to it. As for the petals in my hair after sleeping ... now it's also clear. Holy Mother!"

Sarah thought herself to be the greatest sinner. Being the hostage of her filthy fancies, she not only stood in her own light, but tarnished the cloister, the place that was sacred for any true believer. It was unbearable for her to pay for the kindness of the convent's inhabitants with such a sophisticated demonology, which seemed to be rooted in her mind.

When Sarah and the cleric arrived at the convent near nightfall, the girl couldn't get to her cell without assistance. She burned with fever. After carrying Sarah into her cell in his arms, the cleric put her in bed. He fussed over the girl and cursed himself for taking her to that hamlet. Not understanding the cause of her unexpected burning ague, the cleric suspected she might have become infected with something dangerous in the dirty dwelling of the peasants, where, by some miracle, survived the infant. The old man frazzled out a doctor, sending for him several times during the night, yet he could not believe the physician's efforts to reassure him.

After a while, Sarah overcame her hard pangs of conscience. Banishing all thoughts of her darling Stranger and bending her knees to the minster, she sank into monotonous, penitential praying. Yet Sarah never dared voice the cause of her pain. She knew it would seem absurd to all.

One night, having awakened to the sensation of the Stranger's presence, Sarah glanced at the stool, where he sat quietly. As usual, his dark eyes absorbed the girl's green look.

"Are you waiting for my prayers?" Sarah asked with an irritated quiver in her voice. "Let's do something less kinky. I'll allow nobody to defame my faith!"

Sarah got out of her bed resolutely and approached her celestial love. She stopped beside the Stranger, inspecting his spellbinding, long eyelashes, which shivered in response to her closeness.

"Why do you never talk to me?" the girl demanded, realizing she would always have only a monologue with such a mute interlocutor. "Indeed. Why converse? I'm within your grasp wholly. But I'm not going to fulfill the wishes of some dumb illusion. I'm an ordinary woman, and your emphatic eyes are not quite enough to make me fall in love with you. Why raise my desire if you can't satisfy it?"

Suddenly, Sarah gave a tug at the twines of her hard linen bed gown, which hid her body up to her toes, like a massive sarcophagus. The chemise fell upon her feet.

The imperturbable Stranger stared at the naked girl as before. Except for his light breathing upon Sarah's skin, he seemed an immovable mirage.

"Come ..." the temptress uttered, endeavoring to see in the man's dark eyes even a hint of lust. "I don't ask your love ... just prove that you are real. Don't I deserve a human happiness on this damned Earth instead of your illusory love?"

The Stranger remained unmoved, and Sarah approached his face with her lips slightly parted. But the girl realized she would lose her consciousness if she merely touched him.

"Well," she whispered crossly, "if it comes to that, I'll uproot this absurd love out of my heart ... even if it will be damned after all!"

The fire of icon-lamps flinched ominously. Shadows scurried across the walls.

Sarah started back from the Stranger. His amazing eyes were now horrendous, empty holes, where hellish darkness blended with its fire. But the girl could not move. The cross-shaped scar bled freely, and blood curled and hardened like lava on the floor.

Now Sarah realized it was her insuperable pride that had precipitated the avatar of Angel to hell. The earth girl was now at the mercy of a powerful afreet occupying the incredible energy of the celestial. The Stranger, the only creature able to protect Sarah from the inexplicable bleeding out of her palm, now indifferently waited for her inevitable death.

By force of habit, Sarah opened her mouth to whisper a prayer. But to her surprise, the hellish entity also uttered something. The ghoulish vibrations penetrated Sarah's brain with a wild pang. The girl squeezed her head with her hands and closed her eyes as blood suddenly flowed from her nose and ears.

With no hope of salvation, Sarah knelt on the floor in the puddle of her blood. She hadn't the strength to even squeeze her head more. Suddenly, her hand sensed the flower petals that were knotted in her hair after getting out of the bed.

Clasping the cool petals to her bloodstained breast, Sarah felt their tender delicacy as if the waft of Angel's wings touched her body again. It carried her back to the superlunary appointments with her Stranger, who now was helpless before the fit of her pride.

Despite her physical collapse, suddenly Sarah sensed an unbelievable energy germinating within her. She rose from the floor, as if by dint of the same powerful wings. In a blink, she attained the entity and pressed her bleeding palm to the Stranger's empty eye-sockets. At the same time, a sizzling force threw the girl toward the opposite wall.

Naked upon the cold stone floor, Sarah collected herself with difficulty. But she sensed the tender tapered fingers interlacing with her own as the bleeding ceased. She opened her eyes and smiled, seeing the Stranger's usual wistful look fastened on her.

"Sorry... I was mistaken," the girl whispered, losing her voice. "You can't be real. People never have such Heaven's Love in their eyes."

The Angel listened to Sarah's words, sadly observing her useless struggle with approaching unconsciousness. But suddenly, the Stranger bent to Sarah's face and kissed her lips slightly. The girl winced in pain or ecstasy.

"You can, if you want," she smiled ironically, still clasping the Stranger's healing hand. Slipping into unconsciousness, still feeling the Angel's intoxicating breath over her lips, Sarah uttered willfully, "But even after that, you are an illusion."

After awakening in the morning, Sarah felt renewed. The only unpleasant sensation that troubled her after that wild night was some pain on her lips.

Nothing had changed in her cell. Her bed gown was still on the stone floor. Having picked it up to cover her nudity, Sarah approached a small mirror on a wall near the door. She took a peep at its bleared surface and was terrified. Her lips appeared burned.

After dressing in her monastic cassock, Sarah left the cell, her lips covered with a handkerchief. Suddenly, she collided with the old cleric, who seemed to have turned up from the morning darkness of the austere walls.

"Why didn't you come to the matins?" he asked Sarah reproachfully, grasping her shoulders. "I see ... something is happening with you! You have to pray more."

At last the man took note of the girl's half-covered face and saw her eyes, which were like those of a sick dog, staring at him imploringly. The cleric took Sarah's hand with the handkerchief, removing it from her face.

"Powers above!" he sighed, looking at her deformed lips. "What happened?"

"What's the difference now?" Sarah said. She waved impatiently, as speaking was painful. "It was just an unlucky attempt to put out an icon-lamp," she added, comically mangling the words.

The cleric burst into laughter, shaking his sides. Sarah wanted to smile in return but could only wince in pain.

Having settled down at last and wiping his involuntary tears with his hand, the cleric beckoned the girl to follow him. "Let's go ... I'll help you."

The man salved Sarah's lips with balm and muttered tensely, "Indeed, you'll drive me, the old sinner, to the grave with your malarkey. To kiss a hot candlestick, my God! However," he added didactically, "to offend angels is really far-reaching."

Sarah glanced up as if ready to curse, regardless of the sacredness of the place. But her burned lips reined back her impulse. She suddenly licked the man's finger, which was still treating her lips. The cleric withdrew his hand from her face in confusion. Sarah squinted at him cunningly and whispered, "Please, never tell me about angels ..."

Tossing on her bed all night, Sarah now begged for her Stranger, but he didn't appear again. The girl's soul withered without his eyes. Her exalted faith turned to gray, gloomy suffering and doubts in God's Absolution.

At last, the self-contradiction of Sarah's soul reached its peak.

Sinking into the everyday cloistral routine, Sarah thought with despair, "I can't stay here. It's true; my nature is too hot for such a place. The secluded atmosphere just stimulates my absurd fancies." It seemed a reasonable justification for Sarah's fear to accept her destiny. At the same time, she intuited that her illusory love would unlikely trouble her any more.

Now Sarah felt like a prisoner. Sometimes, she memorized her stupid, fleshy pretensions to her celestial sweetheart. They were so happy in that sacred place, regardless of the difference of their physical nature. Nobody would know of her empyrean love ... just God, in the all-seeing eyes of whom she would remain a constant imperfection.

Day after day, living among the poorly educated nuns, Sarah understood that she couldn't develop pure love for people like the unpretentious, kind women did. For the first time in her life, Sarah was surrounded by people with little regard for themselves. The nuns' serenity and fearless accepting of the inclemency of the sublunary world finally took down the girl's pride.

Sarah at last made up her mind to inform the cleric she was leaving the cloister. After the news, the thunderstruck man didn't find strength even to get angry with the unbalanced girl, whose peculiar mind so charmed him. The cleric didn't say a word in response. He just shrugged his still strong shoulders. A stinging tear, invisible to Sarah, disappeared into his thick, grey beard. There was no choice for the man but to solace himself with his worldly wisdom.

Parting with Sarah at the huge gates of the convent, the old cleric was distressed. Clasping Sarah's hand after his farewell blessing, he uttered with sad irony, "Don't forget our cloister. I think you had a chance to be proved in its holiness."

"Absolutely," Sarah whispered, dropping her eyes, which were filled with pent-up tears. The girl hated her contradictory nature, compelling her to lose the favored few who loved and appreciated her unusual mind.

After a pause, the cleric shook his head.

"Even so, if you feel alien to this world, you'll find the way to escape it. But finally, you'll see that the elemental harmony of the Earth is the same objectification of God's Love as your abstract spiritual reality."

The bus stopped at the gate. Finding no words to express her mixed feelings, Sarah hugged the confused cleric, and then hurried onto the bus. Highly emotional, she refused to concede her error even now. Flicking tears from her cheeks, the girl refused to look out the window, where the desolate figure of the cleric disappeared into the cloud of road dust.

Sarah's life became routine. Living with her parents and brothers in their ordinary flat, day after day, the girl struggled with the actuality of her place under the sun.

Only in her dreams, the severe walls of the Orthodox citadel arose in her mind. Buried in the golden wheat, against the azure sky, the convent shined with its silver crosses. The old cleric, who was the greatest exotic of that place with his kindness and wisdom, stood by the huge, oak gate. He waited patiently for the girl's return; she was the personification of his faith in the innate integrity and generosity of human nature.

Earthly love ...

The telephone rang.

"Hello!" Expecting no calls, Sarah grasped the receiver nervously.

"Excuse me ..." a man's voice said hesitantly. "I seem to have dialed a wrong number."

"Very likely," Sarah answered indifferently and hung the receiver. But the unknown fellow phoned repeatedly. His polite manner was so touching that Sarah couldn't angry. The next time, hearing the same embarrassed voice on the line, the girl burst out of laughing.

"You have an unusually feminine voice," the caller said softly.

Having forgotten whom he was trying to reach by phone, the fellow now described to Sarah the nature of the Black Sea shore, his native land. Sarah, who had never longed for any earthy exoticism, heard him leniently.

The boy's name was Vlad. After speaking exclusively by phone during a couple of months, Sarah invited the fellow, who was from a small seaside town, to visit her town. There was always a place for friends in her crowded flat.

On a cool October morning in 1992, Sarah entered the waiting room of the three-story city railway station. She wore a blue blazer and dark trousers tucked into argent knee-boots with stiletto heels, making her ordinary legs looking like those of a model. The girl examined the capacious room, with its enormous, wall-sized windows. The view through one of the windows was of the platform, and another opened onto the city sights. The hall was deserted at this early hour, but Sarah studied the inquiry office; Vlad should have been waiting for her after his arrival, as had been arranged. But only a few people sat on tip-up seats, not far from the inquiry.

Because Sarah had never seen the fellow she was meeting, she made up her mind to keep the arranged place. Sarah approached a huge timetable hung on a wall not far from the inquiry. Examining the timetable, she emphatically ignored a plain boy sitting not far from her. But he scrutinized the girl almost admiringly. Sensing some discomfort with his fixed gaze, Sarah cast a glance at him and shifted her eyes immediately to the timetable.

Still able to see the fellow with her peripheral vision, Sarah noted his peculiar appearance. His exaggerated chest seemed unnatural, contrasting with his thin legs. It prompted some unpleasant sensation of the person's physical deficiency. But most loathsome for Sarah were his hands: small, nearly childish, with stumpy fingers.

Involuntary, the tapered fingers of her celestial Stranger came back to her memory ...

Suddenly, Sarah realized that this was the boy whom she was meeting.

Sarah slowly shifted her lackluster eyes at the fellow, who was catching each of her gazes. "So ... you are Vlad," she pronounced with a perplexed tone, as if she had met a Quasimodo. Growing weak in the knees, Sarah helplessly took a seat not far from the fellow. The girl, who admired the power of human spirit and intellect, was shocked by the corporal defects of the boy.

Ignoring the voice of her insight, which seemed to be trying to protect her from folly, Sarah shamed herself for such inhumanity; it was disgraceful for a Christian. In fact, the boy was alone in the unknown town because of her ill-fated invitation.

"Yeah, it's me," Vlad mumbled bashfully. Such reaction at his appearance seemed common for him. The boy fidgeted in his seat, as if fearing Sarah's response when he stood.

"Well ..." Sarah drawled, barely able to collect herself. "Let's go to my place. I guess you must be tired from all this traveling."

Vlad felt how strongly his self-respect was hurt. He knew that females didn't regard him with favor. But now, he wanted, as never before, to do the impossible by winning the girl's favor. She was so beautiful. The keen intuition of a physically defective outcast told Vlad that Sarah, so arrogant and unapproachable at first sight, could be facile in the hands of a clever man.

Having caught a bus, Sarah willfully stared through its window. She curtly answered Vlad's reserved questions concerning the places of interests in her town. Meanwhile, the girl longed to remove her heeled high-boots. They made her appear to be a giantess beside a Pygmy.

In the end, Sarah thought as she gazed through the window of the bus at the avenues of her town, as if she were seeing them for the first time, *I'm not obliged to stay with him. He'll be a guest for a couple of days and go away ...that's all.*

In Sarah's dwelling, Vlad quickly grew comfortable. Sharp-witted and conversational, he impressed Sarah's parents, provincial intellectuals who at first were dazed by their daughter's strange taste.

Several days elapsed, and Vlad was still in Sarah's flat. The girl was nearly used to the handicapped fellow, who unobtrusively shadowed her everywhere and was at Sarah's disposal at any moment. Sometimes it seemed he had been always living in her home. Ingratiatingly agreeing with her about everything, Vlad seemed ready to fulfill any of her wishes. Sarah didn't realize she was a hostage to her own open-heartedness.

At last, they became intimate. Sarah's sexual sophistication was beyond Vlad's comprehension. She seemed to be trying to drown in wild sex a pang of her heart. However, Sarah's religiosity was still a barrier to her hot-blooded sexuality. Realizing that only a church wedlock should keep Sarah in his bed, Vlad was ready to get married to her in accordance with the rites of all world religions, separate or all together. But casting her lot with Vlad seemed grotesque to Sarah.

After another unforgettable night together, Vlad at last offered the girl his hand. But in return, he heard her quite a frank answer: "Get married? No ... that would be for life, and I'll not be able to stay with you so long ..." She wanted to add "without loving you," but restrained the last words in her heart. Sarah regretfully watched Vlad's anguished grimace, as if somebody had cut him with a knife. Slight waves of compassion swept over her soul.

Suddenly, she recalled Serge and Oleg, who were the only men able to make her even a little happy in this world. Why did she again reject the plain boy? She couldn't love him, but the fellow's affection for her and his homely appearance promised an uneventful family life and stability. The boy's corporal defects aroused Sarah's pity. She suddenly felt as if it would be easy for her to reject herself for the sake of another person's happiness.

Vlad's insistence was rewarded.

Marrying without love was a smashing blow to Sarah's Christian faith. Nevertheless, she believed the sacred ritual of the religion would correct the imperfections of her strange marriage. Beyond that, she would be rid of that endless obsession, her inexplicable love for the illusory Stranger.

After legal and conformist marriages following each other, Sarah and Vlad settled down at Vlad's native seaside town. But neither the exotic place—which was full of sun, sea, mountains, and rampant tropical plants—nor the hot southern nights in the arms of her husband could fill her heart's emptiness.

Now Sarah sensed that her marriage was too hard on her soul. She didn't love Vlad. In fact, she had married only to help her husband to overcome his inferiority complex. But Vlad didn't recognize Sarah's motive. He didn't even suspect that their marriage was just her immolation for the sake of his love for her.

Upon learning of her pregnancy, Sarah was peacefully happy. Her physicians confirmed that her health was good. At last, her life should find its true purpose.

Sarah continually pondered the fatal error of her marriage, which she couldn't correct being bound to her husband by church vow. She could only reconcile herself and live for her future child, who, in any case, would need his father.

After opening her eyes on an early March morning, Sarah slightly touched Vlad, who was sleeping near her. The man awoke and glanced at his wife absently.

"It's impossible!" Sarah whispered, fixing her eyes on the ceiling. "It can't be true! It's not time yet ..."

Then she cried out and lost consciousness.

Sarah awoke in the snow-white labor ward of a nearby maternity hospital. The hospital was built on the site of an ancient Moslem cemetery. Currently, the facility was closed, due to a rampant bacterial infection; the hospital doctors were embittered by the unexpected problem of Sarah's abrupt arrival. But the woman's unstable state forbade her transportation to other hospitals, which were more than two hours away.

In great pain, Sarah moaned weakly. In reply, a woman's baleful look clashed with hers. Those almond brown eyes flashed with such hostility that Sarah was terrified to learn that the woman was a physician.

"Harlot," she whispered in Sarah's face. "It's easy to sin, but not the same to harvest!"

Sarah stopped to endure another pain.

"Impressive ... funny company for my first child-bearing," she pronounced, restraining a moan. Trying to overcome the doctor's irritation, Sarah whispered, "So, you're Archangel Gabriel, who has come to bill me for my sins. Very glad to meet you!"

As she struggled for the life of her child, which was rushing to be born so early, Sarah heard only vulgar swearing. She'd heard the words so many times before, but now the foul language seemed to be killing her. The words cut her like a thousand knives.

"Listen here!" Sarah uttered at last, exhausted with pain. "Why is such language used in your hospital?"

"Oh, what delicacy!" the dark-eyed doctor smirked. "Indeed, it's unbelievable for the floozies of our seaport."

With more pain approaching, Sarah could only close her eyes and clench her teeth, ignoring the fury germinating within her soul.

At last, the small, crying body of Sarah's newborn daughter appeared in the hands of a young obstetrician, who was assisting the doctor of uneven temper.

"Oh! So little!" the obstetrician exclaimed, squeamishly inspecting the neonate's bloodstained body, which was slightly blue with beginning asphyxia. "What will we do with her? Not even one medical device is functioning now." The doctor's only response was a withering stare.

Sarah's eyes were wide with horror. She clawed hold of the doctor's arm.

"Please," the young mother whispered, choking with despair and squeezing the doctor's arm. "Save my baby. I know any hospital has a specialized ambulance car. I'll pay … I'll pay as much as you say."

The doctor yanked away her arm and measured Sarah's flat body with a cold once-over. "It's not a big loss. You'll give birth again."

Sarah could no longer restrain the fury bursting from her inwardness. She wasn't able to forgive such people, who turned the sacred moment of her childbirth into a crucifixion. As never before, Sarah sensed how far was her nature from the ideal of Christ's All-forgiving …

Ready to leave the labor ward, the doctor paused. She glanced coldly toward the mute patient, whose left hand hung and bled slowly upon the floor. But that wasn't the object of the doctor's curiosity.

Sarah's eyes were peculiar, filled with deep darkness alternating with sinister gleams of fire …

Expecting no movement from the exhausted patient, the doctor studied Sarah, trying to understand the unusual phenomenon in her eyes.

At last, the doctor smirked and whispered, "Chippie! You got off easy ..."

Immediately, Sarah grabbed the doctor's long dark hair and reeled it up on her bloodstained hand.

"Much worse," Sarah hissed with some otherworldly voice. "I'm an Angel's spawn! I always pay for my sins. Now it's your turn!" The doctor uselessly tried to unclasp Sarah's suddenly steely hand. Despite the doctor's struggles, the distraught young mother indifferently squeezed the hair of the bitchy Gorgon, making her welter in the puddle of blood on the floor.

Sarah found herself lying on the same labor table. She was still hemorrhaging. It was so silent everywhere that she couldn't believe such peace existed in nature. Sarah was deeply shocked by all that had happened. Thoughts about the destiny of her newborn daughter pained her. But she believed God would never abandon her child. It was impossible. She had felt that Almighty Love so many times, and the power of this Empyrean Love was always the immanence of her soul.

The young obstetrician-assistant entered the labor ward.

"Come alive!" she addressed Sarah with swagger. The girl threw a ragged hospital dressing gown on the patient's body. "Two hours have passed ...wake up!" she ordered, ignoring Sarah's amusing attempts to get up without help.

Having stood up at last, the silent patient dressed in the hand-me-down. Sarah tried to regain her Christian patience. She didn't wish to beg for indulgence of the people, who couldn't give it to her; they were indifferent the sufferings of fellow creatures.

Rocking with strong giddiness, Sarah shambled beside the obstetrician toward the wards located in the sole functioning unit of the hospital. But their destination was across a road. Seeing the bloodstained woman on the road, passing drivers barely controlled their vehicles.

Suddenly, Sarah stopped and examined her left palm, where she could see the barely discernible tracks of her recent bleeding. Several of the doctor's dark hairs were glued to Sarah's palm.

The obstetrician paused and glanced back at Sarah with vexation. The patient stood still, wistfully inspecting her palm. Fitful spring wind impermissibly fanned Sarah's ragged hemline.

"My bleeding," she whispered, having cast her imploring glances at the girl. "Who stopped it? It couldn't happen by itself ..."

The obstetrician shrugged. Lightning up a cigarette, she leant with her back against a huge tree near the road.

Sarah's heart revived upon the hope that the celestial Stranger had been near. How poignantly she hankered for his life-giving look after three blank years living without him!

Meantime, drawing upon her cigarette, the obstetrician scrutinized Sarah's legs, which were covered with blood. "Your bleeding? It hasn't stopped yet."

But Sarah waved off the girl, realizing the obstetrician didn't understand her question. Sarah stared at the spring sky. Her soul was filling with the blessing of Heavenly Love and immortal hope.

"Besides," the obstetrician said, interrupting her meditation. "First of all, we have to hunt down the doctor. She inquired about your plans concerning the dead body of your baby. Will you bury it by yourself or leave it here?"

The earth reeled under Sarah's feet.

"What?" she whispered in dread. Her blank eyes shifted at the obstetrician madly. "Repeat again..." Sarah uttered with difficulty, barely moving with her tongue.

But now the obstetrician rushed up to the patient, catching her collapsing body. The girl placed Sarah on the cold earth under the same huge tree.

The patient's eyes were vacant. Some impenetrable mist separated Sarah's mind from actuality. A single, wild sensation seized her core: she, a young and healthy woman, had outlasted her newborn daughter. And that tender breath had saved neither by the Holy Spirit nor with Sarah's belief in His Mercy.

A month elapsed since Sarah had imprisoned herself in a hostel. Eating almost nothing and wishing to see nobody, she stayed in bed or loitered about the room. Vlad, returning from his work toward evening, spoon-fed his heartbroken wife. He was anxious about her attenuate figure and sunken green eyes, which were reducing her femininity. But Sarah coldly ignored him.

One fixed, desperate question distressed her mind. "Why did this happen to me?" But there was no answer. Orthodoxy, which once protected Sarah's mind from destruction, became useless self-delusion. The death of her daughter was as absurd as it was unnatural. In comparison, Sarah's own end would be a mere trifling. Her hatred of the cruel human world grew stronger. Yet Sarah could find no way to kill the sensation of God's Varity, which existed inside her. This intuition of God always lived in Sarah's soul, independently of her religiosity. In contempt of logic and good sense, she perceived the Spirit of Being with her inborn Gnostic insight. But it made her life on the earth even more senseless.

Two years passed. Sarah now rarely grew hysterical after seeing other happy couples with their kiddies. Her new, troublesome work, which demanded frequent business trips abroad, finally drove depression from her mind. Recollecting Vlad's unobtrusive support after the death of their daughter, Sarah, as before, impersonated a typical wife, combining in her person the features of a passionate paramour and a housekeeper. She didn't think more about loving her husband. It was enough that they had married in accordance of Orthodox rite. She would stay with the weak man to the end of her days, going halves in happiness and grief.

Trying to find out the cause of her advanced labor, Sarah visited physicians' consultations tirelessly. But the doctors, as if having gone into a huddle, harped on about her perfect health. At the same time, they insisted that Sarah receive more thorough prenatal care in the event of her next pregnancy.

Sarah scrupulously followed the doctors' recommendations during the period of her next gestation, but everything repeated as it had the first time.

After sensing the familiar symptoms of her spontaneous abortion, Sarah hurried into the maternity hospital. She was in the seventh month of her pregnancy, and the expectant mother hoped doctors could prevent her advanced labor, which she knew was dangerous for her unformed fetus.

The second day of her stay in hospital seemed endless, with vexing treatment and trivial chatting with women in the same ward. Keeping to her bed and aimlessly beholding the ceiling, Sarah was uncomfortable in the four-post bed, which resembled a hammock with its sagging lattice frame. She was sleepily listening to the conversation of the in-patients. Their perpetual rigmarole lulled Sarah, in contrast with the medics, who were in joyful anticipation of the coming weekend. They drank and laughed in a room not far from Sarah's ward.

It was quite early to go to bed, but the hospital surroundings were so disgusting that Sarah longed to doze off at once.

Suddenly, her eyes opened and her hands clawed hold of her bedding. Pain pierced her abdomen. Sarah cried out unwillingly. Her neighbors in the ward interrupted their conversation and glanced at the uncommunicative new patient with surprise. Feeling her pang wasn't over, Sarah smiled tensely when she saw the women's alarmed expressions.

"Nothing ... it's all right," she whispered through clenched teeth.

But the pain only grew and made Sarah toss about in agony. The doctor on duty, who was located with difficulty, was drunk. He perplexedly watched Sarah's writhing. At last, he informed the woman in labor with his thick voice, "Everything is under control! We'll keep your pregnancy!" Several injections were given to Sarah with the aim to stop the process, which had already gotten out of hand. She lost all sensation of space.

Now Sarah found herself on a labor table with a powerful spotlight overhead. Wracked with pain, she saw two more intoxicated physicians, together with the first, who was already messing about Sarah. Two young nurses assisted the doctors, and the drunken company exchanged remarks merrily.

"Thank God, they don't use foul language," Sarah thought abruptly between the fits of pain, involuntary recollecting her previous childbirth. Inwardly, she was glad the drunken doctors, flirting with the nurses, paid almost no attention to her suffering.

After five hours of labor, Sarah lay motionless on the labor table. Being absolutely worn out herself, she listened to the doctors' scoffing cues. They replied to the laud comments of the nurses, weighing Sarah's newborn son, "A boy, two and a half kilo ... with nappies"

Sarah broke down finally. The same, inexpressible ennui overcame her soul again. Even there, in maternity hospital, new life seemed debased for having been touched by human hands.

"Is it over?" Sarah asked weakly, addressing one of the doctors, who had still been standing between her spread legs. The man glanced at her apathetically.

"Not yet," he answered coldly. The doctor had sobered up a little, but he still spoke with difficulty. "You'll fly now," he added and nodded assent to another physician with a syringe in his hand.

Before Sarah opened her mouth to clarify the doctors' intention, the physician injected some medicine into the patient's drip bulb. Pitch darkness and deathly silence reigned over Sarah.

She flew unbelievably quickly. The direction of her levitation couldn't be changed. Sarah slowly realized that she didn't feel her body. It seemed not to exist.

"Body! My body!" Sarah cried. She sought any slight connection with the material world, but her mind was locked in the trap of the other reality. In response to her quest for materiality, Sarah sensed only a thin web tying up her knees. But the sensation was obviously false. Realizing the futility of coming back to tangible reality, Sarah's consciousness appeared in another environment.

An awesome sight opened before her mind's eye. Huge vertical movement, resembling a gigantic, shining torsion spiral, appeared before Sarah. Having forgotten about her long-suffering body, she perceived the grandiose whirling structure with her strange inward vision. Fulgent ribbons gyrated on the invisible pivot and pulled into darkness, creating a powerful vortex.

"Souls ..." The thought or sensation came to Sarah from the outside darkness, which seemed to become the new way of her perception of the reality. It simply distilled the information from the Mind of the Universe, and Sarah's human consciousness was no longer hers.

The core of the gigantic gyre became dark, forming the crater of a black hole and absorbing everything around it. The Galactic Apocalypse, engulfing the shining ribbons with unbelievable speed, developed before Sarah. Despair seized the aerial structure of her soul, dismembering the smallest corpuscles.

"It can't be true ..." Abysmal darkness answered Sarah's desperate attempts to save her soul. "Even the quarks of my soul are fissioning ... something super-physical ... why does my mind not appeal to my devoutness? If only an Angel's look for the last consolation ... but nothing ... just cold physics." The darkness mechanically repeated Sarah's desperate thoughts.

But then the dismal environment was abruptly silent. It just transformed her soul into a black, amorphous mass mixed with plasmic fire.

Suddenly, a maelstrom picked up the disembodied creature, which had not long ago been a pure human soul, and engulfed it into the yawing abyss of the Space hole. Sarah's soul finally fused with otherworldly darkness. Her intolerable regret of senseless human suffering was expressed by the universe, sounding from everywhere. "Hell ...only hell is real."

Sarah's eyes roamed madly across the tiled, white walls of the recovery room.

"Only hell is real," she said again, in delirium.

"Dearie, do you hear me?" Sarah's attending doctor, who had

been delivered to hospital during the night, addressed the woman. But she didn't recognize him.

Sarah saw the man's alarmed face, but she didn't understand his words. At last, she awoke to her surroundings and attempted to rise. But the doctor stopped her impulse with his hand. Replacing vials with antibiotics from his pocket into the pockets of Sarah's robe, he said, "It's for injections! Take them to avoid infection!" As if trying to strike through her mislaid mind, the doctor repeated the phrase several times, sawing the air before Sarah's vacant eyes.

Having hazy recollection, whereby she appeared in a cold, empty ward on the ground floor, Sarah contemplated its chipped walls. Keeping a bed covered with bedclothes of dubious cleanliness, she lent an attentive ear to the words of a nurse busying herself in the ward.

"Take a rest," the portly nurse said, as if speaking to herself and guessing Sarah didn't hear her. "I'll come in toward the morning and give you an injection."

"What's happened to me?" Sarah's silent question suddenly stopped the woman, just as she had opened the door to go out. The nurse glanced back at Sarah's pale face. "So, you have awakened from your stupor," she pronounced, eager to go away and get some sleep in a room warmer than Sarah's.

"Nothing special," she answered Sarah's question quietly. "Just apparent death. Doctors were drunker than usual, and they overdosed narcosis to you. But you are still alive, so thank God."

The nurse went out, slamming the door loudly. Obviously, she was assured that nobody would be troubled there in the small hours.

Despite her fatigue, Sarah couldn't sleep. Every inch of her body ached and shivered with drug intoxication. She barely sensed her left palm, which was slowly becoming wet and sticky with blood.

"Damned bleeding," Sarah thought, constantly shivering and uselessly balling her hand into a fist. Her scar bled through her squeezed fingers, more and more.

The fathomless, dark eyes arose in Sarah's misted mind, warming her heart and irritating her at the same time.

"You," Sarah thought, despairingly sinking in her drug delirium again. "Just a hallucination ... you appear neither on the earth nor in Erebus. You always were just my senseless, excruciating illusion of love. Leave me in peace. I have found the sense of my existence in this damned world without your Angel's love ..."

Losing consciousness, Sarah could feel nothing more, including the tender, tapered fingers with their usual, styptic effect, brushing over her bleeding palm.

Sarah was awakened by the nurse, who had promised to come with an injection at dawn. Having done her job without saying a word, as if Sarah was an anatomic dummy, the nurse hurried out. After staying alone, Sarah apathetically watched the cold, March sun slowly rising beyond a latticed window. Finally, she slightly overcame her intoxication and sensed the coldness of the room. A thermometer hanging on a ragged wall displayed just 10 degrees above zero on Celsius.

"It's just a cellar," Sarah thought, more tightly wrapping herself in a thin, camel blanket, which couldn't warm her. She recollected her night shiver pityingly, because it warmed her more effectively.

Suddenly, the door was opened and three young women-inpatients appeared. Sarah glanced at them indifferently. She uselessly wrapped herself in the blanket as before.

"What are you doing here?" one of them asked, scrutinizing Sarah's shivering figure and bloodstained legs, which weren't covered by the blanket because of its small dimension. "Indeed ... blood is a problem here," the women continued without waiting for Sarah's answer. "There isn't any shower for washing here."

Keeping her bed, Sarah listened to the woman's chatting without interest, as if she were still under the influence of drug. But the cold was not the problem troubling her now. Sarah's heart ached with the thoughts about her newborn son. If he was all right, she should not be left alone in the cold ward. It was impossible to bring a neonate there. The young mother longed to clasp to her breast the sole reason for her existence.

Seeing Sarah ignoring their presence, the women gave a wink to one another. All together, they suddenly seized the shivering Sarah, making her stand up with their assistance.

"What are you doing?" Sarah asked weakly. She could barely stand on her feet with the women's support.

"We'll bring you to our ward. It's the only heated one on the floor," the woman answered crossly. "Or maybe you have superhuman health to remain in such cold?"

"Maybe," Sarah echoed perplexedly, hanging weakly on the women's shoulders. She was deeply touched by the sympathy of these strangers for her.

Two days elapsed. The women who had taken Sarah to their ward were discharged from hospital with their neonates, and Sarah stayed alone in the one heated ward on the empty ground floor. Nurses appeared there seldom, not to mention doctors.

Two endless days Sarah drove crazy with suspense about the destiny of her newborn son. Being weak, she couldn't even go upstairs. Wandering about the ground floor like a lost soul, Sarah hoped to catch her doctor, who seemed to have forgotten about the patient's existence.

The following morning, the young doctor, who seemed cheerful and not bothered by the problems of his patients, came to Sarah's ward. Seeing the woman's gloomy face, he asked merrily, "Why are you so upset? The worst is over!"

Sarah gazed at him as if she didn't realize where she had been staying. Most likely, it was a madhouse. How could a doctor, a man of non-typical intellect, be waiting for positive emotions from a mother knowing nothing about her newborn child?

"Where is my son?" She seemed ready to strangle the man, who scoffed at her parental feelings.

The physician glanced at Sarah suspiciously and moved slowly to the door. But Sarah suddenly blocked his way. She glared at the doctor. "You won't go out until you tell me about my son!"

The doctor looked up and down Sarah's exhausted figure. "If only you weren't so dirty ... in any other circumstances, we should spoon with you ... but now, if my memory serves me right, your husband promised me to pay after your childbirth."

"What? Is that the reason you are keeping me alone on this cold floor, and telling me nothing about my child? I'm not obliged to pay you and the other drunken idiots who nearly ended my days!" Sarah tried to attack the doctor with fists. But the fellow suddenly burst out laughing and intercepted her weak hands.

"Your son is fine. He has a good appetite, which is very important for his viability," the doctor pronounced with his usual liveliness. He squeezed Sarah's swollen nipple and several drops of breast milk oozed out of it. "Besides," he whispered, still playfully petting her filled breast and breathing in Sarah's face, "your son is a prematurely born child; you have to breast-feed him as long as possible." Being thunderstruck with long-awaited news about her son, Sarah felt her legs give way, despite the doctor's unequivocal attempts to dispel her postpartum depression.

The woman was sliding with her back over the door, almost squatting at the doctor's feet.

"What are you doing? Your sutures! You can't sit down until you are fully recovered!" the man said as he picked Sarah up.

He bedded the sobbing patient, who hugged the doctor like a friend. Carefully covering Sarah with her blanket, he muttered with embarrassment, "What's up again? Indeed, hysterics are just my luck!"

Wondering about Sarah's reaction to the good news about her son, he said reproachfully, "You mustn't be alarmed. It may be bad for your lactation." His last phrase calmed Sarah better than any nervine.

Soon, Sarah and her newborn son were back home in the small, rented flat, not far from sea coast. However, the greatest surprise was waiting for the young mother there. Usually attentive to Sarah, now Vlad looked for any reason to get away. The woman remained alone with her son, who constantly cried, demanding attention and care. Sarah accepted everything, realizing all responsibility for the life of her weak child. But Vlad began to live his own life, ignoring the most vital needs of his family. He seemed weighed down by fatherhood. The burden of caring for her preterm infant, aggravated by the disorder of family life, fell heavily on the woman, who had gone through a hard childbirth and apparent death not long ago.

Sarah's son grew up to be a healthy and clever boy, but after two years of working so hard, Sarah felt her health failing. She feared her son would be without any care if she took to bed.

Meantime, Vlad grew further estranged. Sometimes after visiting his son and wife, he disappeared from the flat quickly. But he always brought to Sarah's mind that he loved her and their common child as always. Such declarations looked cynical against the background of the man's factual indifference to his family.

Even after five years of their living together, Sarah couldn't imagine her husband's ability to betray her at this difficult time in their lives. She realized it bitterly, but too late.

Unable to further endure her husband's lies, Sarah and her two-year-old son returned to her native town. There, she felt better than she had in the strange land. But their Orthodox wedding didn't ease her mind. Sarah still hoped that her family life would be saved. She repeatedly took her son to Vlad, not wanting them to become estranged from each other. It was the greatest horror for Sarah to see her son as a fatherless child.

The power of hell

August 2001 was the height of the holiday season at the small seaside town, where Sarah and her son visited so often. Noisy disco and alluring bars, which were chock-full with attractive, sun-tanned men, didn't impress Sarah. Every day, she toiled along in the small bar located on the seashore that belonged to her husband. When his wife and son arrived, Vlad rented a flat for his family. The flat was located far from the sea, on a mountain. Vlad visited his family rarely, so Sarah was forced to visit the bar of her husband. But nobody waited for her and her four-year-old child there.

Appearing in her husband's small, neat bar, the woman sensed derisive glances from the young waitresses, who were laughing over Vlad's amorous adventures behind her back. Most painful for Sarah was to see that the narrow-minded, plain man—her husband—imagined himself an Apollo. And it was though, after Sarah's hapless response on his fleeting attraction to her. Vlad couldn't understand that his new fancy girls just used his income for their temporary aims, appreciating him not a bit.

Weary of the waitresses' private jeers, Sarah left. She spent all day long on the beach with her son, only in the heat of mid-day hiding with her sleeping child in shadowy Exotic Park. Sarah pretended to herself that she would never see that damned town again. But scrutinizing the cherubic features of her sleeping boy, she drowned in tears. She was really helpless to give her son anything within a hair's breadth of a normal family life.

After returning to her rented flat at night, when the town burst with the roars of audio systems rumbling at numerous discos, Sarah bedded her boy. Staying in bed near him, she listened to his spasmodic breathing. The damp climate always put Sarah on guard. But she was assured, as if her child were born in that region, that he would be fine.

She was wrong.

Once morning, Sarah's son was barely breathing. She was horrified with his unnaturally swollen bosom. A doctor who examined the child diagnosed bronchitis. After prescribing some medicines, he advised Sarah to return to her hometown.

But when they got there, the fits of strange disease remained. Sarah stopped sleeping at nights again, keeping an ear to her son's unsteady breathing.

Haunting the hospital, Sarah tried to clarify the reason for her son's aggravated health. But she heard no good answers, and was directed to keep using the medications—which did not work.

"Why the lingering bronchitis?" Sarah asked one of the many physicians she'd consulted.

The woman-doctor glanced at Sarah with a withering look, as if she saw a filicide bringing her child to such a condition.

"Bronchitis? No, dear! It's bronchial asthma. Besides, it's one of its hardest forms. If I were you, I'd never rely upon a miracle. It's not such a case."

Embarrassment became despair, shrouding Sarah's mind.

"Where has the disease sprung from?" she whispered, stricken with grief.

"Heredity, obviously," the doctor answered reservedly, filling in the child's medical record. "That seaside climate just provoked the visual symptoms of the latent illness."

"Heredity..." Sarah repeated, as if in delirium. "But I have no asthmatics in my family!" She recollected her childhood, when a light snuffle was the true trial for her during the frosty winters, after her willful walking with an uncovered head.

The doctor glanced at Sarah in even more amazement. "Really? But your son has a father as well."

"I can't be sure," Sarah said, faltering as she described the disproportion of her husband's body. "Of course, he coughs often, but he is a smoker ..." she added, casting down her eyes and avoiding the doctor's gape.

"Unbelievable!" the doctor sighed. "You have described his asthmatic's chest! Aren't there any healthy men around, to produce a healthy child?"

Sarah flashed an offended glance at the physician, who sermonized to her. "Should I have demanded from my future husband the results of his medical examination?" she asked. She wanted to add that it would be humiliating for him. But hearing her son's hard, choking cough, the woman did not wish to further challenge the doctor. As never before, Sarah realized that it was her child who would pay for her foolish generosity after all.

"How can I help him?" Sarah asked, watching her four-year-old son short-winded and wheezing like an old man. "I'll do everything to heal him," she added. "If it's necessary I'll bring him abroad, to the best clinic."

"That's excellent," the doctor answered, sadly examining Sarah's modest clothing. "But even if you can somehow find the round sum necessary for that, I'd like to warn you against delusion. Asthma is an incurable disease. You might pay in your 'best clinic' for high-quality, careful medical service—but not for your son's final healing. As I said, it's impossible to break his genetic inclination."

Hearing the doctor's sober assessment, Sarah thought she could physically feel her hair going gray. All her hard efforts to raise a happy and healthy child were crossed by one merciless gesture of destiny.

Day after day, Sarah's lively, cheerful son became a slow-moving, wheezy asthmatic. He couldn't walk a short distance without fatigue. His grieved mother watched at the boy's bedside all night long, listening with a sinking heart to his weak breathing.

As her son's health continued to suffer, Sarah appealed to one of the state medical centers. It was located in a big Ukrainian city, several hours from her province.

However, when she arrived in the hospital with her son, Sarah realized again the hell in which she lived. Her son fell into a trap of a ruthless medical conveyer, operating with dry statistics of child mortality and justifying any physicians' acts, as long as they weren't at variance with common norms of medication.

Constantly arguing with doctors and demanding an effective cure for her son, Sarah heard only the official answer: medicine didn't know another way of curing the agonizing ailment.

Staggering after so many sleepless nights, a haggard Sarah loitered aimlessly about the hospital, clasping to her heart her little boy, who had become emaciated. Sometimes, the young attending doctor of Sarah's son looked for the woman and her child all over the big clinic. When he found them at last, he brought the depressed mother to a medical procedure that was the boy's treatment.

Sarah's son, dreading the medication with injections and IV drips, broke away from the powerful hands of the gross nurses, who tried to control him. He cried with a harrowing voice, "Mummy! Don't give me to them! I've done nothing bad!"

Being escorted from the procedure room by the nurses, Sarah clasped her hands as she heard her son's heart-rending moans. Acting upon her ebbing spiritual and physical strength, the woman kneeled on the floor of that limbo of hell. She cursed herself and her ability to perceive her life's greatest nightmare. Now, death seemed to her as the greatest boon.

Regardless of all physicians' efforts, the health of Sarah's boy grew progressively worse. The woman realized the doctors couldn't change what it had been foreordained from above. She felt enmity for the representatives of the most humane profession, which was based on Sarah's previous negative experience.

Once, the doctor of Sarah's son, the same one who always looked for her in the hospital, entered the ward. As usual, he reminded the woman about the procedures that were necessary for her boy. Sarah flashed a furious glance at the physician. He was tall and stately, in his early thirties, as was Sarah. He had quiet, pleasant, Slav features. The man's big, gray eyes reflected a superhuman intellect, scrutinizing Sarah coldly through smart glasses in golden rims. For a moment, those eyes seemed familiar, but Sarah lacked the strength to remember the man. In response to the doctor's dry reminder, she snarled, "Enough! I bring my son nowhere! There is no sense in your medication! It's just slowly killing my child!"

Studying the woman, the doctor readjusted his specs with his long fingers.

"Mother!" he addressed Sarah bluntly, as did the brusque nurses. His cold, rational voice made Sarah convulse again. But she wasn't inclined to analyze her spontaneous sensations. She was absorbed by thoughts of her son's disease. "Did you come here to wear out my nerves? Isn't it quite enough I have been looking for you throughout the hospital, all day long? I have no time to listen to your dilettantism! Be so kind as to fulfill my prescription properly!"

Sarah's mind once more limply ascertained the man's incredible coolness. But her fury was not spent. Sarah leaped up from the bed, which she shared with her son, and darted toward the imposing man. She clutched the irreproachable, snow-white coat that covered his bosom.

"Yeah, I'm not a doctor. But it doesn't mean you may kill my baby with your damn chemotherapy! Look at his urinalysis! There are no healthy vitals in his body after he takes your medication!"

Through his glasses, the doctor couldn't see Sarah's face clearly. She was very close to the man, and everything ran together before his eyes. But the doctor sensed the nervous palpitation of Sarah's body huddling next to him.

Remaining aloof under the stares of the other patients, the doctor said more peaceably, "Please, cool it. I long for your boy's recovery no less than you do. Be patient. Believe me, when it seems there is no hope, it just seems ..."

The doctor paused, noting her anxiety, and then added, "At the end, if I don't suit you, you may change your son's attending doctor for another one."

Sarah released the doctor's coat and sat on her bed helplessly.

His compassion suddenly warmed her heart. The wilted woman sadly recollected how many doctors had treated her son without any result.

Skillfully entertaining Sarah's son, the doctor took the boy for procedures without troubling his mother, who had lapsed into deep prostration.

After arguing with the doctor about her son, Sarah now accepted the intelligent, pragmatic physician. He was always glancing at her with his somber, gray eyes through his elegant glasses. Each day, he carefully examined Sarah's son, whose broken state of health slowly stabilized. She was gratified to see that there might be somebody in the world who wasn't indifferent to the underserved sufferings of her child.

One evening, sitting on the bed in her ward, Sarah glanced nervously at her wristwatch. It was already late, but one more drip bulb was necessary for her son that day. The boy wanted to sleep, but nobody came to call them for procedure. Obviously, the medics had forgotten about her child. After losing her patience, Sarah went to intern's room.

She peeked in and saw the attending doctor of her son, who was on duty that night. The man was reading a book peacefully.

"One more drip bulb is necessary for my son tonight," Sarah addressed the doctor indignantly.

"What?" He stared vacantly at the woman, who had come into the room too silently. "Yeah ..." the doctor said, understanding Sarah's phrase at last. "A drip bulb ... it's necessary." The man glanced at his expensive Swiss wristwatch. "Unfortunately, all the nurses are busy now," he said with air of detachment. "Wait just a bit." And he sank into his reading again.

"And how long is it your just a bit?" Sarah asked. She boiled with indignation. "What shall I do to keep my son awake while waiting for your medication? Can't you settle this damned drip bulb by yourself? Half-taught intern!"

Infuriated, Sarah turned back harshly and directed her steps to the exit. But the doctor loudly tossed his book aside, and Sarah glanced back.

He approached the woman, his eyes cold. "See here! Why do you use such a tone with me? I medicate your son! I do everything for his recovery! But instead of a little gratitude, I receive the only your snubs!" His voice rang with the same rigid coldness, jarring Sarah.

"Oh, sorry!" the woman said, glowering. "Let's talk about gratitude, doc! It should be clarified from the beginning! But you medics never say the exact sum of this so-called gratitude. It's such a game. 'Guess how much the life of your child costs.' I lost my first-born daughter in such a devilish roulette! But it's impossible to always lose, even in your hellish games!"

"I need nothing with you," the man said resentfully. Dropping his eyes, he realized that Sarah had made up her mind to make him pay for all faults of the national public health.

Suddenly, the doctor grasped Sarah's shoulders with his strong hands and turned her round, softly forcing her to go out and following after the woman. "Let's go. I'll handle the drip bulb. It isn't worth such a dramatic speech," he whispered, bending toward Sarah's ear from behind.

After entering a spacious procedural room with several couches and IV stands, Sarah felt her son clasping her hips. He sobbed and looked around fearfully. Sarah embraced him, instinctively cuddling the boy's head to her abdomen.

After preparing the treatment, the doctor glanced at Sarah. She studied him with the eyes of a hunted she-wolf, ready to bite off the head of anybody who would approach her scion.

Restraining his irritation, the physician approached Sarah slowly. Enduring her withering look, he coaxed the woman. "Please, let him go." The doctor's long fingers passed tenderly over Sarah's hand and her son's hair. "Can't you understand that your anxiety is inherited by your child? In fact, he is not as sensitive to pain as an adult. It's just your unfounded fear."

Seeing that it wasn't easy to appeal to Sarah's good sense, as if she were ready to die for her child without moving from that place, the doctor said more resolutely, "Well, let's do what comes next. Leave your boy with me and go out." He pressed his forefinger to Sarah's lips to preempt more of her complaints. "You'll go out to decide in which form you'll express your frenzy at me after hearing the first moan of your son. Is it a go? I'll withstand any of your fancies!"

Surprised, Sarah was intrigued by the chance to get even with someone for the humiliations she had endured in the hospital. Involuntarily, she diverted her thoughts from her son's sobs and relaxed her arms over his head.

The physician entertained the boy with funny trinkets, jocular toys made with the plastic tubes of used drip bulbs. Small patients made them as they were whiling away the dull hours of their treatments.

Having left the room, Sarah stood in the hospital corridor, pressing her back into the wall and closing her eyes. She listened keenly to every sound in the procedural room, the door of which remained ajar. It seemed that if she heard a little cry from her son,

Sarah's heart would tear asunder. But nothing broke the silence except the squeak of an IV stand and the doctor's steps.

Sarah peeked into the room. Her son was quietly lying on a couch with a settled drip bulb. With his free hand, he had been still playing with the toy, which had been placed over his bosom. Meanwhile, the doctor, sitting by the table, wrote down the information about the procedure in a register. He couldn't see Sarah.

At last, the physician went out of the room, casting a glance at Sarah's boy, who was now sleeping. Having shifted his grey eyes toward Sarah, the man ironically scrutinized her motionless figure. It seemed the woman was rooted to the wall with her back.

"So what?" the doctor asked amicably, gazing at the stunned Sarah. "Have you invented something interesting for me? As I said, your son and you interact psychologically. Don't be so afraid of him. If he inherited his father's somatic ailment, it's very probable he also inherited a little of his mother's fortitude to withstand the disease."

"Please ..." Sarah whispered. "I want you personally to cure my son. Otherwise, I won't survive another day."

In a blink, she appeared close to the quite tall physician. Having stood on tiptoes, Sarah flung her arms round his neck and kissed his lips feverishly. She so wanted to believe that the man who had taken pity on her child was well-disposed toward her as well.

Slightly bemused by Sarah's act, the doctor nevertheless collected himself quickly and replied to her kiss. Sensing his strong hands upon her naked body under her light negligee, Sarah almost choked with lust. She had not been close to a man for more than three years. She tried to move away from the doctor's strong grasp. Perceiving her resistance, the man whispered near Sarah's lips, "If my doctor's coat so disgusts you, I can take it off."

"Yes ...no ..." Sarah tried to free herself from the man's

persistent arms, but didn't insult him with the withdrawal. "It's just my emotions. You allowed me to let myself go. I'm grateful to you, overwhelmingly grateful. But I prefer to pay with cash. I hope you'll tell me, at last, how much your kindness costs."

Setting Sarah free and settling down his strong heart palpitations with a long exhalation, the doctor smirked. "Keep your money to yourself. We would be living in the most perfect of all worlds, if it were possible to buy everything."

The doctor's name was Eugene. Sarah endeavored to keep a distance from the man. Casting glances at Eugene's wedding ring, she wanted to know nothing about his private life. The woman just hoped to find some human indulgence for her child. Nevertheless, she had given Eugene a reason to suspect her attraction to him. In fact, his care for Sarah's son really awakened in her heart quite a strong attachment to the doctor.

As he had promised, Eugene settled drip bulbs for Sarah's child himself during the evenings. Once, after the drip therapy, Sarah and the doctor were wending along the faintly illuminated hospital corridor. Eugene brought in his arms the boy, who always fell asleep after the procedure. The strong man freed Sarah from her hard duty of constantly carrying her weak child in her arms. Nevertheless, the boy was already too heavy for Sarah.

The woman idly pored over Eugene's night duties, which seemed excessive. But suddenly she stopped, having gone too far by counting the doors of wards without numbers. Seeing that they had almost reached the intern's room, Sarah addressed Eugene.

"Doc, we have passed by my ward."

"It's nothing," the man answered, carefully correcting on his forearm the position of the head of the sleeping child. "Drop by my room. I have something for you."

The intern's room was small, and the table with a computer, a couch and two armchairs were crowded together.

After placing Sarah's son on the couch, the doctor set her in an armchair with an eloquent gesture. Reclining in another armchair near the window, Eugene produced a bottle of French brandy. Sullenly, Sarah watched the man open the bottle and fill two small glasses on the table.

"What's this?" she asked. Staring at the gargle, the woman involuntary recalled the drunken idiots in doctor's coats who had brought her within an inch of death, almost orphaning her newborn child.

"Brandy," Eugene said in answer to her strange question. "And it's a very good one. It was a gift from grateful patients. Drink. You can hardly afford such an expensive indulgence."

"Naturally," Sarah answered maliciously. "I will not buy it, because I abstain from drinking, and I wish you would do the same."

"Listen!" Eugene said nervously, setting Sarah's glass on the table. His hand had become too numb to hold it. "That's the limit! Do I look like a dipsomaniac?"

"I don't know," the woman uttered, taking in his neatly shaven face and intelligent eyes.

Eugene couldn't stand her mockery longer. "It's impossible to be such a hypocrite as you are! You do not drink, you do not smoke, and you eschew sex. You are simply virtue personified! But there must be some way to relax your nervous system!"

"Me?" Sarah laughed. "A hypocrite?"

She stopped laughing as unexpectedly as she had begun. "In a way you are right," Sarah whispered. She pierced Eugene with a bitter look. "But your list of the ways of relaxation, doc, is too poor. As for me, there is nothing better than knowing honest and clever men, which I considered you before now."

Her words piqued Eugene. He crossly opened the drawer of the writing table. His manners became strained.

"If so, then you will comply with my directions," the doctor pronounced in a formal, dry voice as he uncased the blank of a receipt from the drawer. He was nervously filling up the form with the Latin names of medicines.

Having approached the man, Sarah looked tensely over his shoulder. At last, he offered the receipt to the woman and said, gazing at her with disapproval, "Tomorrow, you'll begin to inject all those preparations in the adult department of this clinic. If in the near future you are determined to be a person of diminished responsibility, your tender son will stay without due care, which only you can give him."

Smiling wryly with the physician's fee-faw-fum, Sarah slowly shredded the receipt. In a pointed manner, she took the mickey out of the man, whose stern, hard look concealed his lust under the cover of rage.

"You are forgetting yourself," Sarah sneered in a low tone. "You are my son's doctor, but not mine."

Suddenly, Sarah grabbed the bottle of brandy and began drinking. Eugene's eyes widened nearly to the rim of his elliptic spectacles. Springing to his feet, the man snatched the half-empty bottle from Sarah's hand.

The doctor put it on the window sill and settled himself in the arm chair again, blocking Sarah's way to the bottle. "I should have given you an injection from the beginning."

But not long afterwards, Eugene was amazed again by Sarah's onrush. Having climbed up in his lap without warning, she tried to reach the bottle that was standing behind Eugene, who defended it steadfastly.

"I'll toss it to the last drop," Sarah muttered in thick voice. "It's a crime to leave the diseased children of this department without the only clever-minded medic during the night!" Her woozy eyes studied the anxious Eugene. She smirked, seeing his irresolution. "Besides, doc ... am I looking less nervous now? Don't keep silent! I need your professional opinion!"

As his hands slipped around her graceful waist, the flustered Sarah couldn't inhibit her strong, drunken desire to destroy the man's self-control.

"Oh, doc! I am ready for one more method of relaxation," she whispered with passion, unpleasantly leaning with her knees against Eugene's haunches.

Suddenly, Eugene felt he kept in his hands not Sarah's body,. but just her negligee. She was only in underwear. Having taken off his glasses, Sarah kissed the man's lips with drunken rapture, her fingers sinking into his titian hair.

"Wait," Eugene whispered, addressing the heated Sarah. Nevertheless, he continued to embrace her.

"So ... to wait or not to wait?" she asked, grinning, feeling again his hesitation to release her. "Doc, what are you thinking about? Is it about your family? But it's simply hypocrisy to hesitate at such a moment! This dull living in call of duty! It could drive anyone crazy! So, relax and profit from the occasion! Your nerves will become stronger!"

Eugene smiled bitterly.

"I want to see your back," he whispered, burning Sarah's naked breast with his hot breath.

"So that means, not to wait," Sarah pronounced with a wisp of a smile as she gazed through the impenetrable coldness of his eyes. "In that case, it'll be what I want first. I need your eyes until the first orgasm. After that ...any of your conditions." She brushed over Eugene's shaven cheek. "Of course, your eyes aren't the ones what I actually long for," Sarah whispered, straining her drunken imagination. "But I hope intoxication will help me."

Suddenly, Eugene stood and flung the woman from his lap. Still keeping naked Sarah in his hands, the doctor turned her round abruptly and sat her on his lap, as he had wished, with her back to him. After flinging aside Sarah's long locks, Eugene palpated her spine, detecting the first signs of scoliosis. It had been brought on by Sarah's constant carrying of her child.

Finally having become limp with brandy and Eugene's massage, Sarah whispered, "What are you doing?" She feverishly crumpled the doctor's jeans with her hands.

"I'm groping for your angel's wings," Eugene wisecracked crossly.

"So?"

"Something rudimentary," the doctor answered absently, as Sarah fell asleep in his arms.

Having picked up the woman as easily as he had carried her son, Eugene put Sarah on the couch near her sleeping boy. After bending to her ear, he whispered with some poignant desire, "You see, it should be a walk-over. But once I had already been full to the throat with your drunken rut. There's too much of your false audacity in it." Eugene squeezed Sarah's earlobe with his lips, making her moan in her sleep.

At the same moment, a nurse came in the room. The abashed woman stayed on the threshold and gaped at the doctor, who was bent over the couch with a half-naked Sarah on it.

"What's happened?" Eugene asked the nurse crossly.

"Sorry, doc," The woman said as she shifted her weight from one foot to another, "but a patient needs help."

"Just a moment," Eugene said. He stopped the nurse's unwary attempt to move into the room with his imperious gesture.

Suddenly, he rushed to the door, almost bumping into the puzzled nurse. They hurried to the patient who was in pain.

After awakening in the early morning with a hangover, Sarah saw Eugene sleeping in an armchair. His head was thrown back uncomfortably. Slowly approaching the man, Sarah wondered how to improve his posture without waking him. But having made certain it was impossible, she invented nothing more clever than to pick up Eugene's specs from the floor and place them on his face.

Suddenly, Eugene grasped Sarah's wrist, keeping the glasses just in front of his eyes. His cold, gray eyes opened wide, as if he hadn't been asleep at all. "What?" he asked, piercing Sarah with his otherworldly, hard look. "Has anything happened?"

"Nothing," she said, startled. Having taken his glasses from Sarah's hand, the man set free her wrist.

"It's all right," Sarah mumbled, pacifying either the doctor or herself. She returned to the couch, where her son slept. "I'll take my boy, and you will be able to lie on the couch."

"Are you going out?" Eugene asked sadly, having unwound at last. He watched with bleary eyes as Sarah fussed with her sleeping child.

"Yeah," she answered, ignoring Eugene's impudent gaze. "It'll be better to leave before your colleagues arrive. I hate gossip."

"You are prudish, as usual," Eugene said. He smiled ironically, keeping his eyes glued to Sarah as before.

"First of all, it's important for your moral character." She glanced at Eugene's wedding ring.

The man took a sneering glance at the same direction.

"Oh! So that's why you're nervous," he mocked, trying to

sting Sarah. "Don't be so preoccupied with my matrimonial state. My fifty-year old wife and I understand each other perfectly. She permits me to have lovers."

"Wow!" Sarah's eyes opened wide with surprise. "So, taking into account the disparity in your ages, you are more interesting for her as a personal doctor," she blurted out suddenly.

In a blink, Eugene was across the room. Sensing she had really insulted him, Sarah cast down her eyes. She sensed the man's long fingers trembling near her lips and chin. Avoiding his withering look, Sarah just heard his low voice, which was quivering with fury. "Maybe. But she's the only woman who loves me," Eugene said. Then he abruptly left the room.

Sarah shrugged. Inwardly, she was sorry for her inability to keep a civil tongue. Yet something in his tone seemed to blame Sarah for making him marry an old crone. Or perhaps Sarah had made him ignore the pretty nurses, whom Eugene drove to hysterics with his accusations of incompetence. Sarah couldn't get rid of the fixed sensation she had heard Eugene's voice before. But she wasn't able to recollect when and where.

As if having forgotten about his pique, Eugene continued to be concerned about Sarah and her son, just as before. He constantly asked the woman to spend the time of his night duties with him in the intern's room. Sarah couldn't deny his request, but she always took her sleeping son with her. She dreaded leaving her boy alone, even for a moment. Inwardly, Sarah was glad that a practiced doctor was keeping the bedside of her son with her. It gave her nerves a little relaxation. Therefore, she was ready to entertain Eugene with her chatting all night long, like a fairytale Scheherazade.

Every evening, taking her son into the intern's room, Sarah sensed the mocking glances of other in-patients who did not understand why she was so inseparable from her child. The boy, obviously, prevented her from having a good time with the doctor.

Keeping company with Eugene, Sarah constantly caught the man's unequivocal eyes as if testing her stubborn self-restrain. But as they harassed each other by idle talking, nobody gave up first.

Gradually Eugene saw Sarah as a remarkable woman who had withstood senseless afflictions during all her life, constantly balancing on the margin of insanity.

From her side, Sarah tried not provoke Eugene's sexuality more. His ability to govern his passions awakened in her a deep respect. Sarah couldn't fall in love with such a man, but her heart was warming with the secret hope that she had found a friend. She had abandoned that hope after Serge and Oleg's deaths.

Once, sitting on her bed in the ward, Sarah was engaged in mending her son's clothes. Her boy was lying motionless with his back to her. "Thanks God, he has slept," Sarah thought with relief.

But a powerful urge shot upward from her soul. The woman grasped her son's shoulder and turned him harshly. The boy's body was limply inverted on his back. Seeing his pale face and his deep-blue lips and closed eyes, Sarah shrieked and collapsed on her knees near the bed. Her son wasn't breathing.

Several medics rushed into the ward. Pushing an oxygen mask onto the boy's bloodless face, they struggled to control his mother, who rushed from one doctor to another. Sarah instinctively searched for Eugene, whom she hadn't seen that day. At last, her distraught eyes clashed with his cold ones. Out of her wits, Sarah suddenly knelt in front of the physician, embracing his legs.

"Gene, dear, you are a remarkable doctor!" she whispered, not letting the man to move. "Save my boy! I'll pray for your children to the end of my days." Eugene was startled and furiously glanced at Sarah. The doctor's hands trembled and his thoughts were unsettled by her desperation. As never before, he realized that his attachment to the woman deprived him of his cold logic. But his good sense was necessary for saving the boy.

Struggling to regain self-control, Eugene suddenly picked up the woman from the floor and whispered near her lips, "Pray for your child! I'm sterile."

Meanwhile, other medics took charge. Only two plump nurses were still watching the scene between Eugene and Sarah. They didn't interfere, supposing the couple to be very familiar. Eugene shifted his eyes toward the nosy parkers.

"Will anybody work here?!" he shouted at the nurses, losing his control. Suddenly he pushed Sarah toward them.

"Take her away! Double dose of sedative!" Eugene barked at the fearful women, who nearly fell down as Sarah bumped against their plump bodies. The nurses barely prevented the distracted mother from breaking away with their disgusting, porky hands.

Meanwhile, Eugene joined the other medics trying to save Sarah's son.

Not long after, Sarah, injected with sedatives, sat at the door of the recovery room, where physicians struggled for the life of her child. The woman's blank eyes were staring straight in front of her. She seemed broken, finally. It was impossible to withstand her destiny any further.

At last, the door of the room opened and several medics came out, Eugene among them. His face had become thin and hollow-cheeked, as if he had grown old so quickly. The man nervously felt for cigarettes in his pockets. Suddenly, he noticed Sarah sitting on a chair near the door. He approached her and harshly grasped the woman's shoulders, forcing her up. Looking intently at Sarah's laid-back eyes, Eugene whispered crossly, "What are you doing here?"

Drugged, Sarah stared apathetically at his angry eyes. It was obvious that he felt helplessness in the face of the inexorable circumstances.

"Is it all over?" Sarah whispered, sensing her mind finally separating from her body with her own words.

"What?" Eugene roared. "Did you habituate yourself to death?"

Unexpectedly, he slapped Sarah across the face so hard that her nose bled. "Don't you understand you create this reality yourself? Your mind lives with your unconquerable foreboding of death for everyone you love!"

Having grabbed Sarah's forearm, Eugene almost dragged her along the hospital corridor. Blood from her nose splattered on the floor. At last, they stopped at the fretted wooden fence of a small hospital chapel decorated as a modest Orthodox altar-screen. The doctor pushed Sarah inside that compact space, which was dense with icons, and she collapsed upon the floor.

Lustfully gazing at Sarah's hips, now exposed by her tucked up negligee, Eugene pronounced, "You said you are a devotee of Orthodoxy! So, pray to your God! It's impossible He doesn't hear your praying! You haven't got any ambitions, you don't live with worldly temptations, and you even don't know how to manipulate the man whose help you need. Why should you deserve the neglect of your God, who absolves repenting thieves and killers?"

Kneeling, Sarah's blood mixed with tears over her face. Eugene's slap had returned the woman to her senses. Ashamed, pulling down her negligee, Sarah muttered bitterly, "But it's true. I have been praying all my life long, and He's impervious to my pleadings."

"Angel's spawn ..." Eugene hissed coldly, making Sarah startle. She had heard such words from ephemeral hellish creatures. Sarah dazedly stared at the man who was so shrewd and logical in all his acts, yet now addressed her by the words from the beyond. Sarah intuitively stroked the cross-shaped scar on her left palm. She had her eyes glued to Eugene's penetrating gray ones as if waiting for them to turn into half-dark, half-fiery holes. But nothing happened.

"Why did you say that?" Sarah whispered.

Eugene replied as if his heart were afire, which was so unusual for his reserved nature. "You are an angel's spawn. You have all the pride of a fallen angel. You know, your spirit is strong enough to withstand the war against hell! Most people aren't that strong. But you prefer to vegetate in your endless hostility toward this world. I don't pity you! I pity your son, whose weak spirit and health are in your power now!

"It's easy to find hell everywhere and make a martyr of oneself! You must recollect a moment when you felt your true connection with God. Even the most miserable person has sensed such a state at least once in life. If you'll find just one reason to be grateful to your God, He'll hear you."

Still kneeling on the floor, Sarah set her eyes on the icons that were so close to her heart with their spiritual images. Eugene's words seemed like quotations from the book of her soul, which he read so easily.

"Convent," Sarah said, keeping her eyes upon the icons.

"What?"

"The convent," she repeated. "I was very happy there."

"Excellent!" The doctor rejoiced that he had aroused such pious recollections, averting Sarah's mind from the anticipation of approaching death.

But as before, Sarah could never explain the source of her happiness at the convent. Flashbacks flickered across her mind, obscuring actuality. Sinking into a trance, she didn't notice Eugene's departure. The doctor returned to the recovery room, where his medical skill was as indispensable in physical reality as was Sarah's gift of an innate Gnostic to reach the Mind of God.

Endless Ukrainian steppes stretched across Sarah's mind. The stone walls and silver crosses of the convent stood lonely against plains of ripe wheat. Then all became an expanse of big, white flowers, which unexpectedly dispersed, forming the galactic spiral. In the next moment, the myriads of stars spread all over the space with divine iridescence.

Graceful, tapered fingers brushed over Sarah's forearms from behind. She knew: it was the Angel. The profound expression of his eyes joined her soul within the Mind of God, creating the pure and sublime Love.

A short prayer arose softly in Sarah's heart. It was the prayer of an Orthodoxy martyr, who retained his faith up to his last breath. "Thank you, God, for everything ..."

"Your son is alive." A deep low voice sounded beside Sarah and cut short her trance.

She opened eyes perplexedly. The fascinating Stranger stood before the kneeling woman. His melancholic, dark look captured her soul, as always. Sarah was shocked by his announcement as well as by the ability of her love to converse with her. She couldn't utter a word, as if she had adopted the previous mute conduct of the Stranger.

Sarah's heart jumped. Suddenly, the Stranger squatted and took her left hand. The man was so close—and so real! Sarah squeezed his hand in response. She scrutinized the Stranger's long, dark eyelashes and the slightly disheveled, dark-brown curls covering his high cheekbones. Sarah ached to tell him about her tormenting love for him. But she couldn't utter a word.

The Stranger smiled beamingly, as if he understood her without any words.

"I know, you can't help loving me," his low voice said, warming Sarah's heart. "This empyrean love is just our common nature of celestials."

Sarah awoke to the pungent smell of ammonia liquid. Eugene knelt beside her. Hoisting her from the floor, the agitated doctor shook Sarah with the mad euphoria of a person who sensed triumph over death.

"He's alive! Your son is alive! It's a miracle," the man whispered, pressing Sarah's cheeks to his ardent lips. But sedatives, still in the woman's blood, limited her ability to express emotions again. She simply stared at the doctor through the mist of tears. Instinctively fingering her left palm, which had no scar after the Stranger's handclasp, Sarah whispered in embarrassment, "Yes, I know. Thank you, God, for everything…"

Sarah's son gained strength each day. Realizing it was just a temporary improvement of his soft health, Sarah longed to leave the hospital walls.

She was aware that, after being discharged from hospital, she would see Eugene only when her son's health was in danger. Sarah tried to nip in the bud her attachment to the doctor, to whom she was indebted for the life of her boy. She knew it wasn't time for amicable relations in the everyday routine of the married man, whose *raison d'être* was just to climb the ladder in medicine. Sarah wished to part with Eugene as quickly as possible. She believed their mutual attraction would ebb at a distance.

It was the day of Sarah's son discharge. Approaching the room to gather some papers, the woman noted a key in the lock of the door. Obviously, Eugene had overlooked it in the course of a busy shift. Sarah came in. She took a seat quietly on a stool by the writing table, where Eugene had been already sitting. Concentrating on the paperwork, he ignored Sarah's entrance.

"You forgot the key in the lock outside," Sarah said. Eugene was silent, merely glancing at the woman's knees, which she covered with the skirt of her short negligee. But in a moment, the doctor became immersed with his writing again.

After finishing the work with his bold signature, Eugene handed the papers to Sarah and avoided her gaze.

"It's necessary to stamp with a seal in the governor's room," he said as he approached a window in the spacious room. The man fastened his wistful look far away. Up to the skyline were the multi-storied buildings of a large Ukrainian city. Eugene contemplated the urbanity, drawn in the slush of January 2002, which was unusually warm. He secretly hoped that when he turned back, Sarah would not be in the room. But the woman made no haste to go out.

Willfully standing, half-facing Sarah and keeping silent, Eugene gave her to understand that she shouldn't wait for his sensible, parting effusions. Uncomfortable with his gloomy silence, Sarah wanted to say something warm to the man who had done so much for her. "Thanks, doc. Thanks for your generosity," she said under her breath.

Eugene flinched. "For goodness sake!" he pronounced with irritation, nervously drumming with his fingers over the window-sill. "Generosity is my everyday job."

Being on the point of leaving the room, Sarah glanced at the man, whose fingers had been still beating some rhythm over the window sill.

"Did you finish an academy of music?"

"Yes." Eugene tried to retain his inward balance, which Sarah destroyed by her presence.

"Piano?"

He nodded, but still refused to talk.

"All the same … thank you." Sarah wended her way toward the door without looking at Eugene again.

Clenching his teeth, the doctor nodded, silently accepting Sarah's gratitude.

Suddenly, the door flew open and another physician burst in. Having appeared unexpectedly in Sarah's way, he nearly knocked the woman off her feet.

"Eugene Petrovich! How long will we be waiting for you? You know, it couldn't be the council of specialists without your presence!"

Unexpectedly, Sarah and the man's gazes crossed. Both were shocked. Sarah recognized those Asiatic eyes, which were devouring her with feverish darkness. Silky, jet-black hair cascaded over the man's shoulders. After throwing back an unruly lock that fell on his face, Sarah's former, reckless neighbor, Andrew, studied the woman.

"What gives? By what chance?" he said as he stepped toward Sarah. She perplexedly scrutinized Andrew's arms, which were still covered by the numerous scars he'd gotten after his falling into the mirror in the den. The ugliness of his skin could be seen from under the rolled up sleeves of his white coat.

"Are you a medico?" Sarah asked, not believing her eyes. She restrained her nervous laughter with difficulty. Now Sarah involuntary backed away from the well-cared-for, virile man. He barely resembled the drug-addicted, foppish youngster who had been Andrew 15 years ago. "How is this possible?" she whispered. "At school, you couldn't distinguish alkalis from acid ... and besides, your phobia ..."

"It means nothing," Andrew answered, now standing so close that Sarah sensed dizziness from his hot breathing. It poured over her face like the winds of the sultry, southern lands of their common, hot-blooded ancestry. "As I see, contrary to all expectations, you didn't succeed in life, despite your poring over books in our salad days." Andrew touched Sarah's simple habiliment with the same assumed arrogance he had expressed once at the school disco.

The man straightened his long, dark hair with an elegant gesture, making Sarah shudder internally. His appearance was strangely similar to that of Sarah's illusory Stranger. Suddenly, he cast a cunning glance at Eugene, who had been still standing near the window. "As for my phobia," Andrew said, perking, "it doesn't prevent me from officiating as the governor of the children's department of the clinic. On the subject of immediate medication, I rely on a pro like Eugene Petrovich." He motioned toward Eugene.

"Besides, I recommend him as one of our best doctors. He has never had problems with chemistry."

"I know him quite well," Sarah said with vexation. She had been still moving back from the slowly approaching Andrew. "He was the attending doctor of my son in this clinic until today's discharge. And since you are the governor of the department, I need your seal on these medical documents." Sarah pressed the papers to her breast as if they could defend her from the passion of Andrew's eyes.

"Oops!" The man suddenly flicked the documents out of Sarah's hands and threw them onto a stool. "Have you a child?!" he continued, excitedly measuring Sarah with the pert look of a wild fellow. "Are you not still a virgin?"

Having lost patience, Sarah unexpectedly slapped Andrew, crabbing his face with her sharp fingernails.

"Heck!" he exclaimed as he instinctively pushed Sarah away. Wiping blood from his scratched cheek with disgust and approaching Sarah again, he whispered, "Devilish half-breed! Asian women are slavish at least!"

Having almost snuggled up to the dumbstruck Sarah, Andrew once more shifted his scrutiny toward the motionless Eugene. The ex-doctor of Sarah's son held himself aloof, as before. He watched Sarah and Andrew with apparent disinterest. But he was betrayed by his spasmodically heaving chest. Having noticed it, Andrew smirked. Drying his bloodstained hand against the skirt of Sarah's negligee, he uttered with a grin, "It's true! Eugene Petrovich is not only a foremost authority in physiology, but he is an outstanding chemist as well. It's worth remembering the bang-up drug blend he prepared for you many years ago. Do you remember Aesculapius?" Keeping his eyes glued to Sarah, Andrew suddenly addressed Eugene.

Sarah shivered. She turned back slowly toward Eugene, who vacantly stared, not daring to look at Sarah.

"So, it's you," she barely uttered. Sarah gazed at Eugene, as if she saw a monster. Now she knew why the man's unfeeling voice and cold, rational look were so familiar.

The shocked woman ignored Andrew's hand, which was gingerly touching her hip under her skirt.

"If it hadn't been for that brew, maybe we wouldn't have quarreled with Oleg, and he would still be alive," Sarah said bitterly, recollecting her perished friend. She had always reproached herself for his suicide.

"Oh! It'll begin now," Andrew said significantly. "Sweetie ... you are trying to deduce some very hypothetical interdependence between Eugene's speedball and the blowing out of Oleg's brains. Let's lapse into nostalgia, but in a more pleasant way."

Suddenly he yanked on the woman's negligee. Sarah fought with tooth and nails against his attempts to lay her on the table, and Andrew barely withstood her wild resistance.

"Scoundrels, beasts ... you both!" she cried.

Having controlled Sarah's fighting at last, Andrew burned her lips with kisses. Her body involuntary relaxed in his arms. But suddenly, Eugene rushed to the couple. Having pulled Sarah from Andrew's hug, he pushed the woman away and pressed his friend against the wall.

"Enough!" He leaned heavily on Andrew. However, Andrew seethed with lust. Licking his lips and casting glances at Sarah over Eugene's shoulder, he sputtered, "What the hell! Let me go!"

Sarah, who had already rearranged her slightly torn negligee, stood behind the table. It separated her from the men, who were familiarly clasping each other near the wall not far from the door. She tried to avoid Andrew's hot looks. But the stamps of his voluptuous hands still burnt her body, raising in Sarah's mind the hot flashbacks about her reckless neighbor, who had always sought her intimacy.

Now Sarah apprehended with horror she felt the same lust after Andrew. But they had little to nothing in common. What would join the ex-play-mates? Just that wild passion, which Sarah could feel as keenly as the dark-eyed, indomitable Asian did.

Having tried to moderate his mate in a peaceful way, Eugene suddenly grasped Andrew's shoulders and knocked his back strongly against the wall.

"Hey! Watch your step!" Andrew exclaimed.

"I said, enough! She is not for you."

"Why the mischief? When did you become so monogamous? Have you forgotten you were the initiator of her gang-rape in your house, 15 years ago? But now you are squeamish even about me."

"You also pandered to it," Eugene recriminated coldly. "Besides, no one was hurt but you. But our mutual debts, we always settle perfectly." The power of a mastermind sounded in Eugene's voice. "I suppose you don't want to lose your place in the sun before I leave the service in the hospice and become the head of my private clinic. But I can always find a more clever substitute for your position. You know my potential. You have enough with the females of this medical henhouse, who thrill even to your look."

"We always understood each other. Why didn't you tell me she was here? You know, I always was zealous for her," Andrew whispered, stopping to twitch in Eugene's arms.

Sarah couldn't find a place for her trembling hands. She was twitching with unexpected lust for Andrew, and her look rushed vacantly about the room.

Suddenly, Eugene harshly sank his hand into Andrew's jetty locks and kissed his lips brusquely.

"Does it get better?" he asked after removing his lips from

Andrew's face and staring significantly at his bleary eyes, expressing the unquestioning obedience of a vassal. "So, do your stuff!" Having grasped Andrew's languished body, Eugene pushed him out of the room. At the same moment, Sarah heard a click: Andrew locked the door with the key outside.

"Possessed cretin," Eugene announced, still standing at the door.

Struggling against her vexing attraction to Andrew, Sarah thought with difficulty. The minute during which Eugene stood near the door with his back to her seemed as if it had been a month of Sundays. "Are you lovers?" Sarah blurted out suddenly.

Eugene startled, as if he had forgotten of Sarah's presence, and turned around. He leaned against the locked door, watching with curiosity the obvious signs of desire in Sarah's behavior, which she concealed artlessly.

"Sometimes," he said, which baited Sarah's curiosity. Watching with a wry smile as her eyes rolled with annoyance, Eugene added, "You saw, he is a hot-blooded boy. It's difficult to refrain from temptation."

"Like enough," Sarah muttered confusedly, trying to bypass Eugene's hint at her similar, latent blood.

Inwardly Sarah regretted she had begun the senseless talk, opening the ins and outs of Eugene's private life and undermining her view of him as an intelligent, generous doctor.

Barely enduring his withering look, Sarah sidled around the table. She cast furtive glances at the list of in- house phone numbers posted near an interphone on the broad table.

"Well," she said reservedly, with a gentle hand picking up the receiver. Trying to change the topic of their conversation for more neutral one, Sarah added beneath her breath, "We have to get out somehow. You have a lot of work, and my son is alone in the ward."

"Nothing will happen to your son," Eugene said coldly. He caught each of Sarah's motions and her vagrant look. "An attendant will look after your boy. Andrew will order it to be done..."

"What?" Sarah whispered.

Before she caught a moment to dial a short number from the list, Eugene was near Sarah. He yanked the receiver from her hand and hung it harshly. The doctor clasped Sarah, his strong hands roving over her body. After squeezing her earlobe with his lips, he tickled Sarah's ear with a feverish whisper. "Unbelievable. You are the same, naïve schoolgirl. Do you remember that chemical contest, when you let me to stroke your legs? Did you really believe I needed those formulas, scribbled over your skin? As if it should be possible to learn chemistry without knowing them ..."

Sarah tried to escape the man, who had been the personification of refinement and steadfast self-possession not long ago, but now gazed at her with alienation.

"Andrew was right. I can control you with drugs. And I can reanimate your son. But all that contradicts my true purpose, which is to gain power over you. How do you like it? Nobody in my life have I wanted so poignantly."

"Indeed," Sarah whispered as she choked with weakness, trying to withstand his strength, "so poignantly that you nearly gave me to those dregs in your house!"

"Yes!" Eugene answered maliciously. He picked up the exhausted woman and set her on the table. "I wanted you to be raped! Only then you would accept me. I wanted you to stay with me, but you were so untouchable! After the violence, you wouldn't reject my medical aid ... and so my love, too. You can't reject me even now, after I saved your son."

"Idiot!" Sarah whispered indignantly, losing the last strength to contain the man. Her negligee was on the floor, as was as Eugene's white coat. "I have already replied to your pretension. I haven't wished to repeat it twice."

"Only over your dead body?" Kissing her breast, Eugene languidly quoted Sarah's answer in the den.

"Precisely! Striking memory!"

"Yeah, I try ... My job obliges me to have a good memory. But persons like you will never die without carrying off others in hell."

"What?" Sarah gasped, escaping Eugene's attempt to part her legs. "Wiseacre ... you heard too many of Andrew's tales about deuces and witches!"

"Leave Andrew in peace!" Eugene snapped. His jealousy cut Sarah's ear. "I sensed the power of your imprecation on my own! I can't have my own children or a normal family after your curses!"

"Delirium," Sarah muttered indignantly. It was obvious; Eugene had been deeply hurt by the rebuke she had dropped in his house, many years ago.

But now, Sarah really longed to curse the monster, who had used her grief for revenge. Some oaths invoking hell were upon Sarah's lips, but she could not wish him ill. The endless gratitude to the man for saving her son absorbed Sarah's fury. She realized bitterly that she had been wrong to consider Eugene as her friend. Now she had also lost the only doctor who could maintain the frail health of her child.

"Please. I can't ... I don't want you," Sarah whispered.

Holding her arms, Eugene gazed at Sarah with the cold eyes of a proud man who was accustomed to achieving any purpose, even the maddest one.

"Really?" the doctor asked as he blocked Sarah's attempt to

jump down from the table. "But you have been unbalancing me! You robbed me of my usual self-control! Deeply touched with your foolish sufferings, I pretended to myself to let you go ... but you as if were waiting for Andrew... Don't you see? He is like a sexual catalyst. Especially after you slapped his face. If I hadn't interfered, he would have had you right here, regardless of my presence!"

"So what?" Sarah smirked. She wanted to pique the man's morbid self-esteem. "Should that so perturb your supersensitive heart?"

"There is only one thing that always perturbs me. I must be the first in everything!" Eugene snubbed the woman, making her regret that she had used such a tone.

Tired of standing upon useless ceremony, Eugene tore Sarah's panties from her hips.

"Damn! Do be reasonable!" Sarah exclaimed, back in his clutches again and struggling against Eugene's hands.

"I couldn't let you go now," Eugene whispered, besotted again with lust. "You'll return to me, in any case. It's me who knows how to maintain the health of your son."

"Never! I can't dishonor my marriage!"

Eugene almost burst out laughing in reply. "Oh! It's a valid argument for the foolish mortification of your flesh! But taking into account your Asian blood, your self-control couldn't be stronger than mine."

Sarah finally understood: the genius savior of her son was a sophisticated rapist at the same time.

Eugene suddenly stopped tormenting her. He just wistfully brushed over Sarah's naked breast, casting glances over her shoulder. "It's true. I can't. I love another man ..." Sarah said softly, still naively believing she had somehow persuaded the man to leave her in peace.

Suddenly, Sarah felt another pair of hands grasping her

forearms strongly from behind. Taken unaware, she flinched and nearly cried out. But anticipating her spontaneous reaction, the man's palm clutched her mouth. At the same moment, a wet, hot tongue raced along Sarah's backbone from below up to her neck.

"Your dream-boy could be only an Angel. Only a bodiless creature could withstand to your passion. You may whisper his name, if it turns you on more. We are not jealous of phantoms." Andrew's whisper burned Sarah's ear from behind.

Having pulled her head back and still clasping her mouth, Andrew peeked into her frightened eyes. Shock almost paralyzed Sarah. She hadn't even heard Andrew enter the room.

The man laid Sarah on the table, which was carefully covered with his doctor's coat.

Having shaken Andrew's hand from her face, Sarah said crossly, "Idiot! What are you doing? It's a crime ..."

"Really?" Andrew smirked, bowing over her face and touching Sarah's breast with his long dark hair. "Love can't be a crime."

With those words, he dug into Sarah's lips with his own. Andrew felt satisfaction with her inability to withstand his sex appeal, which gave carte blanche to Eugene to manipulate Sarah's heated body as he pleased.

It was next to madness: Andrew's lips, being so familiar to Sarah since his greenness, now perverted her. Her impeccability was crushed. The self-contradictory intermixture of tormenting, fleshy delight and hostility to the filthy actuality tore asunder Sarah's mind, sinking her into the darkness of unconsciousness.

Sensing somebody's hand holding her wrist, Sarah opened her eyes.

"Where is my son?"

"In the ward. A nurse is looking after him, as I ordered," Andrew's round voice answered her.

At last, Sarah saw clearly. Sitting on the edge of the couch upon which Sarah rested, Andrew smoked nervously. In his hand, he held Sarah's wrist to measure her pulse. The woman realized she was naked, but covered with Andrew's wrinkled white coat.

"How do you do it?" Andrew asked quietly, inhaling his cigarette. He stared straight ahead. "Two hours without consciousness ... ammonia doesn't influence you ... what is this? Eugene was going to stimulate you with something more drastic, but I dissuaded him."

Sarah said nothing. "Eugene" ... it now seemed a meaningless name. She recalled vaguely the man with his hellish, logical attitude, who had really determined her foibles and seized the opportunity to settle accounts with her. But at the same time, Sarah realized with surprise that a bare mention of Eugene didn't disturb her. Her hatred and gratitude toward the same man seemed to annihilate each other. Eugene's logic was faultless, as usual: the salvation of Sarah's son compelled her to forgive him anything.

Keeping silent, Sarah watched Andrew's gracious gestures, by which he straightened his dark hair. His sexual appeal preoccupied Sarah yet again. Sitting on the couch near Sarah's legs, Andrew suddenly stopped smoking and threw the stub of his cigarette onto the floor.

"You didn't change a bit," Sarah said beneath her breath, referring to his public bar manners.

Still keeping silent, Andrew glanced at Sarah's partly naked hip, visible from under his coat.

"Why did you escape our intimacy? You've always wanted me." Andrew glanced at her eyes cunningly, a ghost of a smile playing over his lips.

"You can't know it, because of your faint. But ... I didn't want you very much," he said, trying to sting Sarah. "In fact, I have to fulfill Eugene's fancies. My prosperity is within his grasp. But as for sex ... I have bags of it without you!" Burning Sarah with his killing, dark eyes, he carefully covered her naked hip with his doctor's coat again.

"But each of your new lovers takes an interest in the numerous, disgusting scars over your body, bringing me to your mind," she retorted. "So you can never forget me."

Andrew once more withered Sarah with his dark look, flashing with unsatisfied, Asiatic rancor.

"You're asking for trouble!" he whispered hotly.

Sarah uttered in a more accommodating spirit, "Have you children?"

"Yeah," Andrew answered half-heartedly, ignoring her friendly tone.

"How many?"

"I didn't count!" He looked away, not wishing to talk to Sarah more. Andrew suddenly flung his doctor's coat from Sarah's naked body. "Go to your son! Your clothes are on the table!"

But Sarah knelt quietly on the couch next to him, examining a small, golden cross over Andrew's scarred bosom. She tried to imagine his hatred for her after unsuccessfully seeking her love, which had cost Andrew his Asian daintiness. Kneeling motionlessly beside him, Sarah delighted in the scent of his smoke-filled hair.

Andrew glanced askance at her. Over the years, his marvelous dark eyes had grown deeper. Andrew's pitch-dark curls, hiding his high cheekbones and his sharply delineated lips, drove Sarah crazy. Her treacherous imagination, fired by her rising lust, searched his face for some likeness to that of the illusory Stranger. Even so, Sarah couldn't love Andrew, however alluring their possible intimacy might seem.

"What?" Andrew asked. With his long, dark eyelashes quivering almost next to Sarah's face, he was surprised that he almost didn't sense her noiseless breathing.

"Nothing," Sarah whispered feverishly. "I just can't understand why God gave such eyes to a scoundrel like you."

Unexpectedly, she pressed her lips to Andrew's, holding his stately torso and pressing her breast to his chest.

"Wow!" Andrew whispered, lapping up Sarah's kiss and trying to sit her in his lap.

"No!" she said, pulling back.

"Indeed ...it's unlikely you'll endure our intimacy now," Andrew said, choked with the surge of lust. "But it's imprudent to think I can control myself." His hands were vehement upon Sarah's feminine curves.

Suddenly dizzy, Sarah kissed him with wild energy, which flowed into her weakened body by the power of the Earth's elements.

Andrew's responsive kisses accommodated the unexpected clumsiness of her lips. Sarah recalled the same awkwardness of Andrew's kisses, which she couldn't forgive him when they were ten-year-old children.

Squeezing his strong shoulders, Sarah whispered lustfully, "Please don't close your eyes." And the man ardently caught each of her glances. Suddenly, Sarah's body trembled.

"Why the mischief?" Andrew whispered, hugging Sarah, who

was now ecstatic in orgasm. "I have still done nothing." Clasping to his bosom her vibrant body, Andrew shook with nervous laughter.

"Sakes alive! I deemed this woman could be solely conquered. But orgasm just after a kiss? Unbelievable!"

Angel's spawn

"... when the sons
of God came in unto the daughters of
men, and they bare children to them,
the same became mighty men which
were of old, men of renown."
(Bible, Genesis, Chapter 6:4)

Dawn rose upon the East at the beginning of a hot, July day,
2006. The rustling of leaves and timid twitter of birds shrouded the
small Ukrainian town with blissful peace. The grandiose summer
sun rose over the concrete buildings of Sarah's town, penetrating
the opened windows of her flat.

Four years had elapsed since the woman and her son had
come home after being discharged from that abhorrent hospital.
As before, Sarah struggled against the incurable disease of her
son, which was made worse by the unwanted medication, as the
boy had developed a drug allergy.

In despair, Sarah searched to maintain the health of her son.

Studying the heaps of medical letters, she gained some success
in treating her child by unconventional, natural ways. Now he
ailed not so often, but even so, Sarah's son remained an incurable
asthmatic. The woman reconciled herself and accepted the doctors'
judgment: it was impossible to change the genetic disposition of
her son.

Sarah had been living alone during the previous four years. She
avoided any pretensions of men on her seeming independence.

She got used to loneliness, no longer dreading it as she had in her youth. Peace became the only long-expected reward for her tired soul.

Sleeping, Sarah rolled from one side to another. Her flat, overlooking the East with its three windows, was already sunlit. Suddenly, melodious chimes could be heard. Sarah opened her eyes, listening to the bells of the Orthodox church, which was situated in front of her windows and calling congregation to Mass every morning.

Gazing vacantly toward the summer sun, standing in all its magnificence, the woman felt inexpressible bliss: her son's breathing was pure and regular. The peal of the bells awakened in her memory the convent and the old cleric, who believed she wouldn't escape her monastic destiny, even living in the world. Sarah's vulnerable nature, which was that of an idealistic recluse, did not belong in the cold pragmatism of material reality.

Having closed her eyes, the woman smiled to herself, recollecting her recent visit to the "Italian" Cathedral, her town's main Orthodox church. Adding to the disorder of her lonely life, Sarah had been living in her conformist marriage for seven years whilst all civil relations with her ex-husband had stopped long ago. She had still been flattering herself with the vain hope that her husband would return. Not for her sake, as she had never loved him—but because of their common child, whom Sarah longed to see at least a little happier.

Every time she approached the church to settle her single status finally, Sarah always went away. Drowned in tears, she couldn't annul the sacral ritual, which she believed should protect her fireside against any evil. But it didn't keep her family even from the most banal devotion.

Nevertheless, the day before, she had come into the cathedral as if by accident. To her great surprise, an archbishop took Sarah in immediately. Having heard about the attractive woman waiting for her estranged husband for many years, the chief cleric was surprised by her devotion. But Sarah just dropped her eyes before the old man, who wore the glaring, golden vestment of ancient Byzantine monarchs. She could tell nobody that she had never loved her husband, and her devotion was mere fidelity to her Orthodox vows.

The archbishop signed her papers, freeing Sarah from her Orthodox obligations: a scratch of the cleric's pen abolished Sarah's sacraments of eternal love with the father of her son.

After leaving the archbishop's room, Sarah shifted her wistful eyes to a young cleric sitting by a table and staring at a computer monitor. Obviously, he officiated as a receptionist; he had been absent when Sarah had first come to the archbishop.

A sarcastic smile played over Sarah's lips as she observed that office interior, in which the Orthodox cleric looked very funny. His long, yellow cassock with the golden stitching of ancient Byzantine style clashed with the man's jeans and sneakers, flashing under his long skirt that almost reached the floor.

Sarah settled straight her thin kerchief, covering her long, dark-brown tress in accordance with Orthodox rules of modesty.

Soundlessly passing by the table and the dark-haired cleric, she heard his cool voice addressing her: "Have you taken bliss?"

"Yes," Sarah said, pausing before the table.

"The bliss of a marriage?"

Sarah was at a loss. Thinking the cleric didn't understand why she had visited the archbishop, she mumbled irresolutely, "In fact ... I have just divorced my former, conformist marriage."

"So what?" the cleric asked with the same, dry voice, his eyes glued on the monitor. "You have to take the bliss of another marriage!"

Sarah's irritation increased because the man spoke roughly and without looking at her.

"Really? Very funny! Is it not humiliating for the religion worshiping the Greatest Altruistic Love? Who will make a match with a divorcee? It's adultery, isn't it? Why do you bless this lechery? "

"What?" The man still did not look at Sarah. "It's such fickle persons as you, who lack of ability to love once and forever—you compelled us to adopt this 'humiliating usage!' It's you who pray us to free you from your own Orthodox vows! However, even after that, you have to live a Godly life!"

"I live quite piously!" Sarah shouted. She was furious and thunderstruck with the sermon of this young priest, who was so much younger than she. The man reproached her like a husband who had caught his wife with a lover. "I have already confessed before His Grace! I'll never again marry. Never! Thanks for your blessing!"

Suddenly, the man shifted his dark eyes from the computer to Sarah, whose face was now red with summer heat and spite.

"You?" the cleric asked perplexedly. His countenance and manner had unexpectedly changed.

"Of course, me!" Sarah answered, pertly looking at his marvelous, dark eyes. "However, I haven't the honor of knowing you, and I'm very glad of this fact!"

The man slowly blushed.

"Sorry," he said confusedly, casting down his eyes. "I didn't recognize you at first sight."

"Very likely! It's no wonder, seeing you immersed in delusive virtual reality instead of the accumulation of faith, which is your main mission."

Accepting Sarah's indignation, the cleric repented. "Please, I am sorry ..." As she calmed down a bit, he burned Sarah with his hot look and pronounced apologetically, "It's true. We haven't been introduced to each other, but I always remember you."

The man stood up, amazing Sarah with his charismatic appearance. He was not very tall, but his long, dark hair and fathomless, dark eyes were deeper against the background of his golden, Byzantine apparel.

After approaching Sarah, he bowed and introduced himself. "I'm the son of the den of the Cathedral. I came back here after finishing seminary, not long ago."

Undeterred by his passionate look and the impressive glare of his splendor, Sarah said, "If you just began your service here, you ought to learn to speak with your parishioners more civilly. Otherwise, all your flock will scatter, regardless of your charming eyes and divine voice."

The man dropped his eyes again, as if letting Sarah understand he would accept her sarcasm endlessly.

Finally calm, Sarah left the building for the broad yard of the cathedral. The young cleric trailed after her. Not knowing why he didn't leave her in peace, Sarah quietly asked, "Where do you know me from? We're quite different in age."

The man glanced at her with slight confusion. He paused by a smart sports car parked on the yard. The car resembled a fantastic, intergalactic rocket with its elegant streamlined chassis. The cleric, obviously, wished to demonstrate that God had blessed him not only with his attractive appearance, but with financial well-being, too.

"May I drop you?" he asked, opening the door of the car before Sarah. But to his disappointment, she turned around, ignoring his proposition. The woman directed her steps toward a bench in front of the magnificent cathedral that had always warmed her heart.

The disappointed cleric followed Sarah and perplexedly sat on the bench near her.

"You didn't answer my question," Sarah reminded him wistfully. "Where do you know me from?"

"As a matter of fact," he answered quietly, "You were my earliest love ..."

Sarah burst into laughter. For a moment, she visualized herself as the wife of a young handsome Orthodox priest.

The cleric stared at Sarah in confusion.

"Sorry," she said. Now it was her turn to apologize. "Couldn't you find anyone younger for your flirting? You have bags of girls in your church, who come here not to pray, but to ogle you."

"However, not one of them would dare to be so impudent with me!" the man said feverishly, placing his elegant hand on Sarah's knee.

"I haven't even started yet," Sarah responded, sensing some irritating lust within the heat of the cleric's hand, perceptible through the thin fabric of her skirt.

The chime on the belfry pealed out high noon. Sarah glanced toward the golden domes of the cathedral, which were surrounded by statues of evangelists gazing sternly at the wicked earth from the unattainable skies.

After following her look, the cleric removed his hand from Sarah's knee and crossed himself devotedly.

"Sorry," he said quietly, amusing Sarah with his affected piousness. "I have forgotten that you lived in a convent."

"Me? Nothing of the kind! You are, obviously, mistaking me for someone else," Sarah said. She seemed to be scared.

"I couldn't be mistaken! You were nearly twenty, and I was thirteen when I saw you at the cathedral at the first time. I was stricken to the marrow of my bones. You seemed descended from an icon! Of course, you didn't notice a young acolyte who waited for your coming here as if he were waiting for the appearance of the Blessed Virgin."

"Please," Sarah whispered, sensing even stronger desire from his words. "You are a cleric, yet you blaspheme like ..." Finding no words, she stood from the bench and prepared to go away, to deliver the man from the temptation to grasp her skirt beside the church.

Trying to detain Sarah, the cleric said intriguingly, "Nevertheless, I still remember the council of clerics hesitating to give you the letter of credence for presentation in the convent. There was only one reason for their irresolution: the scar on your palm. They felt it was an ill omen."

Astonished, Sarah flopped down on the bench again.

"Why are you ecclesiastics so eerie?" she muttered with vexation, revealing that her palms had no scars.

Inspecting her palms and ardently brushing over them with his long finger, the cleric pronounced, "But I saw it with my own eyes! Once, when the fire of a taper, which you held, lit up your left palm."

"You are really mistaking me for someone else," Sarah insisted with a sneer, escaping the man's brushing of her palm. "Besides," she said, seeing the cleric's embarrassment, "even if it wasn't me, why is our church afraid of the cross? It's the symbol of our faith!"

"It's true," the cleric answered in a melancholy tone. "But there are a lot of different crosses. We worship the crucifixion. But the cross-shaped scar on the palm of that girl ... was the heathen symbol of the sun. Hell marked the posterity of seduced angels with it."

"Whose posterity?" Sarah gaped at the cleric.

"Seduced angels," he repeated, without a shade of abashment. "There is such a story based on the scriptural plot ..." The cleric was glad he had captured Sarah's attention at last.

"Time out of mind, strange creatures formed a race, getting on with people. The same in physical body, the beings had unbelievable spirit, inherited from their great ancestors, Light Angels. The Angels were tempted by the beauty of Earth women. Strong-willed and exalted, these so-called Angel's spawns had superhuman ability to exist in different dimensions of the universe. But vegetating in the primitive sublunary world, the creatures lost their sense of God's Love. They felt only a lenient compassion upon the imperfect materiality, undeserving of their sublime attachment. The pride of the fallen angel insulated the spiritual beings from God once and forever. The Angel's spawns became the most acclaimed warriors and prisoners of hell at the same time. Hell was on the watch for the creatures everywhere.

"Rushing between materiality and spiritual worlds, the grim nomads of the universe, the Angel's spawns, had no place for their self-defeating, ambivalent souls. So they remained alien from all of God's Being.

"The cross-shaped scar over the palm gave its possessor power. But at the same time, inexplicable bleeding out of the scar threatened the Angel's spawns with physical destruction and final unification with hell. Only the intrusion of Light Angels could protect their fallen relatives against the traitorous dual nature of the scar."

Sarah listened to the cleric, not believing her ears.

"Such heresy!" she whispered sarcastically. "Where did you pick up it? At the end, where is your vaunted fundamentalism? Is this what you studied at seminary?"

"Of course not!" the man said, as he cast down his dark eyes again. "Certainly, I don't share such an apostasy ... but there is so much belief in The Heavens Absolution in this story. How could Our Maker ruin in the waves of Deluge the posterity of the Light Angels, the gist of His Spirit and Love? It's impossible to alter an Angel's nature by human's original sin!"

Sarah listened wistfully. She fixed her green eyes on the majestic Corinthian chapiter of the Cathedral, which looked like an enormous heavenly flower, statuesque in marble forever.

Watching Sarah's fingers involuntarily stroking her left palm, the cleric continued. "Only a look of a Light Angel could awake in the hearts of the half-hellish Angel's spawns that all-embracing love.

"The grandiose feeling returned their lofty souls to the spiritual world. Now, like all celestials, the Angel's Spawn could contain The Almighty Love of God to All Existence."

Sarah had remained silent, apparently ignoring the man's narration. "Well, what next?" she asked suddenly. "Did that girl earn the permeation to domicile in a convent?"

The cleric glanced dazedly at Sarah. He didn't understand why she constantly talked about herself in the third person. "Yes."

"So, how is the convent getting on now? Is it still safe, after harboring such a devil incarnate as she was?"

"Sure!" the man answered, smiling at Sarah's dark humor. "Furthermore, provincial nuns almost apotheosized the girl. She had strange fits of lethargy, which seemed to them to be God's Grace to her. But she didn't stay at the convent ..."

"Indeed," Sarah whispered with bitter sarcasm. "She just remained the hostage of the pride of a fallen angel. Still, it's no reason to cotton with the imperfect, sublunary world."

Sarah rose from the bench, restraining with her expressive gesture the man's impulse to follow her again. Having stepped toward the massive gate of the Cathedral—the semblance of refined bronze lace made by an unearthly Samson—she suddenly stopped and glanced back at the dark-eyed cleric. Her green eyes sparkled. "Tell me! Was it not frightful for you, a thirteen-year old boy, to love such a strange girl?"

"No." The man gazed at Sarah, still hoping she would give him one last chance to entice her. "I longed to taste the love of an Angel, even a fallen one..."

Sarah smirked. "Not everything is worth such a taste. Angel's love ... it's just some inconceivable Platonism, uncongenial to people's fleshy nature."

After turning around, she went out through the opened gate and into the town's bustling main avenue. Sarah wished to never again see the young dissimulator, who resembled a celestial with his appearance, but not with the purity of his mind.

The summer sun rose, packing Sarah's flat with dazzling light. Intently looking at the peaceful face of her sleeping son, the woman sat on the edge of his bed.

His eyes opened, and Sarah smiled tenderly.

"Mummy," the disheveled, drowsy boy whispered. "For three days now I have been asking you to take me to the cinema."

Sarah sighed. "Dear, you know I'm an allergic to cinema. It's just far-fetched, abstracted fancies that enthrall our mind with chimerical characters and candy-floss. We must survive in our actuality such as it is."

"All my mates have already seen the movie. It's funny, about pirates ..." the boy sobbed.

"Pirates?" Sarah rose indignantly. "This is out of the question!"

Seeing her inflexibility, the nine-year old boy was wiping his tears stealthily.

Suddenly, Sarah was lost in thought. Indeed, it was unjustified severity from her side. Her son was whiling away the fourth summer in the hot, dusty town because of her fear to change his environment, which doctors considered might further harm his health.

Pity for the monotonous life of her child overcame Sarah's fear. "Well," she pronounced wistfully, standing by the window and sensing her son's silent sobbing, "we'll go to watch the movie. Now, wash yourself!"

The broiling July sun was in zenith. Dressed in jeans and a T-shirt, with her long curls gathered in a ponytail, Sarah wended over the sizzling asphalt arm-in-arm with her son, who now reached his mother's shoulder. Sarah ignored men's eyes as they glanced over her sharply outlined body, which was accentuated by her clinging clothes. Now she was certain as never before: there was only one man on the Earth whom she loved: her son. But even that sacred love of a mother couldn't free her boy from his incurable disease.

After getting tickets, Sarah was in no hurry to approach the central entrance of the cinema hall, a modern building of glass and concert. Enormous boards with posters were propped up in flowerbeds in front of the building, but Sarah couldn't see what was depicted upon those pretentious placards. She just scrutinized their backsides, standing apathetically under the cover of a branchy lime-tree that protected her son and her from the merciless sun.

"Let's go inside!" Sarah's son insisted. In a moment, he was already jumping before one of the huge placards.

Slowly approaching the big board, which had been placed in a lawn among big, white flowers, Sarah stood motionless, her eyes opened wide.

The marvelous, dark eyes of her empyreal Stranger were derisively staring from the enormous picture. The long-haired, dark wig of the pirate's image, tied with a scarlet bandana and interwoven with elaborate pirate's frippery, just increased the inimitable charm of the man, whom Sarah loved—yet she had never believed in his existence. His dark look, simultaneously icy and passionate, absorbed her mind.

Having noticed something inexplicable happening to his mother, Sarah's son came up to her. Now nervous, the boy fearfully watched tears slowly trickling over her cheeks.

What have you done? Sarah thought, inwardly addressing her celestial love, who had suddenly incarnated in the famous actor. *I always cherished the hope that we'd meet each other... maybe in some spiritual world. But now ... indeed, it's easier for me to get to God with my soul than to overcome this human world separating us forever.*

Sarah couldn't move away from his eyes, the love of which was rooted in her heart.

Suddenly, inexplicable euphoria seized her mind, setting her free from past pain and sufferings. The attachment to the man changed her inwardness, although her love retained for her the same chimerical delusion as before.

Now Sarah sank into some mad love of Actuality, with all its sinful sacredness. She felt strength to remit the world all its imperfection, because of the inimitable look of an angel belonging to a man who lived on the same, erring Earth as she.

Undying, divine music, always pulsing in Sarah's soul ... her pure ideals of human friendship and mutual understanding, the lofty spirituality of Christianity and selfless love to her son—all fragments of her destroyed faith, bringing her to God just a little— were integrated into an organic whole by the power of those dark eyes. That Angel's look filled Sarah's heart with Heaven's Absolution.

Sarah approached the big board, stepping over the flowers that so resembled the snow-white poppies from her dreams at the convent. Her fingers touched the actor's enchanting image, and her legs gave way. Fainting and falling onto the lawn, Sarah sensed only the heavenly aroma of the flowers. Their cool petals gently dropped upon her face and dark-brown curls.

Having burst the fetters of materiality, Sarah's freed spirit darted to the empyrean world. The indivisible quarks of her soul were the rare example of corpuscular integrity. Flowing in the

Streams of the World's Mind, they absorbed God's Truth and Beauty, Strangeness and Charm.

Some amorphous, shadowy, sinister creatures rushed with fire patches about endless space. They couldn't find a way to detach the exalted soul, which was now fused with the Mind of God. They just gobbled, scanning the Astral Universe with infinite radiation.

"Angel's spawn ...you always belonged to hell! Which power is returning you to the Eternal Light now?"

But the Universe replied with the deathly silence of the trustworthy keeper of mysteries. It ignored the spiteful perplexity of the primitive hell, begotten by the united mind of reckless humankind, imagining itself a worthy adversary for God to create new realities. But there was only the true existence of Almighty Love, able to slake the languor of human spirit and return elusive harmony to the long-suffering, sublunary world.

In conclusion...

After his July 2006 visit to the cinematic showing of the much-talked-about pirate trilogy, Sarah's son had no further fits of bronchial asthma. In some inexplicable fashion, the boy overcame his incurable disease.